Taken by a Stranger

Also by
Lin Summerfield

Count the Days
Never Walk Behind Me

Taken by a Stranger

Lin Summerfield

Walker and Company
New York

FIC
SUMMERFIE
L

First published in the United States of America in 1995
by Walker Publishing Company, Inc.

Library of Congress Cataloging-in-Publication Data
Summerfield, Lin, 1952–
Taken by a stranger / Lin Summerfield.
p.   cm.
ISBN 0-8027-3194-5
I. Title.
PS6069.U36T3   1995
813'.54—dc20   94-26335
CIP

Printed in the United States of America
2 4 6 8 10 9 7 5 3 1

For Fiona Spence, with love

(And now that I've finished this, I might as well go back to Cell Block H and watch "Home and Away.")

Taken by a Stranger

▽

1

SHE WAS SO beautiful that he ached. He watched her walking down the street, her fair hair disturbed by the sea breeze, her long legs tanned and graceful, and he felt a real, physical pain.

He had trouble keeping up with her. This street, leading directly to the front, was crowded with August holiday-makers; mostly children with their parents and OAPs on the annual day trip, all distracted by ice cream parlors, amusement arcades, and the inevitable displays of air rings, flippers, and silly hats.

He dodged in and out of pushchairs, wheelchairs, old women with dogs, terrified he would lose sight of her. There was one awful moment when she approached a stallholder, smiling as if she knew him well. But she must have been simply asking directions, for the man smiled back and pointed the way she had been going.

She began to hurry, and in his eagerness to keep up with her he bumped into a small boy, knocking him down. The child began to howl, attracting unwelcome attention, yet he couldn't stop—he mustn't lose her.

Angry voices called after him.

"Hey! That's my kid you've just knocked over, mister!"

"Some people!"

"Manners of a bloody pig!"

He couldn't, wouldn't turn back.

Her hair wasn't blond, more honey-colored, as Francie's

had been. If only she would turn around so he could see that face again. Were her eyes green? When she smiled would she reveal perfectly white, perfectly even teeth? And would that smile make him feel—as he had felt with Francie—that he could do anything in the world?

Please turn around. Let me see you again. Please . . .

They were in sight of the pier now. It was a short pier, with one amusement arcade, one café, and a third-rate theater that put on third-rate shows—people on holiday were so easily satisfied.

The pier at Southend was much longer. Three-quarters of a mile, Marsha used to say, though his father insisted it was longer than that; they had arguments about it. There was also a little train that ran its length every half hour. He and Francie often rode on it, though they usually preferred to walk so that they could stop to peer over the rails and look for jellyfish.

But that was in the better times . . . the times before.

A man with a King Charles spaniel on a lead momentarily got in his way. He swore aloud, but was careful to avoid stepping on the dog.

I'll buy you a dog one day, Francie.

She had always wanted a dog.

He was close to her now. Perhaps too close. She wore a blue bikini top with white shorts, and he could see a birthmark on her left shoulder. That was wrong. She shouldn't have a birthmark; it marred her perfection.

He might have stopped following her then, but chance, which had so often played a vital part in his life, caused her to turn around at that moment, allowing him to see her face clearly for the first time.

She had a broad forehead, the hair growing to a point in the middle—a widow's peak, he believed it was called—giving her face a classic heart shape. He gasped. She could have been Francie's twin.

I'll buy you a dog one day, Francie. And one day I'll . . . And one day . . .

He was so close now that he could hear the slap of her sandals on the pavement. And he could taste salt from the sea air on his lips. Funny how salt tasted like blood.

He had tasted that before.

They came to the end of the street and only now could he glimpse the sea, a dull green expanse that gave an illusion of being higher than the land. Did she swim in the sea? Jellyfish were a common sight at this resort, and the water itself was supposed to be below the standards set by the EEC for health and safety. The beach was quite good, long and broad with very fine, dry sand, for the tide seldom covered it, even in winter. He could imagine her running along that beach, barefoot, her hair tangled about her head, laughing into the wind.

She crossed the road cautiously, although traffic was light at that time of day. There were horse-drawn carriages taking holidaymakers for rides along the front, an odd, battery-powered vehicle shaped like an elephant and driven by a man in a clown's costume advertising the circus, coaches coming to collect day-trippers from all over East Anglia. But there were few cars.

He followed her down a narrow path between the mini-golf course and the pedal boat lake, breathing in the mingled smells of sea, doughnuts, and hamburgers that somehow made him drowsy and hungry at the same time. He was thirsty, too. Lunchtime and the two pints of lager he'd had with his sandwich seemed a long, long time ago. It wasn't as if his afternoon had been energetically occupied, either. A stroll through the shops, half an hour in the job center—surely someone wanted a casual laborer in a seaside town at this time of year?

"You're much too late," he was told. "All the casual work is snapped up in May. You might try the Jolly Roger café, though. They always want someone to wash up. Know where it is?"

He nodded and slouched out. Dishwashing wasn't for him. He wanted an outdoor job—deck chair attendant, maybe. Something like that. Well, there was always apple picking, and that was a job he enjoyed. But whatever happened, he had enough money to see him into the new year. After that—who knew? He certainly wasn't going to touch his father's money. Dirty money, that's what that was.

He had gone to sit on a bench outside The Shipmates' Arms to concentrate on his plans. Some farms started picking much earlier than others, and if he used his head he could find six weeks' work. Maybe even two months'. He'd sleep in the camper and live off pub food if he was too tired to warm something up on the tiny cooker. It wasn't a bad life if you were prepared to rough it and to work hard. He was used to doing both.

That was when he saw her. She was gazing into a shop window—no, staring was the word. She was staring like someone mesmerized; at what he couldn't tell and didn't care, for she held all his attention. The way she stood, the way she clasped her hands in front of her as singers in a choir sometimes did . . . So familiar, so well remembered. He could see her face only in profile then, but it was enough, and without pausing to tell himself he was being ridiculous he began to follow her.

Now there was an urgency in her steps. She was late—and also afraid? Past the ice cream stands, past the chalet-style shops that sold buckets and spades, peppermint rock and dried starfish ("A Souvenir from Wheatcliffe-on-Sea"). And everywhere people were idling along, eating Kingcones, nagging their children, kissing their lovers. People on holiday were a generally unobservant lot.

But where was she going?

Ahead, beyond the stands and kiosks, was a row of beach huts, relics of the Victorian Age and a damned good invest-ment at any resort, he knew. They all had nameplates above the doors: Seashells, Seaview, Beachside. Predictable, un-imaginative names. If he owned one he would call it something unusual and original, and he would live and sleep there while summer lasted.

A small boy sat outside one of the huts, Beachside, playing with an Action Man in combat dress. The child's pants were wet. Urine rather than sea wet, by the look of them, and he had smears of something sticky around his mouth.

She stopped there, glancing nervously at the hut, spoke to the boy, and tried to thrust what looked like an ounce of Golden Virginia tobacco into his hand. But he was having none of it. Fractious and sleepy, he whined, "No, no, no . . ." over and over.

As she was about to pick him up, a man in baggy bathing trunks stumped out of Beachside and grabbed her. He was graying and red, sunburned the length of his hairless chest, and he staggered a little, as if either just awoke from an afternoon nap or drunk.

"Where the hell have you been?" he yelled, shaking her. "Does it take a bloody hour to run one simple errand? *Does it!* No, I know where you've been—hanging around the arcade with them boys again! Bloody little tramp!" He snatched the tobacco from her and gave her such a push that she nearly fell on the hard concrete. "Now get out of my sight! Go on—I don't want to see your face again till six a'bloody clock. And God help you if you ain't back to feed 'im! You"—to the toddler—"you get inside and get them wet pants off."

And he disappeared back inside the hut, the little boy following and sucking peaceably on the feet of his Action Man.

She stood there undecided for a few moments, then turned and started back the way she had come. At a safe distance, she suddenly removed her sandals and jumped down onto the beach.

It was growing chilly with the late afternoon, and most people had given up sea and sand in favor of the arcades and cafés. The few remaining made their offspring don pullovers, while only the hardy locals were still swimming.

She didn't appear to notice the cold. She sat watching a large family of Indians, a group that included grandparents

and possibly great-grandparents, without yet realizing she
was being watched, too.

He lit a cigarette. There was time, plenty of time. For
what? He hardly knew. While he was following her through
the streets, he told himself he only wanted to see her
face—Francie's face—just once. Then just once more. Now
more than anything he wanted to hear her voice.

Just once.

Again they were very close. He could see orangey-yellow
marks on her shoulders, old bruises, and one deep mauve
patch on her right thigh.

History repeating itself.

Now he knew. The answer came to him in that moment.
He was meant to see her, meant to follow her. Chance,
Providence, God—call it what you like—had caused her to
turn around and let him see her face clearly at the very
second of his doubt. His purpose was to save her, to atone
for his failure to save Francie. If she was looking down now,
the message could hardly have been plainer. Marsha used to
say there was a time for everything, quoting the Bible, as he
later learned. And if there was a time to make mistakes, then
surely there must also come a time to put them right?

He ran to the nearest ice cream stand, jangling the loose
change in his pocket. An approach. He had to have the right
approach, a feasible story:

*I bought this for a friend and now she's gone off some-
where. Would you like it?*

There was a queue where he could have sworn there
wasn't one five minutes earlier. Kids who didn't know what
they wanted and took forever making up their minds. He
kept looking back to make sure she was still there.

His heart thumped steadily against his ribcage as he asked
for two strawberry splits, and he fought the urge to offer some
explanation to the vendor: for my wife . . . girlfriend . . .
mother. Foolishly unnecessary, and dangerous. Just hand
over the money and walk away.

She was staring out to sea as he approached her. Above,

gulls circled and screeched, and their noise somehow made her seem terribly vulnerable. Overcome by protectiveness, a desire to help and comfort, he bent over her, offering the ice lolly.

"Here . . . Would you like this?"

The child looked up, her eyes narrow, a frown creasing her forehead.

"Piss off!" she said.

2

HE WAS UNUSED to dealing with children. He liked to watch them straggling down the road on their way to or from school, or playing in the park, but he never spoke to them. It just wasn't done these days. Especially for someone with his record. Besides, after a vague curiosity in their play—the strong pack instinct, the youth gang warfare—children held little interest for him. They were a race apart, like the elderly or the mentally handicapped, and to be addressed in much the same way.

He said, "Does your mummy know you use words like that?" and added "dear" uncomfortably .

The child shrugged, eyeing the ice lolly.

"Would you like it? Here . . ."

"Me mum said I shouldn't. She said not to take things from people. Never."

He smiled.

My mother said that I never should
Play with the gipsies in the wood.
If I did, she would say, Naughty girl to disobey.
Your hair shan't curl, your shoes shan't shine.
You gipsy child, you shan't be mine . . .

It was something his grandmother had taught him. He couldn't remember any more.

The child stared at him blankly. "Me mum said I wasn't

to take things from strangers," she repeated, her hand nevertheless ready to snatch the ice.

"If I told you my name then I wouldn't be a stranger, would I? I'm Darren. Here, take this before it melts."

She took it, blew in the wrapper at the stick end to separate paper from lolly, and began to suck. She sucked so hard that she drew out all the coloring at the top, leaving plain ice above the center.

He was content for the moment to sit beside her and watch the sea, because she was content to do the same. There was companionship between them—or so he imagined—and it warmed him.

But moments, warm moments can't last; he knew that well enough to be prepared, when she dug the bare lolly stick into the sand he said, "You haven't told me your name yet."

"I'm not goin' to."

"That's not fair, you know. I told you mine."

"Yeah. Darren. Darren what?"

"Does it matter?"

She shrugged, losing interest. Desperately, he jangled at the change in his pocket. "D'you want another ice cream?"

"No, tah."

"A hamburger, then?"

"Better not. I'll spoil me tea and get wrong."

Newcastle. He had been unsure of her accent until now; Geordie with a smack of East End London. Only Geordie children speak of "getting wrong" when they mean a scolding.

He glanced back at the row of beach huts. There was no sign of the sunburned man or the little boy in the wet pants. "You mean your dad'll be angry?"

"Me dad? Me dad's dead."

"Oh. Who was that you were with just now, then?"

"Nebby."

"Who?"

"Nebby!" The child pointed to her nose, evidently meaning "nebby" was not a name but an instruction for Darren to mind his own business.

She was a loudmouthed, cranky little devil; a disappointment to him. But voices could be softened, foul language and a cranky temper could be governed. She did have poise—after a kind—and cared about her appearance. He could tell so much by the way she kept fussing with the bit of ribbon in her hair. Given time, he might make a little lady out of her.

What was he thinking of? What time did he have, and what business was it of his anyway? The conviction that he was meant to follow her in order to atone for Francie was already beginning to fade, along with the nebulous idea that he could watch over her from a distance. Tomorrow was Thursday. Probably she would be going home at the weekend. And the bruises—well, kids got them all the time, didn't they? They fell in the playgrounds, got into scraps with other kids. It would be madness to assume that every child with bruises was being knocked about at home. Not every child.

"Nicky," she said suddenly.

"What?"

"Me name's Nicky. Well, Nicolle really. Me dad said Mum were going through her French phase at the time." She laughed, appreciating the joke. "Then she decided she didn't like it, and now no one calls me anyfing by Nicky."

"I thought you said your dad was dead?"

She looked at him as if he were being deliberately slow. "He is. But he wasn't then. See?"

"Yes, I see. And where's your mum now?"

"What's it to you? You don't 'arf want to know a lot. She's in 'ospital."

"Hospital. The word's hospital."

Nicky yawned, shivered a little. She should have a cardigan, he thought; her flesh was goose-pimpled. "You're cold. Can't you go and get a woolie?"

"Why should I? I'm not cold. Might go for a swim in a minute."

"Don't be silly. The sea's getting rough. Look, there's no one swimming now."

The wind had changed direction, sweeping rain-threatening clouds across the coastline and sending even the hardiest scurrying to the warmth of indoor entertainment.

"Well, I want to swim." She got up, slipping on her sandals, for the beach was streaked with shingle and broken shells. "I'm gonna go in."

Darren glanced back at the row of beach huts once more. They looked deserted now, wintertime deserted. There was nothing welcoming or even remotely homelike about Seashells, Seaview, or Beachview now that the blue-gray doors were closed against the weather.

"Nicky, don't be silly. It's too cold. . . ."

He followed at a distance, not wanting to alarm her. And there were still plenty of people about who would notice if she started making a fuss. He was acutely aware of his appearance: scruffy in faded jeans cut off at the knee, dirty sneakers, and a T-shirt that bore the words STUFF THE POLL TAX. His brown hair was sea-air dry, unmanageable, and needed a trim. And the peaked cap he wore over it was adorned with Nazi swastika badges. A casual observer would note that he was too young to be Nicky's father and too dissimilar in features to be her brother. The more perceptive would recognize him as a man on his own.

He followed slowly, with difficulty. Only children and the superfit could move easily on such fine sand. To everyone else on a beach the laws of gravity seemed to have been amended.

She kicked off her sandals at the water's edge and waded in up to her calves, arms folded tightly against her chest. Of course it was far too cold, but he was watching and she didn't know how to back down without losing face. Witnessing her indecision was painful, for it was so like Francie. She had been an obstinate little madam, too.

Painful but fascinating. He waited, wondering, longing to know how she would resolve the situation. She didn't have to. Watching the waves rushing back at the sea caused her to lose her balance and she fell, soaking her white shorts. She scrambled up, screaming, and ran back. "Jellyfish!"

Clever, he thought. A clever way of salvaging her pride—and convincing with it.

"Nicky—"

She was already halfway to him, and for a moment he almost held out his arms, but she suddenly sat down on the sand with a sodden squelch a few yards away, sighing as if overcome by tiredness.

"What's wrong?"

"Nothing. Only them bloody jellyfish. Six of them, there was. Seven."

"Don't exaggerate."

"I gotta go." She jumped up, tugging at her wet shorts. "Gotta go. See yer."

"Nicky—"

But he let her go because he had no choice. Probably she would be in trouble for getting her clothes wet, another clout—and there was nothing he could do about it. He stood staring out to sea so that he wouldn't know the exact moment when she disappeared inside that beach hut. Overhead the gulls screeched, mocking him for the fool that he was. Fool to follow a child who reminded him of his murdered stepsister but who, in all probability, was a practiced little liar and juvenile contrickster.

A dead father, a mother in " 'ospital"—God, he had told tales like those himself once. He had haunted tube stations on warm Sunday mornings, switching on the waterworks for likely-looking couples who provided him with pocket money.

Once, he had bought a dressing table set for Francie with the proceeds. A cheap, tawdry set of pink plastic and glass diamonds comprising brush, comb, and a hand mirror with a picture of dancing nymphs on the back. It was the best he could afford, but he loved her and he gave it grandly.

His father beat him. Not just because he assumed the boy had stolen either the gift or the money to buy it, but because he viewed his son's action as a form of weakness, even effeminacy.

Perhaps the old man was right, he thought, wandering along the beach away from the huts and toward the pier. He had never had a normal relationship with a woman. A series of one-night stands, culminating with that girl in Ipswich—he couldn't even remember her name now—whose accusations had landed him in prison. Women. You never knew what they wanted, probably because they didn't themselves. All that business about them always saying No when they meant Yes wasn't a joke; it was a fact of life. They teased you and gave you the come-on. Then . . . Well, he wasn't going to make that mistake again.

Men didn't interest him either. There had been an older boy at the home, Barry, who once climbed into his bed and made him do things. Afterwards he had scrubbed and scrubbed his hands until the skin was raw. But he could never scrub away the memory of how it felt when Barry made him touch down there. It was warm, clammy, and bone hard, like an extension of vertebrae. It reminded him of the cooked turkey neck his mother had given him to nibble on one Christmas Eve.

No, he had no feelings for other men. He wasn't gay. Besides, there had been Francie.

He sighed. He knew he ought to go back to the camper, parked outside the railway station as he'd planned to catch a train to London and spend the evening there. By driving off now, getting as far away from Wheatcliffe-on-Sea as possible, he would be doing himself one hell of a favor. Yorkshire appealed to him; Haworth and the Brontë country. He would visit the pub where Branwell Brontë sat drinking himself to death, and maybe he would do the same.

Somehow, he imagined life must have been easier in those days. Of course, they had things like tuberculosis, and if that didn't carry you off, then you worked yourself into the grave. But at least you didn't have damned social workers at your back every time you got had up for disorderly behavior. And if you were sent down, that was it; His Worship didn't ask for psychiatric reports so that the past could be raked up and rehashed to explain why you went wrong.

"Darren Gillespie is a victim of our times."

"Darren Gillespie is to be more pitied than blamed."

God rot the lot of them—and their pity. They wanted you to get in trouble again, especially the social workers, because it made them indispensable. Well, they were the unbalanced ones, the social misfits. They took up that line of work to gain power over people. What was the latest Rottweiler joke?

Question: *What's the difference between a Rottweiler and a social worker?*

Answer: *With a Rottweiler you have a fifty-percent chance of getting your kid back.*

It was raining. Not heavily, but enough to rouse him from his thoughts. He felt the tension drain from his facial muscles—for he had been scowling—and gave himself a mental shake.

Yorkshire. Yes, that was what he'd do. He'd wander the moors, lose himself, and find consolation in the times when no one thought happiness was a birthright.

That decided, he walked back across the broad beach, now deserted, thinking it might be a good idea to get a snack before returning to the camper. Driving on an empty stomach wasn't good for concentration. The rain wasn't going to last. Already there was a patch of blue sky in the east, and the wind had dropped. His spirit began to revive. Jesus, he must have been mad that afternoon. The episode was distant in his mind now, like a half-remembered night when he'd had too much to drink and woken with a feeling of shame and a sour taste in his mouth. It was wonderful how a few solid plans could buck you up.

His wallet felt reassuringly fat in his pocket. Enough to see him through for a while, and there was no way the notes could be traced. People were fools not to put their money in banks or a building society. Still, this particular fool was dead, and probably no one, not even that sister-in-law of his, knew he'd kept his life savings in the house.

Darren bought a double burger with onions, a can of Coke, and twenty Embassy. As an afterthought, he also bought a copy of the *East Anglian Daily Times* to read while he ate. Sitting on a wall overlooking the mini–golf course he first skimmed the pages, absorbing the headlines quickly. There was no "Man Robbed As He Lay Dying," no "Charley (80) Dies As Heartless Thief Steals His Life Savings."

In fact, Charley had been dead for some time when Darren entered the flat.

No one knew the old man had so much money, 2,100 pounds and 42 pence, stuffed under the mattress. Poor old Charley lay half in, half out of the bed, while the wind howled outside, the television screen flickered silently, and pound coins dropped onto the bare lino. Darren had only called to see how he was.

Cheers, Charley. You won't need it now.

He turned back to the front page and began to read thoroughly. A voracious reader since childhood, Darren could get through anything from *Mayfair* to *Mein Kampf*. Printed matter was there to be read, just as food was there to be eaten, air to be breathed, and authority to be scorned. Now he read the regular features, the kids' section and the readers' letters along with the news.

Fatal mistake. He sat there too long, and just as he realized how low the sun was in the sky he heard her voice—close to him, in his ear.

"Will you take me to the funfair?"

Nicky. She was dressed in black trousers, a thick green sweater, and held a black jacket folded in her arms. She had put her hair up in a ponytail, and the style made her look younger, he thought, like a doll come alive.

"Will you?"

"No, I won't. I thought your mother told you not to speak to strangers?"

"And you said if you told me your name—"

"Never mind what I said. I think I'd better have a word with your mother." He made to get up, thinking she would be afraid of a scolding—or "getting wrong" again—and leave him alone. But she said:

"I told you, me mum's in 'ospital."

"Oh, yes, so you did. And what's the matter with your mum?"

"She's got somefing growing in her stomach."

Darren smiled, softening. The child was at least ten; had no one explained the facts of life to her? "You mean she's having a baby?"

"No. She's got cancer."

She wasn't lying. He could tell she wasn't lying.

"I'm sorry."

"Yeah." She smiled. "But she'll be okay. Miss Miller at school said people don't die of it anymore. Not much, anyway. Will you take me to the funfair?"

"There isn't one."

"Yes, there is. Over there." She pointed in the direction of Dartwick, a resort three miles north, which had lost its reputation for family holidays in the sixties when Mods and Rockers descended on the front to brawl. There was a funfair, a rather grand one it used to be, similar to the Kursaal at Southend. Probably it was nothing special now.

"That's miles out," he told her. "And what about your—your guardian, or whoever he is?"

" 'E won't know. I'll tell him I were on the pier. Then he won't mind."

"Are you sure about that?"

Madness. It was total madness to even contemplate taking a strange child to the fair without her guardian's knowledge.

" 'Course I'm sure. Aw, go on! Please? Please?"

"You can go another day."

"I don't want to go another day. I want to go now. You have to be in the right mood to go to funfairs."

"What do you mean?"

"I dunno. If you won't take me I'll go on me own." She meant it, too.

And what would she do when she got there? Scrounge money off total strangers so she could go on the rides, he supposed.

"Look, I'll take you, but only if you—" The memory of that ill-tempered moron who had Nicky in his care stopped him going on.

Francie, you must always tell us where you're going, who with, and what time you expect to be back.

"Only if you're sure your—he won't mind. And we mustn't stay too long."

"All right. I promise, I promise! Please take me, Darren. Will you? Please?"

They set off, two kids conspiring mischief, to catch the bus to Dartwick, Nicky coltish and trusting at his side like a teenager on her first date.

On the upper deck of the open-topped double-decker he almost came to his senses.

He was taking away a child without her parents' knowledge and permission. He was *abducting* a child. Temporarily, perhaps, for he planned to return her by eight. But abduction all the same.

Nicky chatted away as if to an old friend. The sunburned man was her stepfather, the little boy in the wet pants her half-brother; her mother had become ill after the child's birth. They lived in Bethnal Green, East London, though her mother was originally from Newcastle upon Tyne. Her name was Nicolle Gurney, she was eleven, and her best friend was called Emma-Kate O'Reilly.

Darren absorbed all this without realizing it. What was most obvious on the bus was the child's acute loneliness.

Oh, how well he understood that.

"If anyone speaks to you," he warned as they got off the bus opposite the entrance to Dartwick's funfair, "just pretend I'm your brother. Otherwise, people might think . . ."

She gave him the kind of look children always reserve for adult density. Then she grinned. They were in cahoots.

She wanted to go on all the rides, to all the sideshows. And she had a voracious appetite for funfair junk food. Darren didn't mind. He had more than enough money to stick to his original plan to tour about a bit before the fruit picking began and still give the kid an evening of fun.

Tomorrow he would be miles away, en route to Yorkshire, and the time and space to make more plans.

"Let's go on the merry-go-round," Nicky begged, tugging his arm. "Please?"

"You'll be sick after all that candy floss."

Yet he wanted to ride it, too. There was something unbearably sad about merry-go-rounds. Those painted wooden horses with their wide-open eyes and flaring nostrils, forever going around and around to the pop songs of a year ago. You rode them with your lover, your dearest friend, your children. Sad to sit astride one of those wooden horses when its partner was empty.

"All right," he said, and they stood waiting for the ride to slow and finally stop, while all around the noise of the fair and the smells of hamburgers and sawdust, candy floss and oil made Darren feel unreal and slightly sick.

He helped her up the steps under the glowing lights of the painted canopy and gallantly let her mount one of the outer circle of horses. His was white with a red saddle, hers dappled and with gold. She hugged the wooden neck, jingled the reins, and turned to grin at him.

"See? You have to be in the right mood."

"And are you?" He had to shout. The wails from the ghost train, screams from the roller coaster, and the noise of machinery made conversation difficult. He didn't catch her answer, and the merry-go-round man was ready to start up.

The fairground began spinning about him; the shooting gallery, dodgems, ghost train, hall of mirrors, and shooting gallery again. Rising and falling, she rising as he fell. And Jason Donovan was singing:

> *. . . There's a flame in my heart,*
> *and when you come back to me . . .*

He read her lips, "I love Jason Donovan!" and he laughed with her. The companionship was there, not imagined, as it had been earlier on the beach. The ache was there again, too.

Darren felt giddy. Drunken-happy giddy. Nicky was laughing wildly, oblivious to everything, perhaps even to the voice of her beloved Jason.

> *. . . Oh, how the fire will burn.*

Then they were slowing down, rising and falling in slow motion, and Jason had given way to Kylie Minogue.

"Darren, Darren, can we go again?"

"No, no more. I think we'd better be getting back." He glanced at his watch—and felt hot little prickles of fear on the nape of his neck. It was ten minutes to ten.

"Aw—"

"Nicky, it's nearly ten o'clock. You'll be in trouble. Come on, now." He lifted her off the horse and started to drag her toward the fair's exit.

"Can I have a Coke?"

"No."

"But I'm thirsty. Aren't you thirsty?"

He was. And if he didn't buy her a drink she might start cutting up and draw attention to them both. On the other hand, there were remarkably few taxis in Wheatcliffe-on-Sea, and by the time a bus came along it might be closer to eleven than ten. Had that awful stepfather of hers already noticed she was missing and gone on the warpath? Or worse, telephoned the police?

"All right. We'll have a Coke, then it's straight home."

Home to the camper and safety. What an idiot he'd been.

He'd sleep there for the night now; no sense in moving out at this hour—and with a stomach full of junk. A thought occurred to him as they left the fairground with their ice cold drinks.

"Where do you go at night, Nicky. Have you got a caravan or something?"

"No. We used to, but we flogged it an' now we stay in the hut all night an' sleep on camp beds. You're not supposed to because there's no bogs, but who's to know?" She took a long pull at the Coke, swallowed a belch. "I wanna be sick."

"Oh, shit!"

"Only joking. Can I have a fag?"

"No, you bloody can't! Now come on!"

Her ponytail was half undone, and she removed the bands, shaking her hair free. She looked prettier that way, after all, he decided. "Darren?"

"What?"

"See you tomorrow."

"I'll be gone tomorrow."

"But I don't know anything about you yet."

He was beginning to feel nervous, exasperated. "And that's precisely why you shouldn't have gone off with me."

"You spoke to me first," she reminded him.

"Well, I was wrong. I should have known better."

They crossed the road to the bus stop, the child clinging to his hand because "I don't like roads when it's dark."

"Nicky," he said, squeezing her arm hard to make her pay attention. "Don't you know what can happen to little girls who speak to strangers?"

"Yeah, yeah, yeah. I've heard it all before. From me mum, me teachers, Uncle Tom-bloody-Cobbly. There was even some prat come to the school dressed like a clown an' went on about it."

"Well, it didn't sink in, did it?"

"You wouldn't hurt me."

"Jesus!" He could have shaken her, could have slapped her or done something so ugly she would never forget it. "Jesus

Christ, child! How the hell do you know that?"

She looked at him calmly, like one used to being shouted at. "I just know." Childish instincts at work, perhaps, but still he persisted.

"Nicky, you can't always tell the good men from the bad, you know. People don't go around wearing labels."

"There's the bus! Hey, Darren, do you believe in women's lib?"

"I suppose so. Why?"

"I'll pay our fares."

That was so like her.

No, it was so like Francie. She'd always had a tremendous sense of fairness, of not taking without giving something in return. Once, when Mrs. Tokely made her a dress for the school party, she had spent a whole week scouring the streets and pestering people for cigarette coupons because she knew the woman was saving them for a carriage clock.

He let Nicky pay.

"Darren," she said as they sat in the lower deck of the too-brightly lit bus. "Tah. An' Darren—?"

"What?"

"You're like me dad was. If you 'ad a beard, you'd be just like him."

"*Had*, girl. *Had* a beard." He glanced around at the other passengers; teenagers, most of them, and too preoccupied with their holiday romances to notice anyone else.

He found himself staring out of the bus windows looking for police cars. One did actually pass them, going back in the Dartwick direction, but it appeared to be cruising, on the lookout for drunks and troublemakers, probably. As they approached Wheatcliffe he grew more nervous. Suppose someone had seen him going off with the kid? Someone from one of the beach huts who knew her? The law could have been on the watch for more than four hours.

Nicky seemed nervous, too. Several times he saw her sneaking a glance at her wristwatch. It was now nearly ten-thirty.

When they got off near the row of beach huts, he was expecting the worst: half a dozen cops, organized search parties, and some anonymous voice to shout from the crowd, "There she is! There's the bloke that took her!"

But Wheatcliffe nightlife was proceeding normally, the racket from the amusement arcades being dominant. Everywhere, overtired, overexcited children were screaming for "Just a bit longer! Just another five minutes!"

"I'll see you across the road," Darren said, taking Nicky's arm. But she held back. "Come on, now, Nicky. Don't be bloody awkward."

"No."

"What do you mean, 'no'? Do you want to get me into trouble?"

She shook her head. Yet when he tried to pull her along, she wrapped her arms around a lamppost and clung to it. A group of passersby stared at them curiously, which only flustered him more.

"Okay, cross the road on your own, but be careful. 'Bye, Nicky."

He started to walk purposefully along the road, not looking back. Maybe tomorrow he would return to the beach huts, just to make sure she was okay before he set off for Yorkshire. Right now he could do with a drink. A very large one.

When he left the pub at almost eleven-thirty, she was there waiting for him.

3

"I SHOULD GIVE you a good hiding. Do you know that?"

Nicky shrugged, gave him a deliberate, guilty grin. Evidently she thought herself and her escapade very funny.

"What happened? Haven't you been home at all?"

"No."

"Nicky, don't you realize how late it is? Your stepfather—" He thought of the old bruises on her shoulder. "Won't he be mad at you?"

"Ain't going back. Not till me mum's out of 'ospital, anyway. Can I stop with you till then?"

Darren was suddenly hot, and there was a momentary stillness somewhere deep in his chest. This was how he had felt when Francie died.

"Of course not! I told you, I'm off tomorrow."

"You can take me with you."

He grabbed her shoulders and shook her, shouting, "I can't! Go home, you bloody stupid kid! I don't want you with me! Can't you get that through you head? *Go home!*"

Nicky, so obviously used to being shouted at, started to cry. "I thought you liked me!"

"I do like you, but—" He let go of her. A drunken couple swayed out of the pub door, too far gone, probably, to notice a crying child and the unshaven young man with her. Still, better be safe . . .

Darren led her to a low wall outside the lounge bar and made her sit beside him. "I do like you, Nicky. I like you a lot. You remind me of someone I used to know. That's why

I spoke to you in the first place, and why I agreed to take you to the funfair. But I was wrong. You have to go back to your stepfather and little brother. I can't take you with me because you don't belong with me." She sniffed, scowled at him, and he had a struggle to find the right words. "More than anything, I'd like to have a daughter like you. And then we could go away somewhere until your mum was better—"

"So why can't we just pretend?"

He fought the urge to shout at her again. She was only a child; he had to appeal to her dignity. "Nicky, you're a big girl, almost grown up. You ought to know by now that pretending is only for babies. And besides, if you didn't go back home tonight you stepdad might call the police, and then your mum would find out and be worried. You wouldn't want that now, would you?"

"No. But Mum won't be worried. I could let her know I was okay. I could send her postcards."

"What about your stepdad?"

She stared down at her feet, silent and obstinate. No wonder at that, Darren thought; she must be afraid.

A plan began to form in his mind. If he were to take her back to the camper, just for the night, then in the morning it would be relatively easy to leave her somewhere near the beach huts on the pretense of going off to buy hamburgers for their breakfast. He'd do a fast disappearing act, and by the time Nicky realized he wasn't coming back, had returned to her stepfather—and probably a couple of police officers—he'd be miles away from Wheatcliffe-on-Sea. It wouldn't matter then what story she came up with to explain her absence.

No, it was a stupid idea. The minute she got home she'd drop him in it; not deliberately, of course, but kids like her were always intimidated into talking when the law was involved.

Nicky started to cry again. How odd that she resembled Francie even more closely now. She didn't screw up her face as kids usually did when they were bawling but cried like an adult (or actress?), aware that she was being watched.

"Now you stop all that nonsense. You hear? You're going home."

"I can't find me way back on me own."

"Look, it's only down the end of this street and then you're on the front. You'll see the pier—"

"No-oo! I don't want to go back to him. He ain't me dad. I want me dad!"

"Your dad's dead, Nicky. You told me so."

Then she really began to bawl, a noisy, uncontrolled howling that appalled him. Other people were drifting out of the pub, and this time they were sober enough to notice.

What else could he do? If he ran she would probably be able to keep up with those long legs of hers. If he dragged her into the pub and dumped her on the landlord as a "lost kid," she'd give him away.

"All right, come on. And for God's sake stop that bloody racket."

The racket subsided but didn't stop as he hauled her to her feet and tugged her along in what he hoped was the general direction of Wheatcliffe station and the camper. The town was settling down for the night, and Darren realized that anyone out with a child at this hour was bound to be noticed.

"Where we going?"

"Back to my camper. Where d'you think? Stop sniveling and keep quiet unless you want to get me arrested."

"Do you know where we are?"

"I've got a vague idea. We've got to find the railway station. I'm parked there."

Nicky sniffed. "We came by train. It's near McDonald's, and that's down here."

"You sure?"

" 'Course I'm bloody sure! I know this place, don't I?"

Darren remembered her asking directions that afternoon but said no more. He was frantically working on the plan to dump her in the morning.

*   *   *

The camper was the only vehicle still parked outside the station. It looked suspicious standing there in the dark, and Darren wondered if some cruising cop hadn't already seen it and radioed back to the station to have its number plates checked. Probably a great many of the vehicles stolen by teenage joyriders ended up abandoned in seaside towns.

"That's only a van!" Nicky said scornfully. "Our caravan was bigger than that. Where will I sleep?"

"Stop whining, child. There's a seat in there that opens out to make a bed. You can sleep on that and I'll kip on the floor."

First, though, he had to park somewhere else; find a nice quiet side street, preferably residential, where the camper wouldn't attract attention.

He unlocked the door and switched on the light, vaguely surprised that everything inside looked just as it had that morning. A half-eaten pork pie on the tiny table, yesterday's paper on the floor, and the bucket he used for water to wash in cold and soap-scum-lined in the corner. The last time he had seen these things he was safe, just a guy who had gone wrong, paid for it, and was now a law-abiding young citizen on the lookout for work. Fourteen hours later he was that most hated and feared of all men, the Child Abductor.

"It stinks in here," his guest said. No wonder, for the pork pie, unwrapped the previous evening, had been exposed to the stifling air in the camper all day long. Darren flung it out of the door and, for the want of something better, shook drops from his aftershave bottle around the place to freshen it up.

"All right now?"

"Yeah. Darren, do you live here?"

"No. I've got a flat in Peckham, but I like to travel about looking for work. It'll be apple picking time soon, so I'll do that for a few weeks."

"Haven't you got a wife?"

"No. Sit tight, Nicky, I'm going to find somewhere else to

park." He watched her in the rearview mirror as he started the engine, and he knew now why she wasn't afraid of him; she was even more frightened at home.

He headed north, to the outskirts of the town, and at last found a quiet, dimly-lit lane leading onto a cemetery. There he parked the camper, switched off the ignition, and turned to the business of child-minding.

"Do you need the toilet?" he asked, aware that children did very often.

"No, tah. I went when you was in the boozer."

"Are you hungry, then?"

"No, tah."

"A drink?"

She shook her head, and Darren suddenly remembered to draw the curtains, ill-fitting orange curtains that not only shielded the camper windows but also acted as a partition between the driver and front passenger seats and the rest of the vehicle. Now he was enclosed, trapped with this young girl. The perspiration trickled down his forehead, irritated and itched.

"I'll fix the bed for you, then," he said, still planning, scheming, how to get rid of her in the morning.

She watched as he wrestled with the settee, tugging out the underbelly to make a bed. He slung cushions on it to serve as pillows and a traveling rug for a blanket.

"There. Will that do? Now, you go to sleep and we'll decide something in the morning."

"Turn your back."

"What?"

She glared at him. "I can't go to bed like this, can I? Me mum says only tramps sleep with their clothes on. Haven't you got an old shirt I can wear or something?"

No, he hadn't. Not a clean one anyway. A trip to the laundrette would be top priority tomorrow. Once he was free. "Just take off your trousers and pullover, then. I'll shut my eyes. Promise."

"You better."

That was how Francie used to be. "Don't look," she'd say when they were changing into their swimsuits, "Don't you dare look, Darren." He used to laugh at her, telling her she didn't have anything he hadn't seen before. And the smart-mouth answer was invariably:

"Not on this particular model, you haven't."

He would make a great show of covering his eyes with his hands and then peek through his fingers. He liked to look at Francie's body.

She was so small, so perfect.

Nicky.

As she tugged off her trousers, her back turned prissily to him, her underpants slipped over her bottom. She pulled them back immediately, but not before Darren saw the marks on her. Someone had beaten her severely—and with a stick or cane. His experience told him these wounds were not fresh; a fortnight old at least, and possibly inflicted on the same occasion as her bruises.

She slipped under the traveling rug, all smiles now and apparently wide awake.

"Who do I remind you of?" she asked.

"Just someone I used to know."

"But who? Tell me!"

"She was my stepsister, Frances. Francie. That was why I followed you. Because you look like her."

"Is she dead?"

"Yes." How easily he could say that now. "Yes, Francie's dead."

"We got something in common," Nicky told him cheerfully. "You had a stepsister and I got a stepbrother. No, half-brother. That's different isn't it?"

"Don't you miss him?"

"Our James? No. Why should I? I . . . Darren—?"

"What?"

"If you had a beard, you'd be just like me dad."

"Your dad had a beard?"

"No." The look said that all adults were fools, and she

went on to explain with her child's logic: "Your chin is
different. If you had a beard—well, that'd hide it, and then
you'd be just like me dad."

Darren rubbed the offending chin. Really, growing a beard
wouldn't be such a bad idea: It would lend him enough years
to pass as Nicky's father. . . .

"Tomorrow you're going home," he said firmly. "You
understand that, don't you?"

"Yeah. Darren?"

"What? Go to sleep, for Christ's sake!"

"Can I have a drink?"

"I thought you didn't want one."

"I'm thirsty."

He swore. There was nothing in the cupboard but a
Castlemaine four-pack, and that would be unpalatably
warm.

She pulled a face. "Yuk! It's 'orrible!"

"Well, that's all there is. Take it or leave it."

She took it, guzzled, and belched like an old man. "Cat's
piss."

"Go to sleep."

"Darren . . ."

"Christ Almighty! Now what?"

She grinned. "Tah."

"Go to bloody sleep!"

Her grin became a smile; the smile of love and gratitude,
of friendship, and it hurt him.

Why was it that someone who needed you had such
power?

Nicky closed her eyes, the epitome of obedience, her arms
clinging to the cushions. He waited, listening to her breathing until it became deep and regular.

"Nicky—?" he said softly.

She was asleep. The swift and sound sleep of a child. He
could gather her up in the rug and take her somewhere, leave
her on the steps of Wheatcliffe's police station, get the hell
out of it. Right now.

He switched the camper's lights off and drew back one of the curtains so that he could see her by the streetlamp.

Oh, Francie, I'll make it up to you.

He watched her throughout the night. When she became too warm and tossed the rug off in her sleep, he covered her again.

A toothbrush. She would need a toothbrush. And a change of clothes. He vaguely imagined himself walking into Marks and Spencer's to buy jeans and T-shirts, and maybe a pretty slide for her hair.

Madness. He told himself this was madness. For nothing short of total insanity could lie behind such a plan.

She stirred slightly, made a whimpering sound, and once again Darren felt the odd, momentary stillness in his chest. Suppose she woke, became frightened, and started screaming to be taken home? Children always panicked when they realized they had taken their scrapes too far. He sat close to the bed, ready to clamp a hand over her mouth if she started cutting up.

But Nicky didn't wake, and Darren decided to let her stay uncovered, as that was evidently more comfortable for her. Funny how children all had that same smell about them; a pleasant, warm smell. Funny, too, how in a couple of years' time her little girl's body—now so like a little boy's but for that one detail—would alter so drastically. He liked her the way she was: perfectly formed, neat, smooth, and without a trace of hair but for the thick, honey-colored mop on her head.

He would have liked to touch her, just her forearm, no more. Or perhaps her hand. She had beautiful hands; beautiful but oddly powerful, with the long fingers often associated with musicians and artists.

Darren had once wanted to be an artist. He still kept the picture of a red Indian chief in magnificent headdress that had won him a national children's art competition when he was only ten. His teacher was thrilled and pronounced him "tremendously gifted," but Darren's father did not approve.

"That sort of thing's for girls. You'll be doing bloody knitting next, you little shit."

Then, after it happened, there was no one to encourage him anymore, and he lost interest in painting.

Perhaps Nicky was gifted in some way, too. She was bright, observant, yet immature for her age, as highly strung and clever children often are. What chance would she have with a dying mother and that slob of a stepfather? She'd finish up in a kid's home, as Darren had; and then she could forget all her ambitions and dreams, get herself a dead-end job, a shithouse of a flat, and wait for someone to come along and marry her.

For Nicky life would be a vicious circle.

But if her mother was really going to die . . .

No, there were probably aunts and uncles, grandparents, older cousins: someone to give her a good home. Darren rubbed his forehead. He hadn't drunk all that much today, but the typical stabbing pain of a hangover headache was beginning to nag at his left temple.

If only he could go back in time just twelve hours. Or better still, to the hour when fate put it into his head to stop at Wheatcliffe rather than go on to Clacton or Walton. He finished the can of lukewarm lager and opened another. It didn't help his headache, and Nicky slept on and on.

At last, as it was growing light beyond the orange curtains, he stretched out on the floor beside her bed and managed to fall into a light doze.

It was raining when he awoke. Nicky sat looking out of the window, fully dressed and absently trying to use her fingers as a comb.

"Here, use mine. It's quite clean."

She took it from him wordlessly. No "tah," no grin, and she wouldn't even look at him properly. When he asked if she was hungry, she just nodded, still watching the rain on the windows.

"I haven't got much in the cupboards, Nicky. No cornflakes, nothing like that. We'll have to go out and get something." He looked at his watch. Almost nine. The cafés would be open if not the hamburger stalls. And it was raining; he couldn't dump her outside in the rain.

"Come on. Comb your hair and get your jacket."

"We going home?"

"After breakfast."

"Only if you come with me."

"Jesus Christ, I can't do that! Your stepdad must've called in the police hours ago, and I can't afford to get into more trouble with the law. Nicky—" He placed his hands on her shoulders, squeezing hard, trying to get through to her. "Nicky, I've already been in prison once, and I think I'd die if I had to go back there. That's what'll happen if they catch me this morning. I've kept you here all night. That's called abduction and it's wrong. They'll put me in prison again—"

"But if I tell them, it'll be all right then, won't it?" Her eyes were wide, very frightened. Afraid—for him.

"No, I don't think so. It's still abduction of a minor, and they can send you to prison for it. Look, if I've got you into trouble with your dad—"

"He ain't me dad. Don't call him that."

"All right, all right. Your stepfather, then. I'm sorry if I've got you in a row. I should have brought you back from the fair earlier. But you've made the whole thing much worse by following me, so you must take some of the blame, right?"

"Yeah." She snatched up her jacket, which was slightly too small, and tugged herself irritably into it. "Come on, then. An' I wanna bacon sarnie for me breakfast."

Two bacon sandwiches and two cups of tea meant he had to change the first of old Charley's notes. He told himself again that there was no way they could be traced, but still he felt uneasy about it. The tenner was old, grubby, and long past the state where paper currency is withdrawn. It smelled, too.

"Blimee, mate," the café owner remarked, "spending yer

granddad's life savings or what? Noah must've bought his timber with this."

Darren gave the man a tight, nervous smile. "All I've got, I'm afraid. Might be tatty, but it's still a tenner, right?"

The bacon sandwiches were greasy, the tea tasted stewed, but Nicky wolfed hers down and asked for more. Now was his chance. Finishing off his own sandwich, Darren ordered her another, figuring he had at least fifteen minutes to get away.

But before that there was something he had to know—and some advice he had to give.

"Nicky—" He spoke softly so that the café owner and the two old men who were the only other customers shouldn't hear. "Nicky, I want you to tell me something. I noticed some bruises on your body. Has he been hitting you?"

The child drew invisible pictures on the table with her fingertip. "No-oo."

"Are you sure?"

" 'Course!"

Well, he supposed it wasn't at all uncommon for a kid to deny her stepparent was hitting her. Battered children often felt that they were to blame: He had read that somewhere.

"Nobody has the right to hit you, Nicky. If someone is hurting you, then you must tell your teacher. Don't be afraid. It doesn't have to be your form teacher, but anyone at the school who you like and feel you can trust. Do you understand?"

"No one's hitting me. I fell."

"All right. Here's your sandwich. Eat that up while I go to the loo."

Now. Now was the time. If there wasn't an exit near the lavatories, then he'd have to climb out of a window. The café was in a side street, so the chances were he wouldn't be seen by too many people. And if he were unlucky, well, holiday-makers being what they were, he would probably be mistaken for someone who couldn't pay for his breakfast and simply get laughed at.

Once in the men's he found that he really did need to go, and emptying his bladder, the capacity of which seemed to be about four gallons, took too much time. Too much thinking time.

There was a door in the passage that opened onto an alleyway. He could just leave, he thought, peering out: just saunter away, whistling as a young man might after a good breakfast. He took a step into the fresh air, and the tune that entered his mind was that wretched Jason Donovan song, "When You Come Back to Me."

Perhaps if he had one last quick look at her, make certain she was safe . . . The café owner would see she got home to her stepfather. He crept back, opened the inner swing door a fraction so he could see her. She had her head turned away and seemed to be staring at a badly painted seascape on the wall while her hands toyed at her hair.

The madness swept over him once more, and this time it was that awful, intense kind of madness that dismisses all questions and reason.

Darren Gillespie marched back into the café and grabbed her arm. "Do you want to go home or do you want to stick with me?"

She smiled; a big, bright smile that revealed perfectly even teeth and put the light of mischief and conspiracy in her eyes.

"Come on, then. Let's get out of here."

He led her through the streets of Wheatcliffe-on-Sea, back to the camper, his mind a torrent of plans that, even in temporary madness, refused to run too far ahead. All the while, he was on the lookout for police cars, half expecting someone in uniform to approach him with the words:

"Excuse me, sir. Are you a relation of this child?"

He couldn't know that another two hours were to pass before Nicolle Gurney was reported missing.

4

ALAN RALPH AWOKE at eight, early for him, even on holiday. But then this wasn't a holiday, not in the proper sense of the word, but an escape.

He looked around the beach hut, red-eyed and fuddled. James was still asleep; sea air had that effect on the kid. At home he'd have been up and running around by five at the latest. Hyperactive was how that bitch from Welfare described him, and recommended a diet free from all additives. Those people always thought they knew the lot, but the last straw was when she suggested a child psychologist for the girl. Alan had booted her out and told Lisa finally and forever that she was not to let her into the flat again.

"I know she's been good to you, Leez, but I won't have anyone interfering over the kids."

Now Lisa was . . . was not going to live much longer (he couldn't bring himself to use the word "dying" even in thought), and Alan knew he would be forced to accept help. He didn't quite see himself as a househusband, even if he were prepared to go on the Social. James was far too much of a handful: not yet fully potty trained, always in mischief, and he was going through a phase when his vocabulary seemed dominated by "I want" and "gimme." And then there was Nicky.

Alan stared at her camp bed. It was unmade, of course. As usual. He never fussed about that, though: after all, she was the one who had to sleep in the damn thing. But the heap of blanket looked exactly as it had yesterday. He tried to remember the previous evening. Nicky had come in at five to feed James and get her own tea, then changed her clothes and gone out again. He had taken the boy to the only pub in Wheatcliffe that turned a blind eye to kids in the saloon bar. There he had got steadily drunk, bought half a bottle of Bells, and returned to the beach hut to consume a meat pie and most of the whiskey.

It was ten o'clock, and still Nicky wasn't back. She had a wristwatch, she knew the rules, and yet she went on calmly defying him. Well, this time she'd gone too damn far. Alan Ralph wouldn't have let a sixteen-year-old behave the way she did, hanging round amusement arcades, staying out all hours, giving cheek. Not if that sixteen-year-old had been his own daughter. For Nicky he tried to make allowances, but there had to be rules. You had to draw the line somewhere.

By eleven James was getting droopy. He sat on his bed with his Action Man, a bag of crisps—and probably wet pants— holding his ear the way some children do when tired. In a few moments he would be asleep. Alan, more or less comatose, wouldn't have heard Nicky come in, wouldn't have awoke if he'd fallen out of bed.

Had she been back and gone out again? Alan went through her clothes, but only the things she'd had on yesterday evening—black trousers, matching jacket, and green pullover—were missing. His first feeling was one of relief, for on the two occasions she had run away before, she took clothes and a supply of food. There was no food missing this time. The new loaf of Mother's Pride remained un-opened in the cupboard, the biscuits were still there, and the crisps. So she hadn't run away, which made sense of a sort, for what child runs away at the seaside?

His relief became anger. She'd defied him once too often, and now she was going to be sorry: No more pocket money, no more going off on her own, and if she gave him any lip she'd have a hiding into the bargain.

Alan dressed. That is, he put last night's shirt back on

and replaced his sandals with sneakers because his socks were beginning to smell a bit. Then he put clean pants on James and gave the child a Rich Tea biscuit for his breakfast. He would have liked to dump him on the people in the next hut, but that would have involved too much explanation, so James was placed in his pushchair and wheeled along to the pier.

The arcade was already open but deserted, apart from the woman who sat in a kiosk and gave people change. Most of the machines here were Space Invader type, incomprehensible to anyone over thirty, supposedly addictive, and Nicky's favorite. She spent hours playing them, scorning the moving-shelf machines, where a skillfully dropped penny might win you a dozen, and the sophisticated descendants of the one-armed bandit. There was a "crane" in the corner, once popular in the sixties, now fast disappearing from every resort. The prizes in this machine were far superior to the cheap plastic trinkets Alan remembered from his childhood: plushy mascot dogs and cats, teddy bears and monkeys, even a soft gray koala. Nicky had desperately wanted that koala, he recalled. But after three attempts she realized the toys were too tightly packed for the crane ever to pluck one out, and she gave up in disgust.

Alan approached the woman in the kiosk, described his stepdaughter, and asked if she'd seen her.

"Sorry, love." She sounded bored.

"How about last night?"

"I wasn't here last night. Rita does the evenings. I could have someone ring and ask her if you like, only I doubt she'll be able to help. We get hundreds of kids in here, y'know."

Alan nodded. Probably he would get the same answer at every arcade in town, and his best bet was to ask kids, not adults. Nicky had made friends in Wheatcliffe, at least he had seen her with a gang of young teenagers: girls dressed five years ahead of their age, boys swaggering, some drinking lager and most of them smoking. Still, that was the way kids carried on at home and you couldn't do much about it. It was the drugs you had to worry about, though Lisa, who used to prefer her tobacco green and had experimented with one or two other things, told her daughter so many horror stories about drugs that the child would probably think twice before taking an aspirin.

That was what he most admired about Lisa, right from the start, her openness, her honesty. He was especially pleased that she could talk so freely to him about her first husband.

Paul Gurney was slim, sandy-haired, and softly spoken. When he and Lisa first met, at the birthday party of a mutual friend in their native Newcastle, Paul had the reputation of being a bit wimpish. He refused to take the first job that came along after school just for the sake of money to spend in the boozers or on girls. Instead, he stayed indoors at weekends to study and he went to night classes.

But Lisa didn't think he was a wimp at all. He was unlike the other boys she'd been out with, most of whom thought two vodkas a reasonable price for a fumble in the back of the Cortina. The only problem was Lisa's family. They were of Italian extraction, fiercely proud and possessive—and devout Roman Catholics. After months of misery at home Lisa ran away and married Paul. Three weeks later she telephoned her family, thinking they would at least be happy to know she was safe.

"Living in sin!" her mother hissed, and had nothing more to do with her. She wasn't there to celebrate Paul's new job, his rapid promotion, their move into a spacious new flat, or the birth of her first grandchild. It took her son-in-law's death, in a road accident, to bring about a reconciliation; and even then all she could say was, "Well, it's probably for the best."

Lisa grieved, but only as one grieves for the loss of a friend. Any deeper feeling for Paul had long faded, and while she never stopped admiring his drive and ambition, he was so dull. She knew now that her marriage had been an escape from her parents and the girl they wanted her to be. What *she* wanted was fun, dancing, parties—all the things that had been frowned upon in her teenage years.

With Nicky's birth she was bound to the house more securely than ever. But what made it worse, so much worse, was the jealousy she felt over the child's relationship with her father. Paul took her out every weekend, played with her, talked to her, even taught her to read before she started school.

"Turning her into a right little swot," as she told a friend, and realizing perhaps for the first time that she was Paul's intellectual inferior.

That dull Thursday morning when the police came to the door she had been getting ready to see Alan. She wore her best dress, the one Paul bought for her birthday, and not the kind of thing you put on to slop around the house. The young officers stared at her in dismay and confusion.

"It's Paul, isn't it?" she said, and began to cry.

"There's no point waiting any longer," Alan Ralph told her. "It's been over a year, Leez."

"I know, love. But I keep thinking about his parents. And then there's Nicky . . ."

Alan disliked the effort of reasoning. He wanted a straight yes or no without the dithering. Still, if you wanted something badly enough you had to make the effort. And he wanted sweet, pretty Lisa with her girlish sense of fun, her energy.

"Look, his parents wouldn't want you to stay a widow all your life, and neither would he. As for Nicky, she'll come round. Kids always do. She needs a dad."

At last, Lisa agreed and married him. Even her mother was pleased; Alan Ralph had no airy-fairy ideas about himself, he worked hard, and a lapsed Catholic had to be better than a Protestant—whatever Father Halloran said.

Paul Gurney and Alan Ralph were poles apart, and while Lisa knew it and was glad, her daughter knew it as well and she shrank from her stepfather.

He was a tall, solidly built man with already thinning hair and a voice that boomed down the street when he came home from work. When he sang, as he often did, his voice lost its East End London accent and took on the twangs of the American South.

Skies are not so black, Mary took me back,
Mary has broken your spell.
Oh, Devil Woman . . .

He worked as a garage mechanic and generally smelled of oil and perspiration. Even when he and Lisa went out together, the smell lingered about him, and he considered aftershave strictly for the poofters. He went boozing regularly, got into the odd brawl, did and was everything, in fact, that Lisa had once despised in the local lads.

Just as Lisa became pregnant again Alan heard of a job going in his native East London. The pay was better, he told her, with plenty of overtime; and what was more, his cousin knew of a flat going cheap in one of the quieter streets off the Roman Road. He could pull a few strings if Alan liked.

They took the job and flat, and two months later Nicky ran away. At first, it seemed that she'd been abducted, lured away from the children's playground by some pervert offering sweets and the promise of seeing some puppies, to finish up one more miserable statistic. The Ralphs faced television cameras to plead for their child's safe return. They had seen other couples going through the same ordeal and were only too aware of how their stories ended.

But later, Alan told Lisa what he had half suspected all along. "I reckon she's run off, Leez."

"Run away? But where to, for God's sake?"

"How should I know? Up West, probably. That's where they usually go, isn't it?"

"But she didn't take anything with her—no clothes or anything. I checked, remember?"

"Not thoroughly enough, love. I reckon there's two pairs

of jeans missing and two pullovers; the one my sister knitted and the old blue one—her favorite. There's biscuits gone from the cupboard—and fifteen quid from my wallet. I haven't been anywhere since she went, except to the TV place, so I didn't notice the money gone right away. Leez, we ought to ring the law."

"No! No—I mean, that'd bring in the bloody social workers and everything else. I don't want them poking and snooping in our lives. Once they're through that door they're here for good. Alan, you must know what those people are like? They'll think she ran away from you, her stepfather, and then they'll be round here every time her school grades go down, every time she falls over and gets a bruise—"

"Lisa!" Alan Ralph's voice stopped her short, frightened her; never had he lost his temper with her before. "She's your kid, for Christ's sake! What does all that matter so long as we get her back safely? No, it's no good, love. I'm going to ring the law and tell them what I think."

Alan telephoned the police, and three days later Nicky was found, tired and filthy, eating a saveloy and chips out of newspaper in Euston station.

Lisa Ralph did indeed receive a visit from the Social Services, but she managed to persuade them that the child had been trying to get to Newcastle because she missed her friends there. "Her dad and I have promised to take her up for a weekend visit," she added.

Nicky's next escapade was shorter-lived, and this time Alan found her at Liverpool Street, about to board a train for Wheatcliffe-on-Sea. She had given herself away by telling her best friend, Emma-Kate O'Reilly, of her plans.

"If you run off again you'll be put in a home," Lisa threatened, "because I can't have the worry of you anymore."

Alan thought that rather harsh, and they had a furious row about it.

"I don't believe it!" his wife had screamed. "You're taking her part!"

"I'm not taking anyone's part. She's your kid, Leez. You

ought to know her better than anyone else. You ought to know how to handle her. Sometimes I wonder if you even care."

Lisa Ralph did care, but she was already terminally ill.

She was finally admitted to St. Veronica's on the third Sunday in August, thin but swollen-bellied, pale, and in a lot of pain.

"Don't bring them again," she told Alan that Sunday evening when he had kissed her goodnight and a trembling Nicky was already propelling her brother through the ward door. "I don't want them to see me like this."

The next time he went alone, leaving the kids with a neighbor. He brought fruit and chocolates, knowing she would never eat them, a bundle of magazines she would never read, and a new nightdress she would never wear.

Lisa glanced at them briefly, said thank you, but couldn't smile. The depression that descended on her after the nightmare of the diagnosis had returned, bringing with it fear and despair because she'd fought and lost. She'd had a lot of faith in alternative medicine: relaxation therapy, something called visualization, and a special diet consisting of nothing but grapes and organically grown carrots. She'd taken up jogging, swimming, and even weight lifting. All for nothing.

They discovered the tumor during a routine examination after James's birth, and an exploratory operation proved it to be malignant; inoperable, they told her, and gave her six months to live. At the time she prayed for a while longer, for long enough to get to know her son and try to bring Nicky and Alan together as father and daughter. Nicky, true to her obstinate nature, refused to have anything to do with him, and Alan gave up trying. And while those two bonus years—maybe years brought about by luck rather than the grapes and carrots—gave Lisa her wish as far as James was concerned, she now felt she had been selfish.

"He'll remember me now," she said. "And that might

unsettle him later on. It'd have been better if I'd died when he was a baby."

"Don't say that, Leez. Don't." He wanted to touch her, help her as she made a halfhearted attempt to run a comb through her hair, but he found he couldn't bear to. God, she didn't even look like his Lisa anymore.

"And Nicky. What's going to happen to her?"

"I'll look after her, love, don't you worry. We'll manage." He felt sick inside; this was the first time he had admitted to the fact that she was going to die. For what do you say to someone who has fought so hard and won so many battles, only to lose the war? You tell them not to be silly, and of course they'll get well.

"I want you to take them both away," Lisa said. "Take them to Wheatcliffe. Make a holiday of it." She reached awkwardly into her locker and pulled out a fat white envelope. "This is a letter for Nicky. I want you to give it to her after the—the funeral."

"Leez—"

Her hand touched his. The fingers were bony, swollen at the joints like those of someone with arthritis, but were still reassuringly warm. "Take them away, Alan. The break will do you all good. And don't look at me like that. I'll see you again. When you come home, bring the kids to the back of the hospital so I can wave to them. I will see you again, love."

So far as her husband was concerned Lisa was right. But she had already seen her daughter for the last time.

Alan trudged around the arcades of Wheatcliffe, pushing an increasingly irritable toddler before him. The child wanted the beach, his toys, and his sister. The only thing those two had in common, his father thought, was their independence, a seemingly total disregard for parental anger, pleasure, even love. It was more pronounced in the boy, who had a tremendous capacity to amuse himself and to shut himself off from whatever was going on around him. He preferred

Nicky's care, though she fed and changed him in a perfunc-
tory manner, performing these chores in much the same way
another child might tidy its room. Alan supposed this trait
to be inherited from Lisa, the girl who had defied her parents
and priest to marry Paul Gurney.

His inquiries at the arcades were met mostly with bored
indifference, and once with outright suspicion, even though
he was careful to explain that the child he was looking for
was his daughter. He wished the pubs were open; a quick
drink might help him clear his still rather hung-over
thoughts—a hair of the dog. The next best thing was a seat
outside The Shipmates' Arms, the same spot occupied by
Darren Gillespie when he first saw Nicky less than twenty-
four hours previously.

Alan checked the contents of his pockets and wallet. He
couldn't actually remember how much money he'd spent
last night, and therefore had no way of knowing if the girl
had "borrowed" any, as she had on previous occasions. But
she had her holiday money, and he supposed there was
enough of that left to get her back to London. And he was
sure now that this was what had happened. She had stayed
out so late that she was afraid to come home, probably slept
in a doorway or under the pier, and caught the first train
back to town. She had no key to the flat, and so she must
have gone to Emma-Kate O'Reilly's place.

Alan had to get Directory Enquiries to find the O'Reilly
number, and when Emma's mother told him Nicky was
certainly not there he had to dial 192 again to find the
number of St. Veronica's. He was sweating by now, and when
the switchboard put him through to D3 and he found
himself speaking to the battle-ax sister, he thought his legs
would give way.

"No, Mr. Ralph, we haven't seen her here." Sister sounded
wary, and he could picture her face; sharp eyes and mouth
like fruit in a mound of overrisen dough. "How long has the
child been missing?"

"I'm not saying she's missing," he said quickly.

"Oh, but I understood you were at Wheatcliffe. Your wife said—"

"Yes, well, I'll ring you back later. Don't say anything to Lisa. I don't want her worried." And he replaced the receiver before she could suggest contacting the police.

What to do next? He had been to every arcade in town, looked in every shop that he thought might attract her, and the only course left was to return to Beachview. If she wasn't there he would call the police. Then it occurred to him that she would be hungry. Knowing her, very hungry. There were only two cafés in Wheatcliffe: one the Jolly Roger on Frontside, the other a greasy little place called Chish and Fips, situated between a baker's and the betting shop. Alan chose to visit the latter first because it was nearest and because that was where the youngsters went in the evenings.

He had little hope of finding her, or of the staff remembering her, but it filled in time and enabled him to delay the moment when he would have to pick up the telephone again.

Two men who might have been truckies sat eating sausages and chips with double bacon and beans under a seascape on the wall. In one corner a young couple were sharing a sandwich, and in another an old man dunked a teabag in his cup. Alan maneuvered the pushchair past tables and found a seat as far away from the other customers as possible. He stomach grumbled loudly, sounding more like a fart than anything, and he coughed to hide it.

Chish and Fips was an almost legendary café of fiction; the kind of establishment you see portrayed in sixties films or read about in sexy paperbacks, but that didn't—or wasn't supposed to—exist anymore. The waitress didn't have a cigarette dangling from her lips or obviously bleached hair, but she slouched. And when she wiped the table her cloth left zigzags of grease. Alan ordered beefburgers and chips—another pigeonholing device—though he was terribly hungry. Sick with hunger and in charge of a child.

When the food came he asked the waitress, who wore the nametag "Sharon" on her blue overall, if she had seen a young girl fitting Nicky's description that morning or the previous evening.

"No good asking me," Sharon told him. "That all? Don't you want tea or something?"

"No. Look, this is important. She's my daughter."

"Then maybe you ought to call the police. See, I've only just got here. I don't start till ten. Tell you what, you eat up an' I'll have a word with the ol' man." She slouched back behind the counter, flat heels slapping the lino, leaving a trail of Lentheric and fried onions behind her.

Alan ate savagely, stabbing at the chips and beefburgers, once or twice offering a tidbit to James, who wasn't interested. Alan Ralph never suffered a hangover so severe he couldn't face food before noon.

"A stomach like stainless steel," Lisa used to say.

Lisa . . . Whatever would he tell her?

The café owner crept up on him, tea towel in hand and sullen, his expression that of a chef at a top-class hotel whose masterpiece had just been criticized by a tart in a fun fur.

"Hear you've lost a kid?" he said, as if speaking of a mislaid umbrella, and Alan described his stepdaughter for what seemed the hundredth time that morning.

"She had her hair in a ponytail the last time I saw her," he added. "But when it's loose I suppose it's about shoulder length."

The café owner studied his face suspiciously. "And you say she's your kid?"

"Stepdaughter. Have you seen her?"

"There was a kid like that in earlier on. With a young bloke, she was. Scruffy, like. Y'know?" He shook his head. "Tell yer what, mate, I reckon you oughta call the law."

▽

5

THE FLAT SMELLED stale, felt damp even in the warmth of late August. He had been absent for one week, yet the place had that deathly, long-deserted air he remembered from when he first returned to it on leaving prison.

Nicky lay fast asleep in the camper, and he was thankful for that; he didn't want to be seen returning with a child in tow. And, if he were honest with himself, he didn't want her smart-mouth comments when she saw his home. He glanced at his watch; just gone half past five. It wouldn't be prudent to hang around too long in case Nicky awoke and wandered out of the camper looking for him, but he must watch the television news.

He entered the bedroom—which wasn't so much untidy as twelve-by-twelve foot of squalor—and dragged a suitcase from under the bed. The case contained one green sock, a copy of the *Penguin Book of Sick Verse,* and a travel clock that no longer worked. Darren rooted through cupboards and drawers, flinging some clothes into the case, others on the floor: jeans, T-shirts and pullovers, a spare pair of trainers, and, of course, about four dozen pairs of socks. Clean socks were as important to him as having money in his pockets: He was only content with a large supply of both. He possessed neither a suit nor a proper shirt, but his cupboards held piles of books. Lost without something to read, especially old favorites, he packed Shute's *No Highway* and a biography of Branwell Brontë along with the sick verse.

In the kitchen he filled a Londis carrier bag with tinned

food and an ancient radio, the batteries of which were held
in place with Sellotape. On second thought, he left the radio
behind. If Nicky's disappearance became national news, as
it surely must, the last thing he needed was for her to find
out about it. He went and switched on the television,
fidgeting through the commercials and waiting with a heart
that seemed to beat abnormally, irregularly fast for the news
headlines.

"German Chancellor says Europe . . ."
"Prime Minister cuts short his visit to . . ."
"And the child missing from Wheatcliffe-on-Sea—her
stepfather appeals for her safe return."

The child missing. Nicky. It was official now. It was real.
While someone translated the chancellor's speech to the
Bundestag, and while the Prime Minister acknowledged the
press before entering Number Ten, Darren stood by the
window looking down on the camper. He wondered how many
people in Princess Royal Road were watching the early-evening
news just now: how many people could look out of their
windows, as he was doing at this moment, and see the
blue-and-white vehicle in which The Child Missing was—
hopefully—still fast asleep.

He turned his attention back to the television, where a
picture of Nicky flashed onto the screen beside the news-
caster. Obviously it was an old photograph, taken a year or
even two years ago, for it showed a plumper child with short
hair and a fringe that hid her distinctive forehead.

"Nicolle Gurney, missing from her holiday home in
Wheatcliffe-on-Sea since Wednesday evening, may have
been abducted by a man in his early twenties," announced
the serious-eyed young woman. *"Eleven-year-old Nicolle,*
known as Nicky, was last seen by her stepfather, Alan Ralph,
at approximately six-thirty PM *outside the family's beach*
hut. But a café owner has reported seeing a girl matching

Nicky's description in the company of a young man the following morning. . . ."

"They came in my caff around nine o'clock," said the man who had served the greasy bacon sandwiches. "Kid about eleven or twelve, fairish hair, quite pretty; the bloke about twenty-three or -four, I should reckon. Looked like he could do with a wash an' change of clothes. They had a sandwich an' a cuppa each—he changed the filthiest tenner I've ever seen—then he buys the kid another sarnie an' goes out back to the loo. He was gone so long I thought he weren't coming back. Seemed to me the kid were nervous—scared, like."

Of course she was, Darren thought savagely. She was afraid he had abandoned her to that stepfather of hers.

The stepfather who now had a name. Alan Ralph.

He was strangely pleased that Nicky had kept her own father's name.

"Then," concluded the café owner, "he suddenly marches back, grabs her by the arm, an' drags her out the door."

The Photofit, Identikit, or whatever it was called these days, showed an unkempt young man with an evil expression, and bore only a vague resemblance to Darren Gillespie. Less resemblance, in fact, than the stepfather bore to the man now speaking on the television. He was neatly dressed in a blue jacket and white shirt, his sparse hair carefully combed. His eyes were restless; not restless with anger, but with the desperation of a man who can take no more.

"I shouted at her," said Alan Ralph. "The last time I saw her I shouted at her. My wife is ill in the hospital. She's got cancer and they can't do no more for her. Now I've had to tell her Nicky's gone missing."

Darren watched the man contemptuously as he whined on about how Nicky had never accepted him, how she missed her own father too much, and how she resented her little brother because she associated his birth with the onset of her mother's illness. He was a good actor, give him that. And Darren felt a momentary pang of sorrow for Nicky's mother. But it was only momentary; the woman must have known her husband was knocking the kid around, just as Marsha knew what was going on with Darren's father and Francie.

What kind of mothers were they? What kind of woman could stand by and do nothing while her husband beat the kids?

"If someone has taken her," Alan Ralph concluded, "all I ask is that they think of her mother. She hasn't got much longer. . . . Please, please bring Nicky back. Or take her somewhere she'll be found. Leave her where someone'll find her and bring her home—"

Darren rose and switched off the television, pulled out the plug. Perhaps he should turn the electricity off completely; he didn't know when he'd be back. There were photographs in the sideboard drawer he wanted to take as well; an old album bound in brown leather with Gainsborough's "Blue Boy" on the front. He wanted to show it to Nicky. He raced around attending to these things, anxious to get back on the road. There were no bills to be paid, no messages to be left. For a moment he thought of Mike Southgate, until recently his social worker and archinterferer. At times he despised the man, on the principle that he despised all social workers. But there were also times when he found himself almost liking him—especially since he'd lost his job; and yet others when he felt inexplicably uncomfortable in Mike's presence. No, he wouldn't leave a message for him. After all, he'd told just about everyone that he'd probably go fruit picking, and it was likely Mike assumed him to be slaving in some strawberry field at this moment.

He decided to leave behind his shaver, forgotten on the bathroom windowsill when he departed for Wheatcliffe a week ago, and grow a beard. To please Nicky. With a beard and a bit of luck he might pass for twenty-eight or -nine; a very young father. Now there was nothing left to do but return to the camper. He paused a moment to look at the flat, his grandparents' flat left to him in Nan's will, and a

strange, numbing feeling enveloped him. He tried to mem-
orize the front room, to photograph it with his mind. It was
the closest he'd had to a real home since Francie died. Sad
in a way to leave it. Sad and cold. Standing in the doorway
he trembled, more afraid than he'd ever been in his life
before.

She was still asleep when he returned to the camper,
exhausted after yesterday he supposed. He had taken her up
to Blythwold, mainly for the want of a better idea, but also
to give himself time to think. Blythwold was not a great
attraction for holidaymakers, despite its stretch of unpol-
luted sea and fine beach. Affluent Victorians had built their
houses there or sent ailing relatives there to convalesce, and
it had not lost its reputation for the chilly North Sea winds
that probably killed a good many of them off. There were no
amusement arcades or funfairs at Blythwold, nothing for the
children but an adventure playground and a bubble gum
machine on the wall outside the post office.

Nicky would almost certainly have grown bored with a
week there, but one day was all the time Darren felt able to
spare. He needed to get back to the flat and collect a few
things that would be necessary to him if he was going to be
away a long time. Perhaps he should consider putting the
flat on the market and starting fresh in another part of the
country. At the end of the day his plans were still nebulous;
he realized that whatever he decided it would always, needs
must, be subject to a moment's change.

They stayed at Blythwold overnight, breakfasted late on
Nicky's scrambled eggs, and finally headed back to London
after lunch.

"I've decided," he told her. "We're going apple picking."

Now, once again heading northeast, he hadn't changed
his mind. The café owner had probably known Nicky from
a description of the clothes she was wearing when she
disappeared (she was now dressed in jeans and a T-shirt he'd
bought her that morning). But who would recognize her
simply from the photograph shown on the television news?

*   *   *

He'd hoped the motion of the camper would keep her asleep at least until they were out of town. But the rush hour, which was closer to three hours these days, meant that he had to keep stopping and starting—sometimes stalling—at the lights, and before long the child was clambering over the seat to join him in the cab.

"Get back, Nicky. Someone might see you."

"No! I wanna sit with you."

"Do as you're told."

"No, I wanna sit here. It's boring in the back on me own."

He fought the impulse to shout at her, reasoning that anyone on the streets now probably hadn't seen the early-evening news. "All right. But sit properly. Put the seat belt on."

"Where we going?"

"Out of town."

She stiffened. He could feel the tension, even though no part of her body was touching his. "I know where we are," she said. "Darren, I know this road. Are we off to see me mum?"

"No." He fumbled with the gear change, causing the engine to roar in response. "We're not stopping. Put that belt on."

"I wanna see me mum! Darren, I wanna see me mum! Stop, Darren! Stop right here!"

He drove on, vaguely recognizing a street that led to Bethnal Green's Roman Road and knowing that the hospital caring for Mrs. Ralph must be close by. He would have to do some quick thinking if he wanted to shut her up. Or—or should he just let her go?

If he let her out he would be free of her. But then she might give him away; not deliberately, of course, but under pressure from the police. The familiar alleyways of old arguments—hadn't he gone over them already a hundred times in his mind?—but now a new truth.

He didn't want to let her go.

He drove along Roman Road, past the fire station, past the market square, pacifying her demands to stop with a quiet "Wait a minute. Wait." Finally he parked in a narrow cul-de-sac with rows of flats branching away on either side and terminating in a Victorian archway, the entrance to a park.

"Do you know where we are now?" he asked her.

" 'Course I do. I play here sometimes. Our flat's over that way." She pointed vaguely, and Darren felt prickles of fear on the nape of his neck. So close! She could easily find her way home from here.

A small Indian child in a pink tracksuit and riding a squeaky pink bike circled under the archway. She rode one-handed, the other hand holding an ice lolly.

"Jamilla," Nicky said.

"Oh, Christ! Do you know her?" Darren's hand reached for the ignition.

"Not really. Her sister's in my class. Can I go an' see me mum?"

The temptation was strong; and he did, in fact, lean past her to open the door. "Mind the roads."

"Aren't you coming with me?"

"I can't, Nicky. I thought I'd explained it to you, that they'd arrest me. I thought you understood."

"But you'll wait for me?"

All he had to do was say, Yes, he'd wait, then drive away as soon as she was out of sight. But he told himself that would be a betrayal; she trusted him.

"They won't allow you to come back. You'll have to go home to your stepfather."

Nicky pulled the door shut slowly, provisionally. "Me mum'll be worried if she don't know where I am."

"Yes, she will. So, what do you want to do?"

"We-ell, she doesn't want to see me, anyway." She pulled the neck of her T-shirt over her chin and began to chew on it.

"I don't think that's true, Nicky."

"Yes, it is. That's why we went off to Wheatcliffe. She

didn't want me to see her in 'ospital. An' I don't want to. Not really. But she'll worry, Darren."

The child in the pink tracksuit had paused in her aimless circling and was watching them. Did she recognize Nicky? In his desperation, Darren said, "I suppose you could phone the hospital. Do you know which ward she's in?"

"D-three."

"Okay, let's do that. Do you know where there's a call box? In one of the side streets, maybe?"

"Yeah, 'course. Back out an' turn left." She fastened her seat belt without having to be told, obedient as only a child close to getting its own way can be, while Darren followed her directions.

When he thought about it later he could hardly believe the great calmness that descended upon him as he swung the camper once more into Roman Road; how it obscured his earlier panic completely.

He didn't want to let her go.

"Nicky," he began, thinking rapidly as they drove along, "is there someone in your family—a young man of about my age?"

"My cousin Martin. Why?"

"Never mind. Now, where's this phone box?"

He had to dial Directory Enquiries to get the number of St. Veronica's, scribbling it on the inside of his wrist with a leaky Biro. "Are you sure it's D-three?" he said.

" 'Course I am. Will I be able to speak to her, Darren? Will I?"

"I don't know. That's why I'm pretending to be your cousin, so they put me through. Is his name Gurney as well?"

"Yeah, but Darren—"

"Never mind but. Now you listen, Nicky. . . ." He hunched down beside her as if she were a much younger child. "This is the plan, right? You can stick with me until your mum's out of hospital, then I'll bring you back here. That's what you want, isn't it? You don't want your stepdad looking after you, do you?" And when she shook her head, "Then you have to trust me and do exactly as I tell you. If you get to speak to your mother you mustn't give her my name or anything. Just say you're all right and you're with friends, okay?"

"Okay. But Darren, I don't think you ought—"

"Shut it, Nicky." He dialed the hospital and asked for D3, ignoring her as she stamped her feet and pulled faces in an effort to gain his attention.

The voice that answered was cheerful and young. She would go and ask Mrs. Ralph if she wanted the telephone trolley brought to her bed, but Mr. Gurney would understand if she didn't feel up to speaking under the circumstances.

Darren juggled single-handedly with his loose change, lining up ten-pence pieces ready, while Nicky tried to snatch the receiver from him. At last he heard voices in the background, and then:

"Martin! Is that really you? Surely you can't afford to phone all the way from Adelaide?"

Adelaide? Darren glared at Nicky.

"Mrs. Ralph, it's not Martin, and I have someone here—" Then the receiver was snatched from his hand.

"Mum? It's me. . . . Of course it's me! No, no, I'm okay. Honest. What? A friend." Darren held his head close to Nicky's in order to hear, at the same time placing his hand on her shoulder to squeeze a warning if necessary. When the pips went he thrust another coin in the slot.

"Nicky, love, where are you?" The woman's voice was clear, but wavery and weak; the voice of a sick and dying person. Her daughter looked at Darren for guidance, and he shook his head sharply.

"Not far away, Mum."

"That man—has he been—you know—doing things to you?"

"No, Mum. He's my friend."

"Let me talk to him. . . ."

Darren would have obliged, although reluctantly, because

however negligent the woman had been as a mother she was almost certainly dying and deserved a scrap of reassurance, at least. But Nicky clung to the receiver with both hands, and he would have had to ply her away one finger at a time. Instead, he shouted into the mouthpiece.

"Look, I didn't abduct her, Mrs.—" He had forgotten the name. "And I'll take better care of her than he would."

She must have heard him, but she was silent for a moment. Then, "Nicky, you've been up to your old tricks again, haven't you? And you promised me you'd behave."

"I don't want to come home till you're well again."

"Nick, I'm not going to get well."

"But you're coming home?"

Now there were other voices in the background. Darren couldn't hear what they were saying, but the tone was questioning, and when Lisa Ralph muttered, "Yes, yes," he realized they would try to have the call traced. They were urging the woman to keep Nicky talking while someone called the police, who would in turn get onto the local exchange. But the whole process must take at least four minutes, maybe longer.

He looked up and down the street. It was very quiet with no sign of the old bill, even the mounted version, which seemed to patrol this part of London more than any other. And they were sheltered in the booth by the camper, which he had parked half on the pavement. Still, better not to hang around.

"Nicky, get a move on!" He shook her almost roughly.

"Mum . . . ?"

"Yes, I'm still here."

"You sound funny. Your voice sounds funny."

"I'm just having a bit of pain, that's all. Nicky—"

"I want to come an' see you. You'll bring me, won't you, Dar—" A sharp squeeze of her shoulder cut her short. "He'll bring me, Mum."

"No, Nicky. He mustn't do that."

Again Darren could hear the voices, again Lisa Ralph muttering; it sounded like, "I don't want her to see me like this."

"Nicky, let me talk to your—friend."

"No! No!" She was growing agitated, stamping her feet alternately as if they were cold.

"I want you to go home to Alan."

"No! He ain't me dad! I ain't going home till you're home!"

Darren shook her again. "We have to go now. Say good-bye."

"Mum! Let me come and see you!"

"I've said no. Now, let me speak to whoever it is you're with."

This time she surrendered the receiver easily, a kind of defeat about her.

"We have to go now," Darren said, speaking rapidly and in the London-Irish accent he was familiar with from the pubs in his neighborhood.

"Let her go," Lisa Ralph pleaded. "If it's true what she says, that you're not holding her, then let her go. Leave her somewhere my husband will find her."

"Send her back to him? I've seen the way he treats her."

The pips sounded, and in the few seconds' grace before the connection was broken, he heard her say, "Oh, Nicky, I'm so sorry."

The child was crying. Not noisily, but miserably, and he had to lift her up and push her back into the camper, where she sat cross-legged on the floor and covered her face with one of his dirty shirts.

Darren pulled out of the side street and back into Roman Road. As he passed the fire station he saw a police car speeding toward him, and he was in no doubt whom they were looking for. They were not sounding the siren—obviously, as that would alarm him—but the speed alone was enough to tell anyone their business was urgent. One of the officers seemed to look at Darren as they sped by the camper, and with Nicky safely hidden in the back he did what most drivers do when encountering the law—checked his speedometer and automatically slowed down. It was a natural reaction, and he felt rather proud of himself; a few days ago he would have panicked. He remembered the morning a paper boy had peered through the window of old Charley's flat, seen his body, and called the police.

"I told 'em the old geezer were a mate of yours," said the boy. "That were all right, weren' it?"

"Yes, of course." Darren gave him a couple of quid. Half the neighborhood knew he sometimes ran errands for the old man, but did even one know he kept his savings under the mattress?

The police questioned him twice, probably as a little exhibition of their power, for they didn't hesitate to remind him of his prison sentence. And throughout the interview he had trembled and blustered, not knowing where or how to place his hands. But a postmortem showed that Charley had died from natural causes, and no mention was ever made of his having money in the flat.

Darren had always been one of those people who blushed if a police officer so much as looked at him, even before his arrest. So when he saw the panda car fading into the traffic through his rear mirror, he was amazed at himself for being so calm. Perhaps because he had been so often on hot bricks since Wednesday evening, he was becoming immune to fear. Or could it have something to do with the conversation between Nicky and her mother? It had been a dialogue somehow incongruous with the situation, at least to Darren's mind.

I've said no . . .

Why hadn't the woman said, Yes, come to the hospital? Even if her appearance was cadaverous in the terminal stage of her illness and she really didn't want Nicky to see her, someone would have stopped the child before she reached the ward, and her mother would have known she was safe.

He called over his shoulder, "Nicky, you okay?"

"Yeah." She didn't ask, as he thought she might, to be

allowed up front with him; or even demand to know where they were going.

She would feel better when they were out of town again, when there was some distance between her and her mother. After all, she was content enough to be with him before they returned to London.

He drove northeast, through the suburbs of Gidea Park, Harold Wood, on in to Essex. His stomach was growling, and Nicky must be hungry too: Neither had eaten since two o'clock, and that had only been a sandwich. Darren didn't feel up to preparing a meal now. He was mentally and physically drained, and what little energy he had left must necessarily be saved to concentrate on driving. The best plan would be to find a pub that served cooked meals and had a garden—preferably a large garden with a dozen families present and all too intent on their own pleasure to notice one kid swarming with the rest.

Nicky's head peered around the orange curtains just then to announce that she was "starving."

"Either you're a mind reader or your stomach is."

"When we gonna eat, then? Where are we?" Her face was streaked from crying and grubby, but she seemed perky and quite happy.

"We're in Essex. Just passed a place called Ingatestone. And we'll eat as soon as I find a pub."

"We're goin' in a pub?" she squealed.

"Not in the pub. You're too young. We'll find one with a garden or a room where kids are allowed, right? Wash your face, Nicks. You're filthy."

And once fed, she was going to give him a few answers.

"You've run away before?"

"Twice. Me picture was in all the papers the first time round. I were famous!"

"Infamous, maybe. But why, Nicky? It was because of him, wasn't it? Your stepfather?"

"Yeah. Darren, can I have another Coke?" She looked up

at him slyly, twisting a strand of hair around her forefinger.
Already, he knew this to be the indication of a lie, or at least
a half-truth.

"You wait a minute. You don't go spoiling your supper
anyway. You ran away because of your stepfather? That's
what you're saying?"

"So? That's what *you* said."

"Nicky, is it true?"

She let the strand of hair fall, looked him straight in the
eyes. "Yeah, yeah! I ran off because of him! All right? He's
not me bloody dad an' he never will be! Now can I—"

"Does he hit you?"

"Please, Darren! I'm hungry. I don't wanna talk no more."

There was something adult about the way she rested her
forehead on her hand, a *Weltschmerz*. And she was so
beautiful.

He had ordered chicken and chips in a basket, a lucky
choice as Nicky pronounced fried chicken her favorite (later,
he was to learn that most food was her "favorite"), to be eaten
in the garden of a pub well away from the nearest town. From
their table, Darren could see the landlady busy in her
kitchen, and when he judged the meal to be ready he hurried
to take the tray from her. Pub landladies were a generally
observant breed, and he didn't want her to get a close look
at Nicky.

He let her eat before asking any more questions, and even
then he asked only about her earlier escapades, thinking that
Nicky's disappearance would hardly merit the headlines
when it was discovered she had run away before.

He didn't tell her what was really puzzling him—that
although Lisa Ralph had begged him to let her daughter go,
she was adamant he shouldn't take her to the hospital.
Could it be that she feared the child would be examined for
signs of sexual abuse by him, Darren, and the old bruises
would then be discovered?

He could understand another woman trying to shield the

man who beat her child; she wanted to keep her man and at the same time stop the kid being taken into care. But Lisa Ralph was dying. She had no reason to protect her husband, but every reason to protect Nicky. Why hadn't she taken the opportunity to do so?

$\triangledown$

6

Mike Southgate knocked on the door of flat 23, Princess Royal Road, Peckham, without much hope of getting an answer. The camper was gone from its usual parking spot around the corner, so the lad had almost certainly taken himself off to look for casual work again.

Mike would always think of Darren as a lad, although at twenty-five he was only a couple of years his senior. Unemployed himself since his dismissal, he knew Darren planned to go apple picking and had hoped he might ask him to go along.

It was because of Darren that he lost his job in the first place. Or rather, because of his weakness: A social worker was in that clichéd position of trust, and he—though only in his mind—had abused it. Then he was fool enough to confess his feelings to his superior, Tara Penfold, assuming she would put someone else on Darren's case. Instead, she "suggested" he look for another position.

"You understand, Mike, don't you?" she said. "I'm sorry. Look, if you were to give it some more thought you might decide social work isn't for you. You've got two A-levels and you're only twenty-five—"

"Yeah, I'll think about it." What was he thinking of at that moment was how all the hard work to gain his qualifications had just gone down the toilet.

Six months earlier, it was Tara Penfold who brought Darren into his life.

"Darren Gillespie, just out of prison after ten months for

assault and attempted rape on a young girl in Ipswich. He's a sad one, Mike. I've known him since he was a kid and I can't do any more to help him." She slapped the Gillespie file onto his desk. "I think he resents me because I'm a woman—and old enough to be his mother. I'd like you to take him in your group next Tuesday, Mike. He might—just might—open up to you."

Mike's group of young ex-offenders was newly established and designed to help members understand and describe their problems, also to ease the feelings of isolation experienced by most of the lads. An ambitious project, and until now the crimes of group members were, at worst, robbery with violence. How would they react to Darren Gillespie, who had tried to rape a young girl, a schoolgirl, as she made her way home from a baby-sitting job?

He studied the Gillespie file, and it proved difficult reading, the kind of case that made passive and softly spoken Mike Southgate want to knock seven bells out of someone.

Mrs. Gillespie, by all accounts a lukewarm wife and mother, ran off with a jockey when her son was just starting school. Mr. Gillespie later remarried, to a pretty but shiftless woman who had a child of her own, a girl. She proved unable (or unwilling) to look after her home, her husband, or the children, and she had a reputation that followed her. Darren's father, already a heavy drinker with a jealous nature, took to spending long nights at the pub, coming home three sails to the wind and quite often with fists flying. He took it out on his stepdaughter, Frances, or Francie as they called her. He couldn't look at the child without being reminded that his wife had had a sexual relationship before.

A problem that must haunt many stepfathers, Mike reflected as he read on.

A much happier aspect of Darren's home life at this time was the closeness he shared with his stepsister, Francie. They had got on well from the start. And though Francie often seemed to regard Darren much as any adolescent girl regards her younger brother—as a baby to be petted and bossed around, to be tolerated and sometimes despised—they were friends.

For Darren, the relationship seemed to have been more important, deeper. After his careless mother, his equally careless stepmother, and taunts in between times from girls at school because one of them had seen his father drunk, here was one member of the opposite sex he could trust. And look up to.

It was one of the children's teachers who reported the bruises on Francie, noticed when the girl showered after gym. But it was already too late. The investigation into marks too severe to be accidental began too late.

That night, Gillespie returned home to find his wife absent, his son and stepdaughter still up and watching a late film. They were giggling together, sniggering at a scene where two half-naked women writhed about with a snake while a man peered at them through binoculars. It was smut-comedy rather than erotica, the sort of humor children will laugh at simply because bare tits and bums are funny.

Mike Southgate could hardly bear to go on reading. He tried to skim over the boy's evidence, to absorb only the facts, but it proved impossible.

Darren had been sent to bed, and then Gillespie turned on his stepdaughter, accusing her of being "no better than your slut of a mother." When the girl answered back he hit her. Just a slap around the head, but she screamed at him and swore: He wasn't her father and never would be; everyone knew he was nothing but an old tosspot and he could go to hell.

Gillespie snatched up the first object to hand in the cramped flat, a plaster dog ornament from the mantelpiece, and struck her with it. Only once, on the side of her head. She fell, crumpled, onto the lilac rug and lay in a fetal position, blood trickling from her ear.

Angry at first, and then frightened, Gillespie lifted her up and shook her. He shook her until Darren, who had been watching from the doorway, ran out screaming to the neighbors for help.

They took him to a children's home the same night; led him down a dark passageway past closed dormitory doors where other kids lay sleeping. The housemother recorded that Darren Gillespie hugged his arms to his chest as he walked, as if clinging to invisible possessions.

They wouldn't let him go to the funeral or see his stepmother—he didn't want to see her—and after a WPC had coaxed a statement from him, he didn't want to speak to anyone else.

"Withdrawn," read the child psychiatrist's report. "Incommunicative, hostile."

"A bully in the playground," reported the headmistress of his new school. "Lazy, rebellious, and disruptive in class."

His form teacher, who, like the headmistress, knew little of his background, was more perceptive. "He seems to respond better to men than to women. He's bright but lazy, fond of reading and of animals."

Darren stayed at the home until he was old enough to leave school, and then, with no qualifications and no prospects, took himself off on the first of his countryside excursions looking for work. Tara Penfold heard nothing of him until he returned two years later to the flat in Princess Royal Road left to him by his paternal grandparents. But Darren still didn't settle. Using the flat as a base, he bought a Volkswagen and traveled about taking seasonal jobs wherever he could find them.

What took him to Ipswich Tara couldn't guess, but his next stop was Norwich prison. There were more psychiatric reports: He was withdrawn, showed genuine remorse for what he had done, but no desire to earn the qualifications needed for a decent and steady job, no ambition save returning to his old nomadic lifestyle.

"Probably it's the prison environment that's responsible," Tara Penfold said. "He must have met dozens of old lags in there, all those who've tried to go straight and just ended up back inside. It's a vicious circle for them, and enough to make anyone lose hope."

Mike thought privately that any man who really wanted to make a go of his life after being in prison would do so. Besides, if Darren Gillespie had no ambitions before his conviction, except to drift, he was hardly likely to have them now.

But having read the file through, Mike decided the lad should join his group—if he wished. Whether or not he told the other members about his offense was up to him. They all deserved their second chance. Sometimes their third and their fourth. Especially someone who'd had such a horrific experience in childhood.

He looked so young standing there in the doorway. If someone had told Mike this was a school sixth-former he would not have doubted it, and at first he thought the lad had mistaken the Meeting House—kindly lent by the Society of Friends to the ex-offenders group—for the youth club further along the road.

"Are you Mike Southgate?" Such a quiet, not quite effeminate voice.

"Yes, but are you sure you've got the right place?"

"I'm Darren. Darren Gillespie. Mrs. Penfold said you'd be expecting me tonight."

"You're early. But yes, come in, come on in." Mike apologized for the chilliness of the place. "I've only just switched the heating on. It'll warm up in a minute. Keep your jacket on for a bit."

Darren looked around with only a vague interest at the sparsely furnished room. The acoustics were those of a large and empty house, the air that of an ancient church with piles of musty hymnbooks and proverbial poor mice.

He stood awkwardly, hands in pockets, feet shuffling like those of a nervous schoolkid hauled before the headmaster. He was neat and clean, with new trainers and unfaded jeans, a white T-shirt just visible under his jacket. Neat, but unsuitably dressed for the bitterly cold February evening. His dark brown hair looked freshly washed and fine, a perfect match for the girlish brown eyes. A contrast to Mike, who with his fair hair and blue eyes should have been handsome, and wasn't.

Mike set about making the boy feel at ease—only to find himself rambling.

"We cover a different topic every week, and tonight it's 'How You Feel About Your Victim.' That is, how you felt at the time and how you feel now. Most people don't say much their first time here. So you don't—I mean, if you'd rather just listen, well, that's okay. Then we have coffee, and after that anyone can talk about anything he likes.

"Cold, isn't it? Too cold to snow, as my mother would say. You should have put a pullover on under your jacket. . . ." He broke off, feeling a fool when he saw the smile on Darren's face.

"It's okay. I don't feel the cold."

"Is there anything you'd like to ask before the others arrive?" A shake of the head, still smiling. "All right. Perhaps you'd help me put out the cups, then?"

They trooped in one by one, Mike noticed with his usual pang of disappointment. He had hoped some of the group members would become friends, offer mutual support, but it seemed that having left the Meeting House they all went their own ways; nothing, or perhaps too much, in common. He had taken on more than he could handle but wasn't going to admit it to anyone—least of all himself. And now he had Darren Gillespie in the group.

The meeting got under way with only a brief introduction for Darren and a reminder that as this was his first time he need do nothing but listen.

"I didn't want to hurt him," one youngster said. "He was old, like me granddad. I didn't expect an old man. I guess I just—well, panicked when he clobbered me. I hit him back, grabbed the money, and just took off."

"And later?" asked Mike.

"I thought I'd killed him. He was old, right? Old people can't stand a bash on the head. I didn't want to hurt him. I didn't want to hurt no one. I just wanted the money."

"Why did you need the money, Peter?"

The boy—he was no more than a boy—glared at his hands. "I told you all that last week, I got no job. Never had a bloody job. The money they give you on Social—like, you need a prescription from the doc, right? You have to fill in this bloody form at the chemist's and still you have to pay. They give it to you back when you go and sign on next time, but they look at you like—oh, for Christ's sake! You know!"

Yes, Mike knew. Or thought he knew. You saw what your mates had and you didn't: the stereo, the car, the video. Ninety-odd percent of the unemployed struggled on, and probably always would, without resorting to theft. But for the rest . . .

"How do you feel about your—the old man now?" he asked, eyes constantly flicking back to Darren.

"Glad he made it, I suppose."

Mike went through the questions he had prepared mentally. Would you feel differently if the man you bashed were younger? ("Yes—I mean, no.") But you seem to have some special sympathy for this bloke because he was old? ("I didn't want to hurt no one.") How would you feel if someone bashed your grandfather? ("I'd kill him.") And he felt this was useless, all of it. How could he tell if they weren't just saying what they knew he wanted to hear?

True, these were all first-time offenders, and none had committed another crime since release from prison. But this group had only been established since the beginning of December, and Mike knew that sooner or later the week would come when he had absentees.

"Does anyone have a question for Peter?" he asked, and to his surprise Darren Gillespie raised a hand.

"Do you think you'd feel differently about the old man if you didn't have a grandfather you were fond of?"

Peter, confused, admitted that he didn't know. Then, under the scrutiny of the group, said, "Maybe."

That was the first and last time Darren opened his mouth

during this meeting. After coffee they discussed general problems: the increased difficulty of finding work if you had a record, girl-friends who no longer wanted to know you, the support—or lack of it—from family and friends. Mike hoped Darren would make a contribution to the conversation, but after that one, inspired question, he was content to listen.

Bright, his teacher had remarked. Bright but lazy. Fond of reading and animals. He seemed to fit the description all right; alert, perhaps wary eyes that would be happier focused on a page of print, a voice that would reassure a timid animal, and he sat, or rather lounged, in the manner of one who was basically indolent. It was hard to see in him a potential rapist.

Mike persuaded him to stay back after the others had gone to help him wash and dry the cups in the tiny kitchen. "Well, what did you think?" he asked when the lad silently took the tea towel.

"It's okay."

"Like you expected or not?"

"I don't know. I don't know what I expected. Will they have to know what I was in for?"

"That's up to you. You can always invent something, but lies have a way of being found out. Maybe you could tell me about it first."

Darren shrugged, led the way back into the meeting room. He still hadn't removed his jacket, though the place was now almost too warm, and kept his hands in his pockets when he sat down again.

"What do you want to know?" he said, and his voice was toneless, as if he didn't care or was too tired to resist questioning.

"What we were talking about tonight. How did you feel about the girl when it was happening?"

"I don't remember."

"You must have felt something."

"I don't remember."

"What about now? Do you have any feelings for her now?"

Darren shrugged. "Why should I?" He didn't add, She was asking for it anyway, but that was the message in his eyes.

"How do you get on with women generally?"

"Hey, what are you, a fucking shrink? Why don't you read what that bastard wrote about me in prison? He had it all worked out. I mean, you don't have to be bloody Einstein, right? My mother took off with some prat of a jockey, my stepmother couldn't give a toss. That must mean I've got a pretty low opinion of women, right?"

"I think," said Mike slowly, "that it would be far too simple to draw such a conclusion. Mothers are not the only women in a boy's life. A lousy mother, or even two lousy mothers, doesn't necessarily product a misogynist."

"Who says I am? I don't hate women."

Mike the social worker had trained himself to disguise his natural reactions, to hide all feelings behind an impassive face; but he had no control over his eyebrows, and they always betrayed him. They shot up at this moment.

He would have bet a fiver that no one else in the group could define the word *misogynist*.

Darren rose. "Can I go now?"

"Of course, if you like. You don't have to come to these meetings, you know. It's up to you. Nobody's forcing you."

"Right." And he walked out, Mike willing to gamble another fiver that he would never come back.

But next week he was there, arriving before Mike and even grinning when Mike saw that he had already set out the cups and spooned in the coffee. Once again, he said little and only then when directly questioned. He told the other group members his offense was simply assault on a woman, implying that his intention had been robbery, not rape. And he seemed only mildly interested in what they had to say. Sometimes he looked almost amused by them, superior in some indefinable way.

This was the pattern over the following weeks. Darren was always first to arrive at the Meeting House, apparently eager, yet contributing little. Mike wondered if the lad was actually benefiting from the group or whether he merely came along from a desperate loneliness. Eighty percent of the population of London must suffer from loneliness to some degree, especially youngsters like Darren. He guessed it would only be a matter of time before he took himself off to look for work somewhere else again.

One day as he was leaving the Social Services office—on foot, as his salary didn't yet extend to more wheels than two and he couldn't ride a bike anyway—a blue-and-white Volkswagen camper drew up beside him.

"Hey, Mike! Want a lift?"

Darren looked happier than the social worker could ever remember seeing him.

"Like it?" He grinned, waving a hand behind him. "I had an old heap before, but it wasn't really what I needed."

That was when Mike knew he wasn't going to be around much longer. He accepted the lift with a peculiar, sinking sensation in his stomach. He would miss Darren. In some inexplicable way he was afraid for him, too. And . . . And . . . But he wouldn't permit himself to think about And.

"Good bargain?" he asked cheerfully.

"I reckon so. Take a look back there. Sleeps two—three at a pinch. A cooker, a cupboard, and there's room for a small fridge and a Portaloo. Yeah, I reckon I got a good bargain." He grinned again. "It's okay, Mike, I didn't nick it."

"I wasn't—"

"I bought it with what I got for the old heap and some of my grandparents' money. It's all kosher, right? Now, where d'you want dropping off?"

Mike told him the name of his street, gave brief directions, and sat back thoroughly chastised.

"Not far from my place," Darren said. "How long've you lived in this area?"

"About a year."

"Like it?"

"I've seen worse. At least there's a laundrette down the

street. And the rent's not too bad. Mind you, it's not much bigger than a dog's kennel. Come and see for yourself if you like. I've got a couple of beers in the fridge."

Darren gave him one of his odd, sideways looks. "Okay."

The kennel turned out to be a slightly larger than average bedsit, with a narrow kitchenette partitioned off by a blue curtain. It was spotless but somehow lacked personality; Mike had accumulated few possessions besides clothes to make the place his own, simply because he didn't intend to stay. He had been more or less promised some sizable sum in his great-uncle's will, and the old man was now ninety-two and in frail health. He was fond of his uncle and didn't look forward to his death—of course not—but it was inevitable, and you couldn't take it with you. Better to make a will in favor of a beloved nephew than to leave the family squabbling over it.

Therefore, his present home was temporary, and the only personal effects on display were his late father's travel clock in its shell-like case, a photograph taken at his sister's wedding, and a poster depicting someone's hand reaching up out of a lavatory pan. The two armchairs were not comfortable, the springs having gone after years of misuse by a series of former tenants, but they were as spotless as the aging carpet and the table.

When Mike parted the curtain to get the beer from his fridge, he revealed an equally clean kitchenette; no grease splashes on the tiles around the cooker (this might have been because he seldom cooked), no dirty crocks, no lingering smells save those of cleaning agents and disinfectant. Even the tumblers that he used for the beer sparkled like those in a commercial for dishwashing detergent.

"Not that armchair," he said as Darren was about to sit down. "There's a spring sticking out at the front. You don't want to mutilate the family jewels."

Darren looked blank, then, understanding, he laughed. "You should see my place. My mates call it the municipal tip. If Gran were alive to see it she'd have a fit."

Here was an opening: Darren's grandmother. "You got on well with your gran?" Mike asked.

"She was okay. I was her only grandchild, and I suppose she spoiled me a bit. But then, grandmothers always do, don't they?"

"Why didn't you live with her after—you know—your father went to prison?"

"She wanted me to. I wanted it as well. But Granddad was an invalid, so they wouldn't allow it. That Mrs. Penfold, she was the one who stopped it. Bloody interfering bitch. What qualifies a social worker to say what's best for a kid when she doesn't even know that kid? Tell me that!" He drained the tumbler, which held less than half a pint, and refilled it.

"You must admit, she had a point," Mike said quietly. "Your gran had her hands full enough with an invalid husband, without taking on a small boy as well."

"We would have managed. I could have helped her, but they wouldn't even let us try." He fumbled about in his jacket pockets. "Mind if I smoke?"

"Of course not." Mike rose and fetched an ashtray. "I suppose Mrs. Penfold did what she thought was best at the time. It's not easy when you have literally hundreds of people to deal with every week. Not all of them kids and old folk, either. You'd be surprised—"

"I doubt it. Well, you don't have to bother about me anymore. I did my time and it's over. No one has any claim on me now."

"No, that's true. Does that mean you won't be coming to the meetings again?"

Darren considered. "Maybe. Until summer. Well, it's somewhere to go; free coffee and biscuits, right?"

"You never contribute much, Darren. Don't you get anything at all from the group?"

"Sure. Doesn't mean I have to give my life history in return, though."

"Perhaps it's a mistake not to talk about it."

Darren didn't answer, so Mike asked about his plans.

"Might spend a couple of weeks at the seaside. Then I'll go fruit picking down in Suffolk. That's something I've always enjoyed, but there's still plenty of time. I've got to do some work on the camper first."

"Haven't you given any more thought to finding a permanent job?"

"What as? A brain surgeon? A social worker, maybe? Here—" He took out his wallet and passed two snapshots to Mike. One was of himself as a child, a boy in swimming trunks that were too big for him, wet from a dip in the sea and hugging his arms around himself for warmth. His grin hadn't changed. There was still something of the adolescent defiance and challenge in his eyes.

The other picture was of a young girl, a head-and-shoulders shot. She had fair hair and almond-shaped eyes—and a very striking smile. Not classically beautiful, certainly, but the kind of face it would be hard to turn away from and hard to forget.

So this was Francie.

"Your stepsister?" Mike asked. "She was beautiful."

"Yes, that's her." He took the picture back immediately.

"And you don't want to talk about it?"

"No." He finished his beer and got up. "Better be off now. Things to do."

"Okay. Darren—? If you ever change your mind and want to talk, give me a ring. You've got my number, haven't you?"

Darren never took him up on that offer. He continued to come to group meetings, and sometimes he and Mike went to the pub together afterwards; but their conversation never touched on any subject connected with Darren's past. Mike refrained from mentioning their friendship to Tara Penfold, knowing she would disapprove, maybe even consider it unethical.

Until the day he realized that what he felt for Darren was more than friendship.

Later, he could hardly imagine what had been going

through his mind when he confided in Tara. The liquid lunch may have had something to do with it. That and the intolerable strain Darren's friendship put upon him.

Today as he turned away from the door of flat 23, knowing Darren had gone, Mike Southgate felt overwhelmed by loss, and an odd, inexplicable fear that he might never see Darren Gillespie again.

$\triangledown$

7

"**I** DON'T LIKE IT."

"That's okay, Nicks. It's not your hair." Darren inspected his new style and color in her hand mirror. He didn't like it much, either, but he wasn't going to admit it. Not after all that effort of fiddling with the pre-colorant stuff, sitting around with a wet head for forty minutes and messing up a perfectly good towel into the bargain.

Because it was necessary if they were to pass for brother and sister. This was the story he had decided upon. The beard wouldn't lend him enough years after all, he didn't feel comfortable with it—and it looked stupid. So he had shaved while Nicky was still asleep and trimmed his hair in Jason Donovan's style. Or what he thought was Jason Donovan's style.

Of course she didn't like it. Sometimes he thought she must have been born opinionated.

"You don't look like me dad no more," she complained.

"No, and I'll look a sight less like him by this afternoon. I'm going to dye it."

"Aw, Darren!"

He tried to explain. The beard made him look like a precocious sixth-former rather than the parent of an eleven-year-old. "If I dye it the same color as yours people will believe I'm your brother."

That pleased her, and she didn't start cutting up as usual when he told her she'd have to stay in the camper while he went to the shops.

But he must have left the stuff on too long, because his hair was now several shades lighter than Nicky's.

"I don't like it," she repeated.

"At least it looks natural. Don't you think I look like Jason Donovan?"

"No, I think you look bloody stupid."

He could pass for eighteen quite easily now. The lad who had just left school with a couple of A-levels and was going to pick fruit until the university term started. His young sister (maybe he should call her Vicky) was convalescing after an illness, and their parents had persuaded him to take the child with him because they felt the country air would be good for her.

"That's the story, okay?" he told her. "Do you think you can remember it?"

" 'Course. It's not a very exciting story, though, is it? Can't we make up something else? Like . . . Like—I know! Our parents were killed in a tragic accident, and we're orphans running away from a cruel—"

"No, we've got to keep it simple."

"And why've I got to be called Vicky?"

"Because it sounds like Nicky. Less chance of any mistakes."

She sulked, thought about it for a minute. "What would you have done if my name was Sharon? Call me Karen?"

"Not necessarily. Sharon's a popular name. Nicky is less common."

"Nicolle," she reminded him. "That's very *uncommon*. What's your middle name, Darren?"

He sighed. She was going to be a pest today. "John."

"Tell me about your sister."

She caught him off guard. Since her initial curiosity, demanding to know who it was he said she reminded him of, she had shown no further interest in the subject. And Darren found it hard to talk about Francie without psyching himself up to it.

"Tell me," Nicky insisted. "You said she was dead. What did she die of?"

"It was an accident. She fell. And I don't want to talk about it right now."

In fact, the photograph album he had intended to show her still lay in the drawer under his clean socks. Though he supposed she might have been snooping in it during his absence that morning, hence the renewed interest.

"How old was she when she died?"

"Thirteen. No, fourteen." She'd just celebrated her birthday.

He was drunk again. So drunk he could hardly stand. They hadn't heard him come in because they'd both been giggling at the late film. Who saw him standing there first Darren couldn't remember; but he recalled the fear very well.

They hadn't done anything wrong, anything dirty. Why did he feel that they had?

Cold feet. Cold on the lino.

No, Dad! Not the china dog . . . No, Dad!

But it didn't hit the wall.

"I've changed my mind," she announced. "I like your hair. I like it gold. Where are we?"

"Near Defford. That's where we're going apple picking." He looked at his golden hair in the mirror and decided that he liked it, too.

"Am I going to pick apples an' all?"

"They won't let you, Nicks. Remember the story—you're my sister and you've been ill. They wouldn't let you pick anyway. You're too young."

"But I can help you."

He changed gears irritably. "You'll do as you're told. You wanted to stick with me; well, this is it, mate. This is what we do, whether you like it or not."

"Can we have a telly?"

"We'll see. If I earn enough we'll have a telly."

"Only I'm missing 'Take the O'Neills' and it's my favorite."

A television would keep her quiet: He should have thought of it before.

"Take the what? That Australian thing? Don't think you're going to sit around watching the box all day. That's if I get one."

He turned off the main road, following signposts to Defford, and it felt to him as if they'd been traveling together forever.

"I will get one, I promise," he told her. "At the weekend."

Defford, like most small Suffolk villages, could boast one grocery shop and a pub. There was also a children's playground, though he imagined Nicky, childish one moment and surprisingly adult the next, would turn her nose up at it. He had to stop and ask the way to Elm Tree Farm, then had trouble understanding the thickly accented reply: In this part of East Anglia, accents varied from village to village, so that a man from the Cornards might have difficulty understanding one from Lavenham.

But Rodney Easthill's accent was minor public school. He had the ruddy cheeks of one who spends most of his life out of doors, holes in the elbows of his pullover, and the demeanor, Darren thought, of a gentleman farmer.

"You didn't say anything about a child when you telephoned," he said, evidently displeased.

"She's my sister. She won't be any trouble."

"I hope not, or you'll have to leave. Keep her out of mischief and away from the reservoir. Park round there, on your left."

They found a dozen more campers and caravans parked in the field beside the farmhouse. These belonged to the people who traveled about the country all summer picking fruit and vegetables: potatoes and peas, then strawberries, plums, and apples. Darren put his camper at the end of the row, overlooking an orchard of red-gold apples. These were small trees, like the ones he had passed along the road, but heavily laden. Ladders would be unnecessary, and he was glad of that, guessing that Nicky might be tempted to play on a ladder the minute his back was turned. He had bought her a stack of comics, a drawing pad and pencils, and a puzzle book so that she wouldn't be bored. And he cut a mound of sandwiches for their lunch, peanut butter and banana for Nicky—why did kids like that sort of junk so much?—cheese and tomato for himself, and packed them carefully with two fruit pies, a flask of tea, and a bottle of pop in a plastic carrier bag.

Work began at nine, and they followed the other campers across the road to the Cox orchards. There were several students among the workforce, gangling, acne-ridden boys who scarcely looked strong enough to carry the hods, housewives from the village, and men something past retirement age. Darren spotted the loudmouth in residence immediately—you found one wherever you went; the cock of the walk, the leader of the pack—a small, thin woman in her forties who also camped in the field. She could mean trouble. Well, he and Nicky would keep themselves to themselves as far as possible.

They worked in pairs, and Darren found himself with one of the students. A student of what he didn't say, only muttered something about "the Poly." Darren was ready with his well-rehearsed story, but the lad showed no curiosity and worked sullenly, ploddingly.

"Why can't I help?" Nicky demanded after perhaps five minutes of watching them. "Bet I can pick faster than him."

"Well you can't. It's against the law. Read your comics."

She fussed and fumed for a bit, then settled with her magazines. In between picking and emptying his full hod gently into the wooden bin, Darren watched her. She read as he'd used to do at her age, picking out the best serials and saving them for last. Francie, not a great reader, would turn to her favorites first and go back to the rest only if she had nothing better to do. And Nicky concentrated, read slowly and became involved, which showed she had a great deal of imagination. Even with a well mother and father who didn't knock her around, she was wasted on parents like them. What could they give her, after all? Stability—a word much bandied about and beloved of those so-called experts—was nothing if a child like her was denied the chance to realize her full potential. No, he could give her a better life. And . . .

He loved her.

The love of a brother, a father, a friend. That was it, of course. A grown man can't possibly feel any other kind of love for a little girl—unless he's some kind of pervert. And then it would be lust, not love.

When he looked at her again, the comic had fallen to the ground and she was staring down at the reservoir. That was exactly how she had looked when he first saw her: distant, mesmerized. Did Francie ever look like that? He didn't think so. The thing he remembered best about Francie, apart from her face, was that she was never still.

At ten-thirty, they joined the others for a short break. Darren's inclination was to lead the girl to a more secluded spot, but he fought it, reasoning that this would only attract attention. Better to join in, to chat with whoever sat near them. With her hair swept back from her forehead and secured under an Alice band, the puppy fat gone from her face, no one could think her remotely like the missing child.

Everybody was hurriedly lighting cigarettes, pouring coffee from flasks, and inspecting lunch boxes, so he gave Nicky a sandwich and a cup of tea.

"I want lemonade," she said, predictably.

"If you drink that now you'll have none left for lunch, and the tea will be too strong for you by then. Do as you're told."

He lit a cigarette, leaning against one of the alder trees that acted as windbreaks. His back was beginning to ache, unaccustomed to the weight of the full hod; by afternoon he knew the strap would have made his left shoulder and neck sore, too. It always took a few days to toughen up.

Nicky said, "Don't tell me you're tired already. I bet I could pick apples all day long."

"Well you can't. Are you bored?" He was wondering if it would be safe to let her walk back to the village and the playground.

"No, I like it here." Then she did something unexpected, something that, had anyone at the farm felt any doubts about her relationship with Darren, would have dispelled them.

The overseer, Lesley, gave her an apple to eat.

"It's different from the ones we're picking."

"That's right," Lesley told her. "This one's called a Katy."

"What about the ones in the orchard by the caravan?"

"Oh, they're called Jonagold. They're not ripe yet, though."

"Jonagold . . . Jonagold." She looked at Darren's hair. "That's you, Darren! You're Jonagold." Then she flung her arms around him and clung possessively. She was giggling, for this was both a flirtatious act and a message to any onlooker.

Hands off him. He's with me.

Darren's instinct was to return the hug, though it was mildly disturbing. Instead, he laughed and told her she was a great baby, too old for that kind of nonsense. The action of a fond but long-suffering elder brother.

Lesley smiled at her. "What's your name, love?" and Darren felt the heat of fear radiating from his chest and flooding his body.

"Vicky," the girl answered without hesitating or looking at him. "This is my brother, Darren. We live in Croydon . . ." And she chattered on, telling an intricate yarn that Darren himself could hardly have dreamed up. Her audience of one listened, either truly spellbound or a good actress. Perhaps she had someone like Nicky for a daughter, Darren thought.

Until lunchtime, he worked happily, knowing she was content. Rodney Easthill wandered the orchard, a tubby spaniel at his heels, asking first-time pickers, as he always did, if they were "getting the measure of it." He looked at Nicky's drawing, laughed when the dog jumped up to lick her face and called it a "bloody pest." As long as they behaved themselves, left the trees alone, and stayed away from the reservoir, he had no real objection to children, he told her.

"Keep an eye out for pollinators," he reminded Darren and his partner.

After that, Nicky made it her special task to run along the rows looking for the deep red Spartans, and every little while she would announce importantly, "Next one's a pollinator, Darren."

But his peace of mind was shattered at lunchtime when someone lent him a daily paper. He didn't expect to read anything about Nicky; it was almost old news now, and stories of missing kids were all too commonplace to hold the public's interest for long. Yet there it was on the front page, a single column in heavy print and overshadowed by the confessions of a soap star, "I've bedded two hundred fans" and accompanying photo.

"Have you finished with this?" he asked.

"Yeah, take it, mate."

He folded the paper into a square and stuffed it in his pocket.

Oh, God. Whatever was he going to tell Nicky?

She sensed something wrong. As soon as they were safely back in the camper, the door closed against any intrusion of other pickers parked on Easthill's land, he collapsed onto the settee, eyes closed against her, feeling the newspaper in his back pocket. He could hear her working the pump with her foot as she scrubbed her face and hands at the sink. Then she came and sat beside him, and he could feel her gaze on him.

"Knackered, huh?" she said, but in a small voice.

"Sort of. And don't use that word, Nicks. It doesn't sound nice."

"What's up?"

"Nothing."

She bounced on the seat irritably, trying to make him open his eyes. "Lesley gave me some windfalls," she said, dumping a plastic carrier on his knee. "And she says she's got so many courgettes in her garden this year that we can have some."

"That was nice of her."

"Darren—?"

He looked at her slowly, wrestled the tatty paper from his jeans pocket, and smoothed it out on his vacant knee.

"It's your mum. . . ."

"She's out of hospital? I can go home?"

"She died, Nicky."

She stared at him for a few seconds, then shook her head firmly. "No. No, she isn't. They said she'd be all right."

"Did they? Did they really tell you that?"

"We-ell," her lips trembled. "They said they thought she'd be all right. She's not dead, Darren. She isn't . . ." She glanced at the newspaper.

"Do you want to read it? Or shall I read it for you?"

"Y-you read it."

"Okay." He took a breath and began. " 'Lisa Ralph, the mother of eleven-year-old Nicolle Gurney, the youngster missing from her family's holiday home at Wheatcliffe-on-Sea, died yesterday afternoon. Mrs. Ralph, a patient at St. Veronica's Hospital, East London, had been suffering from a rare form of stomach cancer for two years.

" 'Nicky, described as being tall for her age with fair hair and green eyes, was last seen on the afternoon of Wednesday, August 25th—' "

"No, no!" She snatched the paper from him to read herself; it took just seconds, and then she tore it into shreds and threw them away from her as another child might throw a handful of worms. She twisted around in her seat, fingers gripping the backrest, face hidden.

"Nicky—"

"Leave me alone! I want me mum . . . I want me mum!"

How to comfort a grieving child? Darren, with next to no experience of children and a general horror of bereavement, sat paralyzed. He wanted to say something, to touch her, but was afraid of what emotion that might release. Other campers and caravans were parked close to either side, and if she started screaming it would be the end. For both of them.

He didn't think she was crying, probably that would come later, but if only she would. If only she would move. Seeing her so utterly still, listening to her light and unnaturally rapid breathing frightened him. This must be what it was like waiting for a time bomb to go off, he thought.

At last, as he was staring out of the window, watching the last of the afternoon sun on the rows of Jonagold, he felt her head touch his shoulder.

"It's okay," he said. "It's okay now."

She crept onto his lap and curled up into a tight ball, a fetal position, the way Darren himself used to sleep as a child.

Around nine o'clock he lifted her up and fumbled around in the darkness for the cupboard that held his clothes. He dropped them to the floor and laid her carefully on the pile of sweaters and shirts while he made up the bed. The curtains were still open, and he worried that some of the student campers, on their way back from the village pub, might be tempted to peer in. They were a nice enough lot, and any intrusion was likely to be friendliness rather than nosiness. But it wouldn't pay to become involved; especially not now.

Nicky didn't stir as he lifted her onto the bed and covered her warmly with the blanket. He wouldn't undress her in case it should alarm her when she woke, but he removed her sneakers and socks so that she should be as comfortable as possible.

Now what the hell was he going to do? Lisa Ralph's death wasn't totally unexpected, of course; it was just that he hadn't expected it so soon. He had meant to discuss it with Nicky—preferably when she was in one of her more receptive moods—to gently suggest that her mother may not get well and come home. They could have made their plans together, calmly reached some decisions before the event. He wished he hadn't told her, or at least that he'd put it off until the funeral was over. For what would happen if she wanted to attend? He would be obliged to take her back to London and leave her in the care of her stepfather.

Still, there was one thing he must be thankful for; she

hadn't had time to read the last paragraph in that newspaper report.

Mrs. Ralph's last words were for Nicky. 'Tell her I'm sorry. Tell her I love her.' And her husband, Nicky's stepfather, was quoted as saying, 'It wasn't the cancer that killed my Lisa in the end. It was the bastard who took our daughter.'

Darren drew the curtains and switched on the light. Some people's appetite was dulled by stress, his was sharpened, enraged. He ransacked the larder, buttering half a dozen slices of bread and slathering them with jam. Half a banana cake followed, along with the chocolate digestives Nicky hadn't eaten. Still unsatisfied, but knowing he must leave enough for tomorrow, he started on the apples. Finally, he opened a can of lukewarm lager and downed that.

Now he had to think of the most immediate problems, the next few hours. Lights on all night in the camper might be noticed, but Nicky shouldn't be allowed to wake to complete darkness. He found a night-light, kept for emergencies, and lit that. Tomorrow he would have to follow her lead, see how she felt about going home—certainly try to dissuade her. Then there was the question of work. He couldn't take her with him in her distressed state, but could he leave her alone in the camper? All the half-formed plans he'd made for a long-term future seemed insignificant now.

Late in the night, Nicky awoke. He wasn't aware of her waking, only that he had drifted to consciousness himself, and for a long time he sat watching the flickering night-light. He had been sleeping on the floor as usual, but sitting up with his head resting on the bed, which wasn't doing much for his aching back. When he glanced at her he saw that she was awake and watching him.

"Hi, Nicks. D'you want anything? A drink, maybe?"

She shook her head. "I knew really. I just pretended."

Darren nodded, understanding. "Everyone used to say, Don't

worry, she'll be all right. But I knew. It's like going to the dentist for the first time. You don't think it's going to hurt in the first place, and when they tell you it won't, that's when you know it will."

"That's a good analogy, Nicky."

"Yeah?"

"What do you want to do?"

"Do?" She blinked at him.

"Do you want to go home? For the funeral?"

"No! Darren, don't make me go! Please!"

Of course, he might have realized; sensitive and immature children like her could be terrified of death and funerals. His own father had refused to let him attend the funeral of a favorite aunt for the same reason.

"He'll have nightmares for weeks," he had told Marsha (which was probably true). "And that means wet sheets every morning if I know anything at all about him."

Marsha had agreed. "Buggered if I'm gonna wash sheets every day."

Nicky should remember her mother as she once was, and not as the sick, dying woman he had overheard on the telephone.

"Of course you don't have to go," he told her. "But what about afterwards?"

"I don't want to go home to him. He ain't me dad."

"Neither am I."

"No . . . I know that. But you're like him. You're like him in lots of ways, Darren, even with your hair changed. You even smell like him."

One more chance. He must give her one more chance to change her mind. "What about your little brother? You say you don't love him, but I think you must do. Deep down."

"Why should I? Mum never got ill until he was born. And he's spoilt rotten. He could burn the place down and still not get wrong. I've only got to leave me school bag in the hall to get shouted at."

"How about your friend—what was her name? Emma something?"

"Emma-Kate. What about her? So she's my best friend, so what? I hate her sometimes."

"That's what best friends are for. Sometimes you do hate them, but most of the time you love them, right?"

She looked at him so solemnly that he wanted to laugh. Solemn and wise as an old woman. But not funny; not tonight. "Do you sometimes hate me? Is that what you mean?"

"Of course not! I could throttle you sometimes. But hate you? Not for three million quid and all the noodles in China. Oh, Nicks . . ."

"Then what do you want me to do?"

"Stay with me, Nicky. I can give you a better life than he could. I know he used to hit you. I saw the bruises on you the first time we met."

She drew her knees up to her chest. "He never hit me."

"You don't have to defend him now. You're staying with me, remember?"

"He never hit me. It were me mum."

Nicky, I'm sorry. "Tell her I'm sorry."

"Your mother?" Hadn't he once read that kids like her generally clung to the parent who ill-treated them? "Tell me something. Can you remember when your mother went into hospital?"

"The Saturday before I met you."

It fitted. The bruises were yellow; old bruises. And although Alan Ralph had shouted at her he made no threatening gestures, which he surely would have done if he'd been in the habit of belting her.

"Tell me about it?"

"If you want. Only it's not how you think."

"How do you know what I think?"

She shrugged. "It were only after me dad died. And she always used to be sorry after. She'd say sorry and make a fuss, and say she hadn't meant to but I'd made her angry.

Then when she got ill she'd say I deserved it for making her feel worse than she already did." She sniffled.

"You can cry if you want to, Nicks."

"I don't feel like crying."

"How do you feel, then?"

What a question to ask an adolescent. He expected another shrug of the shoulders, an "okay," perhaps.

But she said, "Relieved. Not for me. For her. And I feel—sort of shaky inside. And hot."

"That's the shock. And it's okay to feel relieved, Nicky." He scrambled up awkwardly and sat on the edge of the bed. "When someone's been ill for a long time and you know they're going to die—well, it's natural to feel that way."

"And I'm scared."

"Oh, Nicks—" Should he touch her? Lift her up and put his arms around her? He covered her hand with his own, noticing how warm she was. Too warm, perhaps. What would he do if she were running a fever—if she became seriously ill?

"Don't be scared, Nicky. I'll look after you. I won't leave you."

"Darren, do you believe in ghosts?"

"Ghosts?" He tried to recall the things that had frightened him as a child: darkness, people shouting, his father. Those were his only ghosts. But he wasn't going to dismiss her fears with a laugh or by telling her not to be silly.

"Well, there aren't many real ghosts. Some people think they've seen one, but it turns out to be all in their imagination. Like my gran. When her dog died she used to think she could still hear it moving about in the kitchen. But that was only because she was used to hearing it. And real ghosts only haunt one place, like the Tower of London—"

"Is there one there?"

"Well—I think so—"

"You know what he—Alan—said? He said only the tour-

ists really know London. The people who live there don't
know it at all."

"He's probably right." He wished she hadn't mentioned
her stepfather.

"Can we go there one day? To the Tower?"

"Maybe. We'll see."

He persuaded her to try to sleep, himself lying down next
to her but outside of the covers. After all, there was plenty
of room. And if she didn't object, then what possible harm
could there be in it? He experienced no echoes of his earlier
disturbance when she'd hugged him, only a vague wish that
she would fall asleep quickly so he might just look at her.
Just look, nothing else. Why feel guilt because you admire
the body, the limbs of a child? Admiring beauty shouldn't
imply sexual attraction. If that were so, half the world must
dream of screwing Mona Lisa or Princess Di.

But when she slept, he found he couldn't disturb her by
moving. All he could see were tendrils of straw-colored hair
across her forehead. She needed a shampoo; not the cheap
stuff he bought by the liter for his own hair, but something
adult and sophisticated. That would please her.

He knew she was deeply asleep by the manner of her
breathing. Funny, he thought, how kids could sleep in the
most terrible circumstances, even the death of a parent. A
kind of safety valve, he supposed, because a child is unable
to cope emotionally in the way an adult might.

Darren himself had no such escape. It may have been
learning about Lisa Ralph or, and more likely, Nicky's need
for comfort; but whatever it was he found himself thinking
about death and dying that night. He had once witnessed a
fatal car crash and thought that the most horrible way
anyone could meet his end. In full public view. Yet it was
easiest to imagine, and he had always felt—felt more pow-
erfully than ever that night—that his would be such a death.

He shivered in the dark, chilly September morning. And
Nicky slept on and on.

8

HOW EASILY LIES come after years of practice. Darren had been in the business since childhood, of necessity coming up with some elaborate tales to deceive first his father, then the staff at the children's home. Now he found that lying required no more effort than eating.

Pickers who came from Defford and the surrounding villages could take their wages at the end of the day if they wished, but those who camped on Easthill's land, and therefore were expected to stay until picking finished, usually collected their money on Friday. Darren, aware that he and Nicky might have to move on at any time, chose the first option, and Easthill was put out.

"It's our grandmother," Darren explained. "She's not been too well lately. I phone from the village every day, and—well, if it looks like she's going to peg out we'll have to go. She's eighty-nine, after all."

"All right, all right." Rodney Easthill wasn't interested in personal problems. As long as people did the work they were paid to do, sick grandmothers, fathers with senile dementia, and delinquent toddlers were no concern of his. And if they didn't pull their weight, they were out, as simple as that. Easthill didn't want to make friends of his casual labor.

He was satisfied with the explanation, but Darren realized this was another angle for Nicky to add to her story.

Her mother's death hardly seemed to affect her. She was slightly more subdued than usual, more thoughtful, and she tended to be clinging, especially after dark. And perhaps it was natural she should take it this way. Her greatest loss had been her father, while she and Lisa Ralph had never been particularly close from what Darren could gather. Some children appeared to reject one parent after the death of the other. It had been the same for him, and Francie was the only reason he hadn't joined the hundreds of other kids sleeping rough in London.

Now he could no longer hide from Nicky the fact that she was news. She wanted to know everything about the paper and television reports, furious that he hadn't saved any cuttings, indignant because they had used last year's school portrait of her.

"I look like a little kid in that one," she complained, "a bloody baby!"

"Well? No one will recognize you from it, will they? You don't want to be recognized—you don't want the police to take you back home?"

"No-o, but it'd be exciting. A real drama."

"Not for me. I'd be in prison."

"No, Darren. No." Her certainty, her absolute sense of her own power, was such that he could almost believe her.

Instead, he said, "I'll look after you. Everything'll be all right."

A simple, ambiguous statement.

The work became easier in a few days. Muscles ceased to ache by four o'clock in the afternoon, and Darren began to miss his evenings at the pub. On Saturday, he left Nicky in the children's playground, drove into the nearest town, and bought a portable color television. A television was what she wanted most, that and her toys and books. In the Dr. Barnado's shop he found a Rubik's cube (unsolved by its previous and probably exasperated owner) and bought that for twenty pence, along with some "Young Adult" novels and a copy of *Jane Eyre*. Then he made one last stop at the newsagent's for another sketch pad, more crayons, an armful of comics—and the daily paper. This he read in the camper halfway between town and Defford.

There were pictures of Lisa Ralph's funeral, intrusive close-ups shot through high-powered lenses of the coffin bearers and of Alan Ralph, supported, as the caption read, by his sister and brother-in-law. Darren remained unmoved by the grief of Nicky's stepfather, and a close-up of the little boy, James, only angered him. What sort of person would take a kid his age to a funeral?

He screwed the newspaper up and threw it from the window.

Nicky screamed when he unpacked the television, wanted it on immediately; and when he had fiddled with the aerial, altered the picture to her satisfaction, she settled down to watch "The Flying Doctors." Fifty minutes of contented silence, and then:

"Why didn't you buy it before? I've missed 'Take the O'Neills.' "

"I've already told you, don't think you're going to watch that thing twenty-four hours a day." But he was relieved that he now had a guaranteed way of keeping her quiet.

"Did you buy a paper?"

"No."

"Aw, why not? You're mean."

Darren looked pointedly at the television, the comics, and the drawing materials, but otherwise let it pass. "I'm going out for a while, Nicks."

"Aw, but I want to stay and watch telly!"

"That's okay. And the word is television."

"Where you goin'?"

"To the pub. Promise me you'll stay put, not go wandering about outside."

She shrugged, bored with the weekend already and probably missing kids of her own age to knock about with. It was just another problem to add to the ever-growing list of problems Darren hadn't anticipated. Going out and getting blitzed at the Seven Bells wouldn't solve those problems, or even make them appear surmountable for longer than a few hours, but you could think with a whiskey in your hand; you could make plans.

He changed his clothes, put on a warm jacket. "I want to find you in bed and asleep when I come home," he told her.

"Yeah. Bring me back a Coke."

He contemplated locking her in, but suppose something happened? A fire, or she was taken ill? "You haven't promised yet."

"Okay, I promise, I promise! Bring me some crisps."

Half of him didn't want to leave her. Not simply because he feared for her safety or that she'd disobey and go wandering off in the dark; he felt guilty for wanting to be alone for a while. He hesitated at the door. Should he play the part she had allotted to him from the start, that of father substitute, and give her a paternal kiss? Or would that alarm her? She was staring at the TV screen, engrossed in some noisy show.

He said, "You'll be all right? I won't be late."

"Yeah."

"I'll bring your Coke and crisps." Somehow it sounded like a plea. He wanted to hear her say, Don't go, Darren. Don't leave me on me own.

Still she sat staring, sulking maybe, he couldn't tell. He closed the camper door quietly behind him and stood listening for a while. When he heard her laugh he walked away, satisfied she was all right, and he didn't hear another door softly closing as he left the field.

Once or twice along the narrow, unlit road into the village he was aware of someone behind him. But Defford was a straggling village, half in Suffolk, half in Essex, with long winding lanes and clusters of houses way apart. So Darren assumed his companion to be a villager. Had he thought he or she came from the campsite, he would have wondered why they didn't speak or call out to him.

In the saloon bar of the Seven Bells he ordered a pint of bitter and a large whiskey. Two old men occupied the seat opposite, making an irritating noise with their crisps and pork scratchings, and Darren might have drunk up and walked out if the nearest other pub hadn't been two miles away and on the main Colchester road.

From the other bar came voices he recognized: the ever-cheerful Ken, foreman at the farm, whose current party piece was an impersonation of Officer Crabtree in " 'Ello, 'Ello"; two Australians, half of a quartet in England for a working holiday; Lesley, the overseer, with her husband. He didn't look their way, not wanting to be drawn into company tonight, and so he didn't realize he was being watched.

Nicky. He had to think of her and how he planned to care for her. Education first. You couldn't just turn up at school and enroll a child; the head teacher would want previous school records. He could educate her himself, and when the time came that she needed qualifications he'd enroll her in a correspondence course. Easy. Too easy an answer? But simple plans were so often the best. And what if she needed a doctor? Or worse, had to be admitted to hospital? A few lies might serve in an emergency, the same story he'd given at the farm. But a serious illness . . . that didn't bear thinking about.

Darren went to the bar and bought another large whiskey. He was vaguely aware of the brown eyes fixed upon him from the other room, vaguely registered the presence of Terry Wallace, one of the pickers camped in Rodney Easthill's field. She was the loudmouthed woman he had singled out on his first day at the farm. Surrounded by a gang of her cronies, her favorite pastimes were telling smutty jokes and ribbing the men. Terry Wallace thought herself a regular wit. Darren could hear her saying, as she often did, "Ooh! Aren't I awful!" and giggling. He shuddered, went back to his seat and his thoughts.

He had made friends, both during his travels and his spell in prison; good mates, some of them, who would do him a favor with no questions asked. He began to make mental lists: who could help him out if he and Nicky needed somewhere to stay, who could lend him money if he was

short, who might lie for him if anyone became suspicious.
What was important now was that he kept his head. And
everything he did must be for Nicky.

Another drink, and another. It was still only nine o'clock,
and the desire to be alone had passed. He was lonely for her.
The old men were gone and two young couples now shared
the saloon with him, while in the other bar someone was
playing the piano. He heard the beginnings of a Saturday-
night sing-song, Terry Wallace's voice leading the rest. The
life and soul of the party. Between verses of "Lily the Pink"
and "Long-Haired Lover from Liverpool" she cackled—predictably—"Ooh! Aren't I awful!" No doubt at eleven o'clock,
when drinkers became sentimental or even downright
maudlin, she would give her cronies a suitable solo.

Darren wanted to leave then. The sounds of people
enjoying themselves made him acutely aware of being alone.
Yet he felt to leave so early would only attract attention;
nobody goes home at nine-thirty on a Saturday night. So he
bought another drink and put his change into the fruit
machine, acting his part with conviction. By closing time he
was having trouble focusing his eyes, and he felt slightly sick.
Whiskey had never agreed with him, but his reason for
drinking it was perhaps the best; he liked the taste.

He bought Coke and crisps for Nicky, cigarettes for
himself, and bid the landlord a slurred good night.

The September air was chilly, misty from the nearby River
Stour, and he worried that Nicky might be cold. The road
back was slightly uphill, no problem to a sober person, even
in the dark, but Darren staggered and almost fell into the
hedge, where blackberries were already ripening. It was only
when he stopped to vomit that he realized he wasn't alone.
Terry Wallace stood behind him, watching, making no
attempt to touch him—which was odd in itself.

"You all right?" she said, in a voice horribly cold for one
with a Scottish accent.

Darren grunted in reply. Was it Terry he'd heard on the
road behind him earlier? She was parked next but one to him

in the field, in an American-made camper she shared with her fat sister and a gangling boy who could have belonged to either of them. And although he'd never seen her watching Nicky . . .

"Why didn't you come in the other bar?" she asked. "We were all in there."

"Didn't notice you." He wiped his mouth on his sleeve.

"Better now?"

"Yeah." What else to do but walk along beside her? He felt empty, frozen over deep inside.

"You shouldn't drink so much," said Terry Wallace. "Not with a little girl to look after. All on her own, is she?"

"She's all right. She's got the television."

"Lesley said she's been ill. Don't you think she'd be better off at home with your parents?"

"That's none of your business."

"Maybe not."

He wished she would either keep up with him or leave him alone, anything but walk slightly behind him as she was doing.

"Where did you say you lived?" she asked.

"I didn't."

"Richmond, wasn't it?"

Oh, God. What had Nicky told that woman, Lesley? Not Richmond, certainly . . . He stopped at the verge, pretending he wanted to throw up again. "Croydon," he breathed at last. "Anything else you want to know?"

"Anything else you want to tell me?"

"What's that supposed to mean?"

Ahead, he saw a solitary light in the farmhouse; behind him, the lights from the village and the headlamps of an approaching car.

"Who is Nicky really?"

He didn't mishear her. She said "Nicky."

"My kid sister. And her name's Vicky." He walked on, moving close to the verge to let the car pass, and she called after him:

"I think she's that kid in the papers. The one missing from Wheatcliffe-on-Sea."

"Don't be bloody stupid, woman. If she was that kid I'd hardly be flaunting her in public, would I?"

"Then let me speak to her." Terry Wallace smiled. That is, she stretched her lips back, exposing her teeth. It was the smile of someone who knows herself to be right and is about to triumphantly prove it. "Let me ask her who she is."

"You'll be wasting your time."

"You've got her well trained, haven't you?"

The lamp in the farmhouse window went out, leaving them in near darkness on the narrow road, with only a few dim lights from the caravans to show them the way.

"You're talking rot," he said. "Want to take more water with it next time."

She took his arm, not roughly, but as a friend might. "If you don't let me speak to that child right now, I'm going to wake them up at the farm and make them call the police. Don't think you can take yourself off, either. I've got your number, don't you worry."

"She'll be asleep, and I won't have her woken up. You can speak to her in the morning."

His head was suddenly, remarkably clear. If Nicky was woken up now she might well be confused into forgetting her story. And Terry Wallace had a motherly, patronizing way with youngsters—he had watched her with the students—which might make the kid trust her. If he got into the camper and drove off now, the chances were he'd be picked up by morning.

Here was another opportunity to get out of the whole mess. He could leave Nicky with this old cow, head back to London where he could do something about the incriminating number plates—maybe get a quick respray job done on the vehicle while he was at it—and then hide out for a few weeks in the very last place the police would think of looking. Wheatcliffe-on-Sea.

The plan, which took seconds to form, took seconds to

dismiss. He thought of Nicky's face, her tears when he told her he was leaving, and he knew he couldn't leave her. Ever.

"All right," he said slowly. "She is the kid they're looking for. What are you going to do about it?"

"Call the police, of course. What do you think?"

Her eyes were round, as a baby's are, but they glittered and snapped, full of loathing. She saw a child molester standing beside her, a monster who had already performed unspeakable acts on a terrified little girl. He longed to shake her, to scream at her:

It isn't like that! You don't understand!

Indeed, he heard himself using those words, though softly, reasonably.

"No? Tell me, then. What don't I understand?"

A little way past the entrance to the campsite and on the opposite side lay the reservoir orchards. Here were the pears: Comice, Conference, and William, heavier than apples and more troublesome to pick, for the stalks had to be left intact on the fruit and the trees were full of earwigs.

"I'll tell you," Darren said, "if you'll just listen. But come in here; we don't want to be overheard by the other campers."

She followed him through the gates; boyish, weighing under eight stones, and still in complete command, she followed him to a stack of empty bins awaiting Ken's tractor. Already the grass was wet beneath their feet, and the mist was now almost a fog. It would be a chilly night, and by morning the trees would be dripping, the ground slightly muddy as the sun rose and warmed it. But Darren wouldn't be there.

"Well?" said Terry Wallace, lighting a cigarette with the wafer-thin gold Colibri she liked to produce with a flourish at lunchtime.

He began the speech he had a long rehearsed for just such a situation—the truth: how the child had attached herself to him, how she was covered in bruises. Then he stopped, looked into Terry Wallace's face by the light occasioned when she took a long pull at her cigarette.

The cock of the walk, the life and soul of the party. She was in command. She didn't care for Nicky at all, but only saw the child in relation to herself as the Heroine of the Year. Pictures in the newspapers, TV interviews, all her admiring cronies telling reporters, "Well, that's our Terry for you."

She wasn't in command now, though. The cigarette dropped from her lips, her hands fell, surprised, to her sides, then rose to claw at Darren's. Now he did at last shake her. He shook her by her neck until the glittering eyes rolled in their sockets and her windpipe felt like a tube of steel under his fingers. For a second he was reminded of the children's home and Barry, who had climbed into his bed and made him touch Down There and of the turkey neck he had been given to nibble on one Christmas Eve. He squeezed then until he felt something give in her throat, and her head fell back, striking one of the empty bins.

Nicky . . . Nicky . . .

He looked briefly at the woman's body, draped over the corner of the bin on which they had been sitting, head hung over the splintery edge so that her hair almost touched the ground, and he felt a curious resentment of her—of it. He needed to be with Nicky, listening to her incessant chatter, watching her prepare for sleep. She was the protecting, he the protected.

Nicky.

Clouds lighter than the black sky chose that moment to part for a brilliant September moon, full and red-gold like a strange sun, and casting a light to give any living being a corpselike hue. He touched her neck where the hair parted and fell. It was warm but lifeless. Once, a long time ago, he'd had a dog that kept having fits and had to be put down. That was how the dog felt when the vet had finished with it: warm as in life, but so still because the blood had ceased to flow.

He couldn't leave her there. Pitying her in death, which is a kind of nakedness, he lifted her easily into his arms—she weighed little more than Nicky—and carried her along the path by the windbreaks and deep into the sloping orchards.

Sheltered from the breeze by the long rows of pear trees, he laid her down beside a bin that was only a quarter full.

They liked to end the day with all bins full. So it was that, if one team had a full bin at ten minutes to four, they were sent to help another group. It often ended with two dozen people scrapping on the same row and getting in each other's way. Still, there were days when a bin had to be left only partially filled, and quite often the job was completed by another team the following morning.

Darren removed her jacket, which was too bulky, leaving her in a red silk blouse and white denim jeans; she couldn't feel the cold. Her handbag—surely she'd had a handbag with her? He'd have to go back for it, throw it in the reservoir or otherwise dispose of it. And her jacket, too, of course.

He leaned into the bin and started scrabbling at the fruit, drawing it high around the four sides to leave a hollow in the middle. They were Conference pears, small, elongated, hard, and stone-cold to the touch. He lifted her in gently, arranging her in a fetal position so that she looked like a child that had gone to sleep. Odd how death gave people a kind of dignity.

Pears were heavier than apples, Easthill had told him; a bin of apples weighing about 705 pounds when full and the pears something like 840. But Darren wasn't sure whether the bins were weighed on reaching BFG, and if so whether a discrepancy would be noticed. BFG, Benthill Fruit Growers, was where all the apples and pears went, he knew. Some were graded, packed, and sent off immediately to shops and supermarkets all over East Anglia, others were put into cold storage, perhaps for Christmas or destined for Europe. Say this particular bin went up to BFG at the end of the week, chances were her body would remain undiscovered for months.

Feeling himself vulnerable in the moonlight yet needing it to see his way among the branches, Darren took off his jacket to use as a hod. He worked quickly, with no time to even think about leaving stalks intact or bruising the fruit—and to hell if Easthill took a quality-control sample from this bin and someone else got the sack. He had to cover her, get her out of sight—his own as much as anyone else's. His shirt was soon wet, he shivered, felt earwigs drop over his hands and down his neck, and once or twice his jeans were snagged by brambles. Despite the moonlight he had to grope to find the fruit, but they were small trees and more heavily laden at eye level and below.

Slowly, too agonizingly slowly, he covered her so that no scrap of the red silk blouse—which had bloody copper hues in the moonlight—was visible. Still he worked on. He had noticed that fruit in a half- or three-quarter-full bin was usually banked up higher around the four sides than the middle. It had to look natural so that Lesley, the overseer, would notice nothing amiss.

At last he stopped, surveyed the results of his work. His jacket was wet and filthy, but he put it on, bundling hers up under his arm. Where to dispose of it? It would float in the reservoir, he supposed, and he couldn't face the work that burying it or hiding it in another bin would entail. There was nothing he could do but take it, along with her handbag, back to the camper.

He'd never had much sense of direction. Even in the daylight he had to follow the others through a maze of orchards at knocking-off time. It was little help knowing that the reservoir lay to his right, and therefore this must be one of the west orchards. In his panic he ran uphill instead of down, realizing the mistake when he came to the row of alders and the young plum trees beyond them. He couldn't, wouldn't go back. Nothing would have induced him to return to that bin; he knew with all the certainty of a childish nightmare that if he did he would see her uncovered again, as though she couldn't keep her mouth shut even in death and must announce what he had done to the world.

A faint orange glow in the sky told him which direction the town lay, and he followed that, running with the bundle under his arm until he saw the sheds, the lavatory, and the bin he and Terry had been sitting on. There was her bag, on the ground where it had fallen, its contents poking rather than spilling out. He picked it up, wrapped it in the jacket, and sat, trembling, on the cindered path.

Suppose she wasn't dead? Suppose she recovered like Half-hanged Smith and staggered up to the farmhouse at three o'clock in the morning?

He began to cry, partly from shock but mostly from fear. Once he'd had a facility—a self-defense mechanism, or a gift—for blocking things out, shutting them from his mind as if they'd never happened. That gift had deserted him now.

Nicky. He had to think of Nicky and how to protect her. They couldn't stay here now, though a sudden departure might not appear suspicious because of the sick grandmother story. But then there was the fat sister and the boy who shared Terry's caravan to think about. Better, surely, to stay at least until midday tomorrow, to be there and seen to be acting normally before they started panicking.

But whatever he did tomorrow he must pull himself together now. He had no idea of the time, couldn't see his watch, but the kid mustn't be left alone any longer: She'd probably still be awake and wondering where he was. She might be afraid.

Quietly, he crossed the narrow lane and crept along the pathway beside the farmhouse into the field where the campers and caravans were parked. Only two vehicles showed a light, his and Terry Wallace's. He bundled the jacket and bag out of sight under his own, where they must stay until he was sure Nicky was asleep and he could retrieve them.

He heard voices from the Wallace caravan, arguing, apparently. The fat sister whined something about "ungrateful" and "couldn't give a toss," to which the boy replied loudly in his thick Scottish accent:

"I dinna care! I inta goin' nowhires this time o'night!"

Softly, Darren opened his own door and found Nicky asleep in bed as she'd promised. The television was still on, but the volume turned so low it was barely audible. He watched her for a minute, called her name, thinking she might only be feigning sleep. But she didn't move, and he went back outside to retrieve the bundle. The jacket he threw into the cupboard immediately—it could be disposed of properly tomorrow; he thought vaguely of burning it—but Darren, always conscious of the need for money, always with a horror of having none in reserve, went through the handbag thoroughly before tossing it aside. He found a bundle of letters, all addressed by the same hand but all bearing different postmarks, a small notebook, a Biro and comb, and all the other junk a woman usually carries about with her. No checkbook or accompanying plastic, but a leather purse containing her last week's wage packet, an untouched eighty-four pounds seventy pence, plus three tenners, a fiver, and some loose change. This went into Darren's back pocket; he then locked the bag up with the jacket and burned Terry Wallace's payslip and envelope in the ashtray.

A moment after the paper had blackened and curled he heard a soft tap at the door; a tentative, apologetic tap. He glanced at Nicky, who had turned in her sleep, her face buried in the pillow.

"Who is it?" he called, his lips close to the door.

"Marianne. Terry's sister. Sorry to trouble you this time of night, but can I have a word?"

Darren opened the door, letting the light fall on straggly brown hair and a pudgy face. She was dressed in a spangled jacket and long blue skirt, as if she'd been out somewhere for the evening. But her makeup was old, worn, with little streaks of green residue in the creases of her eyelids, and the small, spidery veins of someone who smokes and drinks heavily just visible under her blusher.

"Sorry to trouble you," she repeated. "It's just that—"

He let her in, motioning her to keep her voice down and indicating Nicky.

"Sorry. I wondered . . . Darren, did you go out tonight?"

"Down the Seven Bells, yes. Didn't see you there."

"No. John and me went to a club in town, but Terry said she was going to the Bells. Did you see her?"

"A couple of times, but she was in the other bar, too noisy for me in there. Why? Isn't she home yet?" He looked at his watch, surprised to find it was only ten minutes to one. "She was with a whole crowd," he said. "Most of them were from the farm, but there were a few I didn't recognize."

"What time did you leave?"

"Can't really remember. Chucking out time, I suppose. I wanted to get back to see this film." He nodded at the subtitled Polish film that was the late-night offering on Channel Four, trying to look engrossed and only paying her the minimum of attention out of politeness. "Maybe she's gone off with someone to a club in town," he added vaguely.

"Yeah, well, that'd be our Terry."

Still she showed no signs of leaving, so Darren abandoned his pretense of following the film and looked at her steadily. She was obese, quite ridiculous in that jacket and so repulsively earnest that he realized it was all an act; she was using her sister's absence as an excuse to come knocking on his door.

The lies came as easily now as they had with Rodney Easthill. He told her that he'd waited for Terry outside the pub, seeing no one else from the campsite and thinking to walk home with her.

"But she must have gone out the back way. I wanted to say sorry for seeming so unfriendly earlier on. The thing is, our grandmother's ill. And it doesn't look like she'll get better, so I didn't really feel like company tonight. I don't know how I'll ever tell Vicky. She adores Nan." He glanced at Nicky, compelling his guest to do the same.

"Poor kid. Don't you think you ought to take her home, Darren?"

The perfect opening. "That's what I was thinking of tonight. She's really not strong enough to go back to school yet, and she does love it here. But I reckon if Nan's going to die she'll be better off with Mum. So tomorrow I plan to ring up from the Bells, and if Nan's worse, we'll go home."

The fat sister nodded, approving. "And you've no idea who Terry went off with?"

"No, sorry. I saw her empty her glass and say good night to a few people, and that's all. I supposed she'd gone to the loo, but when she didn't come out I didn't hang around. There's—" He nearly slipped up. "There's Vicky to think about, you see."

"Right. Well, sorry to have disturbed you. Good night."

"Good night." He turned back to the TV screen and didn't look away again until he heard the door close.

Interfering cow. Now he'd have to sit through this bloody foreign film until it finished because of her. He looked at Nicky, noticing for the first time that she had taken a can of lager from the cupboard and left it on the table for him. Beside it lay a roughly cut cheese-and-pickle sandwich, only just beginning to get stale and turn up at the corners, carefully placed on his best plate and with a square of kitchen roll folded into a fan for a napkin. He could picture her lying in the bed and smiling as she had last night when he read to her from a kid's joke book, only this time smiling as she thought of him coming home to find her special treat.

He would never leave her.

He tucked the covers around her more securely, although she appeared peaceful enough, ate the sandwich, and drank the lager. No voices could be heard from the Wallace caravan: Nothing could be heard but the muted Polish voices on the television. On-screen, a young woman was arguing with an older man, haranguing him, rather, for he was silently growing angrier until he looked as if he would hit her, or strangle her. Instead, he stormed out of the house. Darren turned away, reached for a book to read.

Books had always been his refuge, his escape route. It was one of the things that singled him out from other boys when he was young, and also aroused his father's contempt.

"He takes after his Uncle Sid," he once told Marsha. "Bloody little poofter."

But reading didn't help him tonight. First, the words made no sense, and then the individual letters became meaningless, like hieroglyphics. He tried to light a cigarette, but his hand shook so much that the paper burned all down one side and the thing wouldn't draw. And he wanted to cry again.

Nicky, I killed someone because I love you.

He wondered, if someone had asked the prison shrink—as they probably had—"Is Darren Gillespie likely to commit a violent crime again?" what the man's answer would have been.

▽

9

HE NOTICED THEM first because they were arguing. Two fat women just off the bus, weighed down by shopping bags with West End names on them, arguing about money.

"He had over two thousand in that flat of his," said one. "He told me so himself."

"And you believed him? Rene, he was an old man. He didn't know whether he was coming or going half the time. Figment of his imagination, if you ask me."

"That's where you're wrong, Lil. I've seen it. Well, I've seen some of it at any rate. Kept it under the mattress, he did."

"More fool him, then. Though that sounds just like our Charley. The old sod."

Mike Southgate, out of curiosity, might even have followed them in order to hear the rest of their conversation, but there was no need; they came and sat on the second wooden bench outside the flats in Princess Royal Road. Mike, hiding behind his *Guardian*, saw that there were many years between the two; perhaps as many as forty. But they were very much alike. Mother and daughter, except that the younger had addressed the elder as "Lil."

"He had his Post Office savings, of course," Lil resumed, "and he left that to me." She prissily arranged her dress to cover her bloated knees, made herself ridiculously proper.

"And he promised me the rest. I need that money, Lil."

"What, so you can go gallivanting off again. Where to this time? Australia? Timbuk-bloody-tu?"

"Jealous or something? You've never got no further than Southend in your life. No, I'm going to the police."

"Over my dead body, you are!"

Mike turned a page of his paper, aware that they were both looking at him. They lowered their voices, but women of their sort can never speak in anything below a stage whisper, and after a few seconds he dared to watch them again.

"You'd rather he got away with it?" said Rene, the younger one.

"Yes, I would. Don't you realize? If the old bugger did have two thousand—and I'm not saying I believe a word of it, mind—if he did have that sort of money in the house you can bet your life it weren't kosher. He was my brother. I knew him all right."

"I know where it came from. Or most of it."

Mike took out his Biro and frowned at the crossword.

"Where?"

"He was collecting Ida's pension for months after she died, that's where."

"That I *will* believe," Lil said emphatically. "But it makes no difference to me whether that young Darren nicked it or not. You're not going running to the law, Rene. They'll find out where Charley got it from and this family's name'll be in the mud. Again. I won't have it, Rene. He was my brother, and I'll deny he ever had a penny in the house. Now then."

Darren. That young Darren. It was a common enough name, of course. Probably there were half a dozen of them or more in this street alone. But Darren Gillespie had known an old man named Charley, now dead, had often drunk with him in the pub on the corner, often run errands for him. The neighbors, including Charley's sister, must have known about it. And if there was over two thousand pounds missing from the old boy's flat . . .

"But that money's mine by rights!" Rene complained.

"How can it be yours when it wasn't even his in the first place? I'll deny it, Rene. I'm his sister, they'll believe me. You're not going to disgrace me, you hear? If you want money you can bloody well work for it like everyone else has to."

"Are you rested now?" Rene asked, in a tone of irritation rather than concern. "Can we go home?" She gathered up most of the bags, there were seven or eight of them, and led the way, the older woman plodding after her.

Mike folded his newspaper and glanced up at flat 23. Darren always seemed anxious about money, but would he steal from an old man? A paper boy had seen Charley lying on the floor and rung the police, who later questioned Darren. But the coroner's verdict was death by natural causes. The heart, perhaps.

Or shock at finding his money gone?

Maybe Rene wouldn't go to the police, not yet. But when Darren came back and she saw him, it was possible she would change her mind. He, Mike, must warn him. Yet how could he do that when he didn't even know where the lad was? Mike Southgate was about to break the law himself.

It worked, and he could hardly believe it. The credit card trick—though in this case it was a plastic library card—actually worked. He closed the door behind him, putting the catch down on the inside, just in case.

The flat was dirty, smelled musty, and he thought Darren might have tidied up a bit before he left. The front room wasn't too bad, but clothes and books lay scattered about the bedroom, while in the kitchen he found the larder door open and a couple of tins knocked to the floor. He went into the bathroom and saw that it was empty of all toiletries; no soap, toothpaste, or toothbrush, none of the aftershave he liked to drench himself with occasionally. Nothing but a roll of Andrex dangling from a broken holder—and Darren's shaver. Now why had he left that behind? With the rest of the windowsill meticulously cleared it was unlikely he had overlooked it.

Mike went into the living room, listening briefly at the front door to make sure nobody was hanging about around the lift, because in that room he was more likely to find some clue to the lad's whereabouts. The old-fashioned sideboard was cluttered. Half a bottle of vodka in one of the cupboards, bits of electrical gadgets taken to pieces never to be put back together again, balls of wool left by Darren's grandmother, family documents and photographs. In the drawers he found bills and receipts, cutlery, screwdrivers, batteries and plugs, several pairs of National Health spectacles (also relics of the grandmother), and scraps of paper that appeared to be personal memos. It seemed that Darren never threw anything out.

Mike took a bundle of these papers and sat at the dining table to go through them one by one. Surely somewhere amongst them he would find something that would lead him to Darren? Old shopping lists, titles and authors of books he must have heard of and wanted to read, phone numbers with meaningless initials after them, even a roughed-out letter to a prospective employer. At last he found a list of numbers with full names and addresses—all of them farms—with their "St dts," by which he evidently meant the date they began picking.

Mike would have to ring them all; only able to ask for a young man called Darren who drove a blue-and-white camper because he knew he used his mother's maiden name and couldn't for the life of him remember what it was. Then it occurred to him that Darren's birth certificate would probably be there among all those family documents.

He turned to the sideboard, steeling himself to go through the lad's personal property for the second time, and noticed something lying on the floor. A photograph. Mike picked it up, recognized Frances "Francie" Gillespie from the snap he had seen once before. Darren must have dropped it by accident.

Such a pretty child. Such a striking smile. And her eyes . . . She looked like a little girl who has just said something amusing to adults, and although she doesn't understand it herself and is mildly embarrassed, she laughs too. And did her face look familiar to him because he had seen it before?

Slightly more chubby and with a fringe to hide her widow's peak . . . Mike covered the forehead with his finger. He was right. Darren's stepsister bore a strong resemblance to the missing child, Nicolle Gurney.

Some miles away, in a flat just off Bethnal Green's Roman Road, Alan Ralph was also gazing at a photograph. Lisa must have looked very like Nicky at the same age. Their eyes were a different color—Nicky's green inherited from her natural father—but of the same shape. Lisa's hair had been lighter and curly, but she had the same widow's peak in her broad forehead: "Touched by angels," Nicky's late grandmother once said, handsomely forgiving her daughter for the mistake of her first marriage.

Alan wished he had photos of Lisa as a child. There were the wedding pictures, of course, and snaps of her taken at Wheatcliffe-on-Sea before she became ill. But that was all. The photograph he held in his hand was one of his stepdaughter with her friend, Emma-Kate O'Reilly, taken only a few months ago in Emma's backyard.

"I'm so sorry, Alan," Mrs. O'Reilly said. "We forgot all about this. It's a better likeness of Nicky than that old school thing, don't you think? You'd better let the police have it straight away."

Why was the woman so irritatingly polite to him now, when before Nicky vanished it was, "Oi, Al," and "How's your Nicks, then?"

He knew why. She suspected him of having something to do with the kid's disappearance—as the police had at first. That was natural, he supposed. Most child molesters are known to their victims, and a high percentage came from within the family. He had read that somewhere, or heard it said on the television. The Wheatcliffe police had kept him at the station for over twelve hours, questioned first by one detective then another, while James was being cared for by a WPC. He told them the same story again and again, and all through his long ordeal the same fears plagued his mind:

Was Nicky dead? How was he ever going to tell Lisa? Suppose they took the boy away and put him into care?

It wasn't until the café owner, having heard a news report on local radio, came forward to say he had served breakfast to a young girl matching Nicky's description in company with a young man that Alan was allowed to leave.

But he had withheld one piece of information, hadn't told them the full story of that Wednesday afternoon.

He'd sent Nicky to buy tobacco from a machine in the pier café, an errand that should have taken two minutes, not two hours, and his temper grew when she didn't come back. It was all too much for him; Lisa so ill in hospital, wondering how he could cope with two kids when she died—especially Nicky. No one could have tried harder with that child.

"I know I'm not your real father, Nicky—"

"No, you ain't."

"And I know I'll never take his place. But couldn't we at least try to get on better—for your mother's sake?"

She stared at him for a moment, four foot ten of dumb insolence, then marched out.

Oh, he had tried all right.

That afternoon he'd had enough. He needed a cigarette, he was thirsty—dehydrated after a daylong binge—and wanted the girl to hurry back and look after James while he went for some cans of beer. When she finally returned he had shouted at her, called her a slut, a tramp, something like that, and slammed the door on her.

A few drags on a cigarette calmed him, and he opened the door again, half decided to call her back, make one last appeal for reasonable behavior for her mother's sake. She was on the beach a short distance away eating an ice lolly, and with her was a young man Alan recognized by sight. He had seen him several times over the past few days, a lonely-looking figure—which was perhaps why he noticed him—incongruous among the holidaymakers, usually gazing out to sea or watching the gulls. Nicky had befriended him, Alan supposed. She was like that, always making new friends at home

in London: old ladies, Indian shopkeepers, an old chap with
a wooden leg and a Down's syndrome boy. She saw everyone
as a potential friend—everyone except her stepfather. This
youngster was typical of her preference: a loner, maybe even
a down-and-out. Alan had never seen him watching children, or watching anyone for that matter, his only interest
appearing to be the sea, the birds, and his own thoughts. So
he was not unduly alarmed. Besides, there were plenty of
people about, and the girl knew better than to wander off
anywhere at the suggestion of one of her "friends."

At first, Alan didn't tell the police about this because he
feared they would think he was merely trying to divert their
attention from him. And when they finally let him leave the
station, he was too stunned and too tired to think about it.
The next day he bought a newspaper and saw the Photofit
picture of the man the café owner had seen with Nicky. Still
exhausted and a little more than half drunk, he came to the
immediate conclusion that this was not the young man he
had seen on the beach.

Now a month had gone by, Lisa was dead and buried, and
still there was no trace of his stepdaughter. Those well-
meaning friends who were trying to prepare him for the day
Nicky's body was found, or the possibility of his never
knowing what had happened to her, couldn't understand.
He knew she was alive. With the instinct supposed to be
exclusive to a natural parent he knew she was alive and safe.
And he wanted her back.

He had found a child minder for young James, a sour-faced
woman who seemed to take the same attitude toward children
as another woman might take toward bacteria. But James, like
the other toddlers in her care, appeared to be happy enough.
He was delivered home at six o'clock each evening clean, well
fed, and usually with a few new words in his vocabulary. So
Alan felt he need not worry about his son's welfare.

But Nicky . . . As the time passed he felt increasingly that
he ought to be doing more. It was what Lisa would have
wanted.

"I have to go away for a few days," he told the child minder. "Could you look after James?"

"Do you think that's wise, Mr. Ralph?" She looked down at the toddler, who was contentedly chewing at the head of his Action Man. "I mean, it's okay by me, of course. But suppose you were—well, needed?"

By the police, she meant. Suppose the police wanted to question him again. Perhaps she and Mrs. O'Reilly imagined he had murdered Nicky and shoved her body up a chimney. He wasn't going to explain to this old trout that he was leaving the little boy in order to return to Wheatcliffe-on-Sea and look for the girl himself. He wasn't going to explain to anyone, because some people couldn't understand, any more than the friends who believed their advice was helping him. None of them had a child that had gone missing.

The resort was closing down for the winter. Amusement arcades and souvenir shops were making one last bid for trade before pulling down the shutters for another season, but most of the chalet-style shops along the front were already closed. The beach huts, too, were locked and desolate; and none more desolate than Beachside. Alan turned away from them because he couldn't bear to look, gazed instead at the fine, dry sand, seldom covered by the tide and now littered with empty cigarette packets and ice lolly wrappers. He could see a few people on the end of the pier, old men fishing probably, and overhead the ever-hungry gulls circled and screamed.

The last time he was here, Lisa was still alive.

He had the photograph of Nicky with Emma-Kate O'Reilly in his pocket, and while he fully intended to take it to the police as a better likeness of his stepdaughter, he would keep it until he had made an investigation of his own.

The owner of the café, the Chish and Fips, recognized him straightaway but failed to identify the girl on the snap as the one he had seen a month before.

"It's a long time ago, mate," he said. "I could see the

likeness to the other picture at the time—could 'ave sworn to it then, but not now. You understand what I mean, don't you? I get so many people come here."

Alan nodded, slightly embarrassed. He shouldn't expect too much, not after so long. But he had to try.

"And the bloke she was with . . . When you helped the police put that Photofit together—"

"Oh, don't remind me," the man interrupted. "They kept me at it so bloody long I began to think they were gonna charge me."

"And was it a good likeness?"

"The best we could come up with."

"That's not answering my question, is it?" Alan looked steadily into the man's face. He was taller and at least five stone heavier, an intimidating figure who would not leave until he had what he wanted.

"No, I can't really say it was, mate. All the features were right, but the expression was wrong. I don't know. I can't explain it."

Alan thought of the lad he had seen talking to Nicky. With his features altered, hardened, could he be the same person? The boy on the beach was a scruffy youth, but not dirty, and with that badged cap he looked like a relic of the late sixties. The cap, of course . . .

"Yeah," the café owner admitted, "that's right, he did have a cap. Took it off as soon as he sat down, though. That's right. And the kid—I mean, the little girl—sat playing with it."

"Playing with it?" That didn't sound like a child afraid for her life.

"Playing with the badges. Swastikas, they were. And I'll tell you what"—he scowled fiercely, proudly—"my father didn't get killed fighting them bloody Nazis so the likes of that little runt could walk around wearing swastikas on their bloody heads."

"The young don't understand that sort of thing," Alan said quickly. "But on the television, you said my daughter looked frightened. Now you say she was playing with the boy's cap."

"She did look frightened. But when the boy went out back to the lav. He was gone so long and I thought she were gonna start bawling. I was about to go over and speak to her when he came back, and then they ran out."

She was frightened of him, Alan; of what he would say when she arrived back at the beach hut.

"He didn't force her to leave with him, then?"

"Well, no. It didn't look like that." He took out a large handkerchief and briefly assaulted his nose with it. "See, everything happened so quick. First the cops and then the TV people. They didn't exactly lead me on but they—well—they sorta made suggestions. I hadn't really had time to think properly. Nothing like this ever happened to me before. I got confused, I suppose."

Alan nodded. Should he force the man to go to the police, admit he had made a few mistakes? No doubt he was confused, bewildered by all the questions and fuss: Alan could understand that. Perhaps his hatred of the Nazi symbol had also affected his judgment when the Photofit was being assembled. And if he did make the wretched man go to the police, sooner or later he would have to admit that he himself had withheld information.

All these doubts had to be weighed against Nicky's safety, his desire to bring her home and be a father to her. He decided to wait a while longer.

"One more question," he said. "Have you ever seen the boy before?"

"I dunno. I might've done. In The Shipmates' Arms, maybe. That's my regular, and there's a lot of young lads get in there in the evenings. You gotta understand, though, I couldn't swear to it. It were that cap an' the bloody swastikas I noticed."

Alan left the café excited, hopeful—and afraid. He was almost sure now that Nicky had gone off with the boy he saw on the beach. She had run away before (something else he had omitted to tell the police), on the first occasion by attaching herself to a drink-sodden "bag lady," an escapade that only came to light when all was forgiven and she began to think of her adventure as something to be proud of. So wasn't it possible she had attached herself to this youth in a similar way, spun him some yarn to win his sympathy?

He looked a nice enough young man. But then, nice young men don't run off with adolescent girls. And there was no law that said a pervert may not have a handsome or even gentle face. Perhaps he was simpleminded; a likely explanation, given Nicky's penchant for the misfit, the handicapped, and the socially inept.

She was alive, he knew that, but for how much longer? He recalled all the horror stories he had read about runaway kids, many of them even younger than Nicky; forced into a life of prostitution by some filthy pimp who picked them up at railway stations, made them dependent on drugs, old women by the time they were fifteen, diseased and often dead at twenty.

That wasn't going to happen to Nicky.

"Yeah, it rings a bell," a barmaid at The Shipmates' Arms told him. "I do seem to remember a lad with a cap like that. He was only here a few days—not even a week, I don't think—but he came in every lunchtime and every evening. If he is the one I'm thinking of, well, I quite fancied him. Oops! Sorry, love. Not your son, is he?"

"No, he's not my son. Can you describe him?"

"Brown hair. Straight, and a bit straggly. Brown eyes. Always struck me like he was deep in thought. Miles away. Tell you something peculiar, though. The last time he was here, the Wednesday night—"

"Wednesday? Are you sure it was a Wednesday?"

The barmaid looked at him as if he'd just offered her a personal insult, so he added, "Well, it was a month ago."

"Oh, well, yes. I suppose it must be a few weeks back now. Only I remember because we had a big darts match on. Grand Final between us and The Eagle and Lamb from

Dartwick, just down the road. We won—first time we've beat 'em in three years—and I got a bit 'ow's yer father. Bit merry, you know what I mean? Anyway, I started chatting young Darren up—"

Darren. The boy had a name now. Darren.

"—asked him for a date. God! Was he a hunk!"

"You were going to tell me about something peculiar that night."

"Oh, yeah. Well, you see, every time he came in here he'd play those old sixties classics on the jukebox. Every night, the same old rubbish. But this time he put on that Jason Donovan thing—'When You Come Back to Me,' I think it's called. Three times on the trot, he played it."

Jason Donovan, Nicky's idol. But did this mean anything?

"Did he have a little girl with him that evening?"

"No kids allowed in here, love. Look, are you the police or what? Hey, is this something to do with that kid that went missing? 'Cos if it is, I can tell you straight; young Darren was nothing like the bloke in that Photofit thing. Nothing like." She banged the change from his pint onto the counter. "If you want to know any more p'raps you'd better speak to the boss."

Ten minutes later, Alan left The Shipmates' Arms. He was sweating, red in the face, his graying hair falling across his forehead.

The boy's name was Darren, he came from Peckham, South London, and he drove about the country in some sort of van looking for seasonal work.

And he almost certainly had Nicky with him.

▽

10

"DARREN, DARREN! LOOK—can we go and see this? Please? Please!" Nicky flung her arms around his neck, squeezing, wheedling, whining.

"What? What are you on about now?" He wrestled free to look at the page of a teenage television magazine that she thrust in front of him.

"Aussie Stars Over for the Panto Season!" screamed the headline, and beneath it photographs of a dozen or so Australian soap stars circled around a map of Britain.

"Look, Darren. Sunny Patterson in *Peter Pan* at the Victoria Theatre, in Barnhearst. She's playing Peter, Darren—"

"Sunny who?"

"You know. In 'Take the O'Neills.' "

Darren sighed. It was her favorite program, a twice weekly comedy series about some awful fictional family in Sydney. Though he had to admit it was funny, the show that ended with an anonymous voice pleading, "Take the O'Neills! Somebody . . . *Please!*" he would have preferred to see her engrossed in something a little more educational, like "Blue Peter" or "Newsround."

"Darren, I want to see it. Aw, go on!"

He tried appealing to her adult half. "Aren't you a bit old for the panto?"

"Have you ever been to one?"

He had, a long time ago. Just before his mother left with her boyfriend, she had taken him and his cousin to see *Snow White*. It was an experience that stunned him and that he never forgot, for it was the last time he could remember being truly, uncomplicatedly happy.

"Yes, a long while ago," he admitted. "When I was much younger than you, though. Much younger."

"Well, I never have. Our class went one year, but I couldn't go 'cos me dad had just died and our mam said it wouldn't look right."

Our mam. She always lapsed into the Geordie dialect when she was excited or upset.

"You really want to go?"

"Can we? I'll be real good, Darren. I'll cook for you, an' I'll read anything you want me to." He had made a preliminary attack on her education, finding that although she could read and write fluently, her general knowledge was poor and her grasp of even simple arithmetic abysmal. ("Stuff sums. You don't need sums to be an actress.") "I'll do anything, Darren, only please let's see *Peter Pan*. I love Sunny Patterson. She's my all-time favorite."

"I don't know, Nicks. Barnhearst's halfway up the country, and—" And he had never set foot inside a theater since his mother took him, didn't know how to reserve seats. "When does this panto open?"

"December fourteenth. Can we, Darren? Can we?"

"Okay. I'll see what I can do." How could he refuse her anything?

"Jonagold." She put her arms around him again, ruffled his hair as Francie used to do when she was in her Big Sister mood.

"Don't do that, Francie. I'm not a baby, you know."

"Ooh, isn't Diddums icckle baby, den?" And she ruffled his hair once more; harder, almost spitefully.

"Francie—"

"Baby! Baby! Bloody little baby! You stop staring at me, you hear? Whatsa matter? You fancy me or something?"

"Nicky—"

"Jonagold, you're gonna have to do something about your hair. The roots are showing. Get some Grecian 2000."

He looked in her hand mirror. She was right; the dark roots were becoming too evident among the blond, and he would have to do something about it if he wanted his hair to appear natural.

They were parked just outside a small town on the Norfolk coast, had been there since leaving Easthill's farm the previous Sunday.

"We have to leave," he told the farmer. "It's our gran. Sorry."

It was lunchtime. He had given Nicky an early meal of chicken with chips and peas—and two glasses of wine as a treat—then set off for the village, promising Coke and sweets on his return. At the Seven Bells he made a point of telling the landlord why he wanted to use the telephone; and he left the pub abruptly, without explanation, a pint of bitter untouched on the bar.

What was more natural behavior for a caring young man who had just heard bad news about his grandmother?

Terry Wallace's sister had called the police, and two officers were at the site when he returned—one didn't even bother to get out of the car. Apparently, women of her age and reputation who suddenly disappear are assumed to have gone off with a man. Darren answered a few questions: Yes, he had seen her in the public bar with a lot of other people, some of whom he didn't recognize; no, he didn't see her leave, and he himself had left before closing time because he had a backache.

His tongue felt like a piece of cracked leather, and he trembled inwardly, but he managed to ask the officer if he would be needed again.

"I shouldn't think so, sir. I'm sure Mrs. Wallace will turn up safe and well."

"Good, because I have to go home this afternoon. My grandmother's just died."

"Sorry to hear that, sir. Perhaps you could leave a forwarding address, just in case?"

Darren provided him with the name he had used at the farm and a fictional address. The fat sister, who had been hovering behind the police officer, even offered her sympathy for the "dead grandmother" and wished him a safe journey, but fortunately she didn't mention the child.

He found her deeply asleep on the settee, breathing loudly, not quite snoring. Her breath smelled of wine, and she didn't stir as he lifted her to the floor in order to make up the bed. This time, he didn't hesitate to undress her; first her sneakers and socks, then her pullover and jeans. She wore a thin, cheap T-shirt in lieu of a vest, and grown-up, silky orange panties that he had bought on special offer at Woolies.

Something was changed about her; something he hadn't noticed the last time he saw her so scantily dressed. A slight swelling around the area of her nipples, a slimmer waist, a firmer abdomen.

He touched her face, traced one eyebrow with his fingertip, and still she didn't wake. It was wrong, he told himself, of course it was wrong. He had got the girl drunk in order to keep her quiet, and now he was touching her. Only her face, but touching her nevertheless. He moved away to find the blanket, and he covered her properly with it, put her slender-limbed, no-longer-childlike body out of sight. While she slept he drove away from the fruit farm, not daring to look at the entrance gate to the reservoir orchards or think about that bin, now almost full among the pear trees, where the body of Terry Wallace lay.

He drove on and on, barely noticing his direction and only vaguely aware that they were heading north. He couldn't return to London. It was too soon after Lisa Ralph's death to take the kid back there. Besides which, he was uneasy over the way she had lately taken to quoting her stepfather: "Alan says if you don't scrub your fingernails, if you eat with them dirty, you'll get worms," and "Alan says if your head itches it means you've got dandruff."

He was afraid to ask if she missed him and her little

brother, or if she missed her home, because if she answered "a bit," he would know it was all over. So his object now was to keep her happy, to spoil her and give her the things Alan Ralph would be unable or unwilling to give. Therefore, when she asked if they could go to see the pantomime in Barnhearst, he at last agreed. It was what she wanted more than anything, she told him, to meet the actress Sunny Patterson. She was so excited; she would do a special drawing for her idol, give her flowers, and ask for her autograph.

"I'm going to be an actress too," she said. It was something she had often mentioned before—usually as a good enough reason why not to bother about arithmetic lessons—and Darren always dismissed it as a passing phase. Most children had grand ambitions at her age: pop stars, first-division footballers, models—only to end up in an office or shop.

"How long have you had this ambition?" he asked, mainly to stop her raving on about Sunny Patterson, which was getting on his nerves.

"Oh, since I was about eight. I saw this film on the telly, *Brief Encounter*, it was called, and I've wanted to be an actress ever since."

Darren was unimpressed. "You'd be up against a lot of competition, Nicky," he told her.

"I know that."

"And you'd be on the dole most of the time. Or waiting tables. Don't you think you could do better?"

"Of course. I've thought it all out." She looked at him steadily, full of confidence. "I'm going to learn shorthand, typing, word processing—everything you need in an office. Then I'll do temping, maybe take typing work at home. Lots of people do that, you know. And working from home would mean I could choose my own hours, and that'd leave me free to train. Darren, bung the box on, I'm missing 'Home and Away.' "

"I trust you'll enunciate correctly when you're on the stage."

"Wot?"

Later, she told him that her father had paid for her to take lessons at a Saturday stage school in Newcastle, where she learned drama and modern dance. But this came to an end when her father died and Lisa Ralph could no longer afford the fees.

"Alan offered to pay for me to take lessons in London," she said, looking thoughtfully at her fingers.

"Oh? Why didn't you, then?"

"I dunno."

"Because you didn't want to take anything from him?"

She nodded. If she were with her stepfather now and he repeated the offer, would she accept?

"Well, maybe—just maybe, mind—you could take lessons again after Christmas."

"You pulling my piss—I mean, you joking?"

"Of course not. If that's what you'd like, I'll see what I can do. But remember, not till after Christmas." He saw in this a possible answer to the question of her education.

Darren had been making more plans since leaving the farm at Defford, and he was now beginning to see that his first instinct, to take her to the country, was unwise. If you wanted to remain anonymous, where better than a city or a large town? People in densely populated areas generally had enough to do minding their own business, let alone anyone else's. London would have been his obvious choice; put the flat on the market and rent another in a different area. But Nicky would be restless in London. She'd want to see her old friends—and Alan Ralph would be too close for Darren's peace of mind.

He thought of Stoke-on-Trent, where he had once found temporary work and even considered settling. He liked the way you could reach the end of a modern street with smart, modern shops and find yourself suddenly looking down upon a row of Victorian terraced houses; it was like living in two different worlds. The people were friendly as well, though Darren had found it sometimes hard to understand their accents and they his. Out of bloody-mindedness, he several times thickened his own, and was amazed to find they mistook him for an Australian. That could be useful.

But Stoke-on-Trent was close to Newcastle-under-Lyme. If he took Nicky there, and she saw the name, would she be reminded of the other Newcastle, her old home and old friends? Yet the family had left Newcastle-upon-Tyne more than two years ago; a long time to a child. Surely the new ties of London were strong now?

"Nicky," he said on impulse, "do you know where Stoke-on-Trent is?"

" 'Course I do." She looked at him suspiciously, evidently thinking the subject of today's attack on her education was geography.

"Where is it, then?"

"Oh, somewhere in Scotland."

"Not exactly." He was relieved. Her ignorance could have its uses. "Anyway, it's a place where I once worked, and I was thinking of going there until after Christmas." Then, as an ace card of persuasion, "It's quite near Barnhearst, actually."

"Oh, yeah, Darren! Let's go, then. Let's go now, can we?"

"Not right now. I've got things to see to. First of all—" He poured a kettle of boiling water into the sink, pumped in some cold—"your hair needs washing."

"Aw, Darren! Not now, I'm reading!"

"Get your head in that sink." He refilled the kettle, put it back on the stove. "I'm not going anywhere with you looking like a saddle tramp."

"My hair wants cutting."

"You want the ends trimmed?"

"No, I want it cut. Will you do it for me, Darren?"

"I might mess it up. Anyway, why do you want it cut? I don't like short hair on girls. You'll look like a boy."

"Who cares?"

He didn't want to cut her hair. She wouldn't look like Francie anymore with it short. But did that matter? So often lately he had looked at her and seen only Nicky. So often she said or did something and he no longer automatically compared her words and actions with those of Francie. Still, he wanted her the way she was, with nothing changed about her.

He said, "Another inch or so and you could style it like Sunny Patterson's hair. It's about the same color, too. Just think, by the time you get to meet her you could look just like her."

"You think so?" She grabbed the mirror, held her hair back, and studied the effect. "We-ell, all right. You really think I'd look just like her?"

"Positive. Only her hair is always clean."

"It's hard to do it in that sink."

"Okay, you win." He propelled her to the sink. "I'll do it for you."

Darren had never washed anyone's hair before, would have balked at the idea of touching someone in what he considered an intimate way. Touching Nicky's hair was pleasurable, seemed to put their relationship on a higher plane—and was also disturbing.

He massaged the shampoo into her scalp gently but firmly with his fingertips, feeling the shape of her head. "Keep your eyes closed," he warned when she fidgeted. He rinsed thoroughly with clean water from a jug, the first time "too hot!" the second "too fucking cold!"

"You watch your language. Okay, that's it. And don't forget to tip the hairdresser."

He toweled her hair until it was damp, then used the cordless dryer he had bought especially for her, brushing as he dried. Her hair was thick and fine, naturally streaked with blond, and very soft when freshly washed. He loved the smell of it, too.

"I like you brushing my hair, Darren," Nicky said. "It makes me feel sleepy, like that wine did."

The wine. No, he shouldn't even think about doing that again. A couple of glasses now and then to make her sleep probably wouldn't do any harm, but somehow it just wasn't right.

"Does it look okay? Do I look like Sunny Patterson?"

"Exactly like." He lowered his head to hers, breathed in the fresh smell of her hair.

"Darren—"

"Where's the hairdresser's tip, then?"

"You don't deserve it. You haven't brushed enough." She grinned. "Okay, here's your tip," and kissed him on the cheek. "Think yourself lucky, my lad. Darren, can we have a barbie?"

For a second, he thought ludicrously of a teenage doll, complete with bridal gown and a swimming pool shaped like a hospital emesis pan. Then he remembered the first night they were camped here. He had thought she was asleep and went out to light a bonfire, on which he quickly disposed of Terry Wallace's jacket and bag. But Nicky awoke, saw the fire, and came out with two large potatoes and two apples, and nothing would do but he let her bake them.

"They'll taste awful."

"No, they won't."

"They'll either burn or be raw."

"No, they won't. Alan once cooked spuds like this on Guy Fawkes night. They were brilliant. Bung them in, Darren." And he had to. But he couldn't eat either the potato or the apple; it would be almost like eating something cooked in Terry Wallace's ashes. Nicky didn't notice when he hid the food in his pocket, and she insisted on calling it a barbecue, or "barbie," as her penchant for Australian soaps had taught her.

"Can we, Darren? Can we?"

"All right." He couldn't, wouldn't refuse her anything. And he wished she hadn't mentioned her stepfather again.

They were camped in a well-sheltered spot, away from any houses or roads, where a small fire wouldn't be seen. Darren scrubbed potatoes, wrapped them in foil, and prodded them into the blaze. "We could have baked beans with them," he suggested.

"And black coffee." The "barbie" notion was forgotten in favor of the Wild West. "And let's sleep out here tonight, Darren."

"We'll see."

Of course they couldn't sleep outside. It was October, cold and damp most of the day, foggy at night; more unhealthy for a kid like Nicky than the crispness of December.

"I love pretending," she said.

"I know you do."

"It's the actress in me. Get the beans, Darren."

"Get the cigs, Darren. Well? Get a move on!"

They were hidden in his bedroom, under the pillow. Francie had thrust them into his hands, ordered him to hide them, and he—as usual—had done as she asked without question.

She and the boy smoked two cigarettes each, neither offered Darren one.

"He's too young," Francie said, and she laughed.

He sweetened her coffee with three spoonfuls of sugar— decaffeinated coffee, of course, and weak, because he didn't want her awake half the night.

"Darren," she said, mouth full of baked potato, "will I have lessons in Stoke-on-Trent?"

"No. No lessons until after Christmas, remember? We've got to find the best place for you, properly qualified teachers, not a bunch of old hacks." He was thinking of Francie's ballet teacher, an old woman who instructed a dozen or so little girls in her phony French accent while her ancient sister banged out three-four time on an indifferent piano.

His plan was to find a stage school that also taught normal school subjects, something like the Corona or Conti. At first, he would enroll her for Saturday classes, making inquiries by letter or telephone and explaining that he was the girl's father, a widower and invalid confined to the house. Her brother would escort her to and from class. After a while, and if she proved good enough, he would telephone again and ask if she could be accepted full-time. Thus her formal education would be taken care of, she would be happy, and the principal would be used to seeing the child with her brother in lieu of a parent. And by then he would have thought of some way to get over the business of school records.

Until then, he must keep her occupied and entertained, let her rattle on about Sunny Patterson and Jason Donovan however much it got on his nerves, however jealous he might feel of her idols. Kids have to have idols, role models, and he supposed Nicky might have done worse in her choice.

"Have we got enough money?" she asked suddenly. The question surprised him, as this was the first time she'd shown the slightest concern over finances. And he, concerned to the point of obsession, was startled into telling her, Yes, of course, and not to worry.

"Eat your beans before they get cold."

"Me mum always used to worry about money."

"Well, we don't have to." Though money had, in fact, been occupying his mind for most of the past five days. He had enough to see them both through for some weeks, though not if he continued to spoil her as he had been doing with new clothes and other gifts: a radio cassette player (complete with Jason Donovan tapes), a gold locket, teenage annuals and novels, a jacket that was too grown-up for her, and posters that were promptly put up in the limited space of the camper.

He refused to ask himself if he were trying to buy her friendship, a pattern begun at Wheatcliffe-on-Sea with a strawberry split ice lolly, because that would have stirred too many uncomfortable memories.

"You can't make someone like you," his stepmother, Marsha, had told him in a rare moment of closeness. "You can't buy friendship, Darren. Francie is fond of you, but she has her own friends, and she doesn't want a little boy tagging along behind her all the time."

And you have to share the people you love, even the one you love best; they can never be exclusively yours.

After Christmas, Nicky would have the chance to meet new people, kids her own age, which was what she lacked at the moment. Only a few weeks to go, but would his money last? He would sell the flat. He'd never liked the area, the neighbors—apart from old Charley—had always avoided him, and he only kept the place for sentimental reasons, memories of his grandmother.

Darren had no idea how one went about putting property on the market, but his need always to know he had money in reserve outweighed his natural fear of being thought ignorant. He would sell the flat, and he would seek advice from the one person he knew wouldn't sneer at his unworldliness, Mike Southgate.

At her home in Defford, Lesley Fielding, overseer at Elm Tree Farm, was telling her husband what had happened that afternoon.

"It was just inside the gate where some of the bins were stacked. At first I thought it was a piece of gold foil." She spooned peas and creamed potatoes onto her plate. "But then I recognized it straightaway. There's no mistaking Terry's lighter. She was always showing it off, every break and lunchtime."

"Gift from one of her admirers," Bob Fielding suggested.

"I wouldn't be at all surprised. But as I told Rodney, she'd never leave the thing lying around."

"So now the police are taking her disappearance seriously?" Lesley nodded, frowning. "What's wrong?"

"I'm not sure. It's probably nothing, but . . ."

"But what?" her husband prompted.

"On the Friday before she disappeared there was one bin left only a quarter full. But on Monday morning it was almost filled. I thought I must have made a mistake, but now I'm not so sure."

"You think someone bumped her off on the Saturday night and then hid her body in that bin?"

"I know it sounds far-fetched—"

"I wouldn't say that. Think about it, love. Not a lot of people liked the woman. You told me so yourself. She always knew everyone else's business—and spread it around. There's a good enough motive for a start. I wouldn't put blackmail past someone like her. As for disposing of her body in one of the bins, what better way? Look, say she was killed where you found her lighter—which seems highly probable to me; a nonpremeditated, spur-of-the-moment job—what could he do with her body? It would float in the reservoir. He might bury it, of course, but only if he had access to some tools." Bob Fielding watched his wife's face carefully.

"You mean someone from the campsite?" she said.

"Who was the one you told me took off in a hurry on the Sunday afternoon?"

"Darren. The boy who had his kid sister with him. No, Bob. I'll never believe he had anything to do with it. I've never even seen him talking to Terry Wallace. Besides, they had a good reason to leave in a hurry; their grandmother had just died." And because Lesley Fielding knew exactly what her husband would say next, she added, "He'd mentioned the old lady several times, said he was worried because she was ill."

"What are you going to do?"

Lesley chased peas around her plate with a fork, her appetite gone. "Tomorrow I'll check the number of that bin, then I'll tell Rodney. I'll let him decide."

11

ALAN RALPH STEPPED on the white envelope before he noticed it lying on the doormat, leaving a wet footprint on the back. Lisa was right; they should have one of those cage things you could fix on the door to catch the post.

Lisa. Odd how often, even now, he still thought of her in the present tense. Always, it was, What will Lisa think about this? What will Lisa say? And it was starting to affect his relationship with James.

"Mummy wants you to eat up all your dinner," he would tell the child, and the response was invariably a certain:

"Mummy gone."

Then he would lose his temper with the little boy. Once, he almost hit him. He had been trying to coax Weetabix into a rebellious mouth when the toddler screamed, "No! No! Nicks . . . Nicks!"

It pained Alan that James should cry for his runaway sister while his mother was apparently forgotten.

He put the child down on the floor and glanced at the letter, supposing it to be from one of his family—no one else ever wrote to him. But it had been delivered by hand, "Mr. A. Ralph" scrawled across the envelope in red biro. Could it be from whoever had Nicky? A demand for ransom money, perhaps? It was unreal and he knew it. People who did that sort of thing went for rich brats, not the child of someone who worked in a garage.

He tore the envelope open, trembling even before he read

the badly spelled, largely unpunctuated, almost hysterical message.

Alan Ralph we know you killed Nicky you murderor. We know she had bruses on her and you did it Filthy scum like you ought to be shot and thats to good for the likes of you. If the police dont get you we will.

Mudrer MURDRER.

He screwed it up, threw it across the room, and glared at his son. The child, who had by now chewed both feet and half the head off his Action Man, smiled in return.

He should have expected something like this. Mrs. O'Reilly wasn't the only one whose attitude toward him had changed since the girl disappeared. He could sense it in their stares every time he left the flat; total strangers seemed to recognize him in the supermarket—seemed even to have gone out of their way to shop at that particular store in order to get a look at him.

Murderer. Child murderer.

Alan retrieved the letter and studied it again, but he didn't recognize the handwriting. Lisa's circle of intimates were in the habit of leaving notes for each other, though as far as he could tell it hadn't come from one of them. He supposed the sender to be a woman; writing anonymous letters was usually a female pastime, wasn't it?

He certainly couldn't take it to the police because of the reference to Nicky's bruises. She'd had a lot that last week at Wheatcliffe, more noticeable as she spent most of the day in her bikini top and shorts, though they had faded to a yellowy orange. Alan knew his wife sometimes hit the girl—kids needed a smacked arse if they couldn't be reasoned with, and never mind what those so-called experts said—but Lisa took it too far in his opinion. He had never raised his hand to the child, not even to threaten her with a clout, though God knew how many times he'd felt like doing so. But who would believe him when he had so often complained down the pub that he felt like strangling his stepdaughter?

Perhaps the author of this note had also contacted the

police. Almost certainly, for it would be senseless to tell the person you suspected of murder what you knew but not the police. They were watching him, waiting for him to slip up and give himself away. That young woman he had seen leaving the child minder's house—too well-dressed and classy to be dumping her own kid in an area like this. Could she have been a social worker going to check up on James? Alan gazed at the little boy, now busy with his toy cars. Every time the child fell and hurt himself he would be in fear of some social worker swooping down like an angry bird of prey with a place of safety order. He had lost his wife and Nicky, and now he felt that the faceless "they" were only waiting for the chance to deprive him of all he had left.

He wouldn't go to the police now to tell them what he had uncovered at Wheatcliffe-on-Sea, for the same reason he failed to tell them about the lad on the beach in the first place. They would think he was only trying to deflect their suspicion away from himself. He would find Nicky. He had a name, Darren, a face, and the knowledge that the boy came from London and traveled about the country looking for seasonal work in some kind of mobile home.

So much to go on and yet so little. He would find her before the police, persuade her to come back to him. Because if he didn't get to her first, convince her they could start afresh, he might lose her forever.

Alan Ralph wished desperately at that moment to have someone, preferably a stranger, to talk to.

Mike Southgate had also been to Wheatcliffe-on-Sea. It was the first time he had visited the resort, and making allowances for the fact that the town was closing for winter, he liked the place. He stood outside the beach huts, remembering that Nicolle Gurney had been staying in one of them when she disappeared; which one he had no way of knowing. But his concern was for Darren, not the child. Convinced they were together and 99 percent certain the lad would never harm a little girl who so resembled Francie Gillespie, he had gone to Wheatcliffe to find the café owner, hot on the heels, as it happened, of Nicky's stepfather.

"You the law?" demanded the owner of Chish and Fips, almost harassed beyond measure by a bunch of hungry youths and an assistant who turned up for work whenever it occurred to her.

"No, I'm a journalist." It slipped out unrehearsed and easily, but failed to convince the man.

"Oh, yeah? It's the other one with bells on, mate. It's about that kid again, ain't it? The second time in as many days. All right, what d'you wanna know?"

"The second time?"

"Kid's dad was in yesterday. I told him that Photofit weren't all that good a likeness, but it were the best I could do. I mean, I know the kid's missing, an' I hate that sorta thing as much as anyone, but sod it, I have got a business to run."

Mike was able to describe Darren with much more accuracy than Alan Ralph. Which was natural; he felt an attachment, an attraction to the lad.

"That's him," said the café owner. "That's him exactly. I'm sure of it now. And like I told the father, I saw him in my local once or twice. The Shipmates' Arms. Here—how come you know him so well?"

This time he couldn't lie. "He's a friend of mine, and I think there's been some mistake."

"You going to the police?"

"Of course." Of course not. How could he see Darren sent down again, this time for a sentence of years instead of months?

Mike left the café hurriedly, wandered about the town until The Shipmates' Arms opened up at six. He sat on the beach, well wrapped against the autumn chill, knowing Darren well enough to be sure he too had sat on the fine, dry sand and watched the waves and the screaming gulls. He licked his lips, dry and salty from the sea air, trying to recall everything he had ever heard or read about the case of Nicolle Gurney.

A mother dying in hospital, a stepfather, a half-brother; a setup almost parallel to the Gillespies. And the girl resembled Francie. Mike took the photograph he had found in Darren's flat from his pocket. Every time he looked at it he saw the likeness more clearly. The child whose face he knew from the television news was chubbier, wore her hair differently, but their coloring was identical: honey-colored hair and green eyes with a pale, flawless skin. Their bone structure was alike, too. Similar enough for anyone who knew and remembered Frances Gillespie to turn and look twice at Nicolle Gurney.

At The Shipmates' Arms he knew for certain: a young man who wore a cap covered with swastika badges, who played sixties records on the jukebox, and who traveled about the country looking for seasonal work. Darren had the Gurney child with him.

Mike spent the next days trudging around the offices of London newspapers and making phone calls. He learned that the photograph of Nicolle was an old one, taken over a year ago. According to the VDU at the office of an East London free paper: *"Nicky's face is now thinner, her hair worn swept back from her forehead, usually under a broad Alice band, showing a distinct 'widow's peak.' "*

The dead girl and the missing girl might have been sisters. Twins, even.

Darren intended to go fruit picking, but surely he'd changed his plans after meeting the girl? What would he, Mike, do in the same situation? Get as far away as possible, hide out in some lonely spot until all the fuss had died down, then take the girl back to London or another large city where they could live in anonymity. Yet Mike recalled a conversation he'd once had with Darren, one of the rare occasions when he spoke openly about his attempted rape on the Ipswich girl.

"What did you do afterwards? The next day?"

"Went back to my job. Carried on as usual. It seemed to me the most sensible thing to do."

So there was a chance he had, after all, stuck to his plans. Mike took the list of East Anglian fruit farms with their telephone numbers from his pocket and began on a series of calls that would surely send his phone bill through the roof. Two farmers told him, Yes, they had employed a youth named Darren for the fruit harvest; one a medical student known in the village, the other a Jamaican boy. Neither of them had a youngster in tow or drove a camper. Darren was a popular name, after all.

Then Mike spoke to Rodney Easthill of Elm Tree in Defford. The man sounded as harassed as the proprietor of Chish and Fips and gave the information grudgingly.

Yes, he had hired a young man named Darren who drove a blue-and-white camper and who had a girl, his sister, with him. But their name was not Gillespie, and they were both fair-haired. They left some time ago—he thought it was a Sunday—because of a death in the family. Easthill added that it was "a bloody nuisance having people coming for a few days and then buggering off."

Pressed further, he said yes, Darren did have brown eyes and was what he supposed you might call handsome. "Dyed his hair? How the hell would I know a thing like that? Now, if you don't mind, I've got a farm to run." And he put the phone down.

That was that, then. Darren and the girl could be anywhere by now. He began making a list of all the places he knew the lad had worked, placing an asterisk where Darren mentioned being particularly happy—Staffordshire and Shropshire seemed to have been singled out as favorites—when it occurred to Mike to wonder why the pair had left Elm Tree Farm so suddenly.

The obvious answer was that someone must have recognized the girl. But if that were the case, surely they would contact the police? There would have been something on the television or in the papers, urging people in the area to be on the lookout for them. Or maybe he had simply gone on to another farm that paid a higher rate.

Money. The boy was obsessed by the fear that he would run out of money: odd, then, that he would never even consider looking for a regular job.

Mike needed money himself. He was still out of work and as little inclined as Darren to think about a settled future at the moment. He had some savings, not a vast amount, but sufficient to keep him modestly while he sorted himself out. After that, well, there was always the Social, or perhaps a loan from his great-uncle, who had more or less promised help if it was needed.

He was already economizing to the extent that dinner tonight would be Marmite on toast, ditto tomorrow's breakfast, with perhaps an egg for lunch. If he was here by lunchtime. For Mike had already half decided to go down to Suffolk the following day, had even washed his lanky blond hair—a task not normally undertaken more than twice a week—and checked bus timetables. A bus, of course, would be cheaper than trains.

His landlady interrupted these plans with the news that "Someone's been ringing on your phone all day long, Mr. Southgate." At first, he misunderstood, her choice of words leading him to imagine that someone had broken into his flat to use his telephone.

She explained. "If you're going to be that popular, Mr. Southgate, I might ask that you take it off the 'ook when you go out all day."

"I'm sorry, Mrs. Burridge."

She softened because she liked him. "Young lady, I suppose?"

"I really can't say, as I wasn't here to answer it. Did it ring many times?"

"Six or seven. 'Bout three times between ten and eleven, once at dinner time, and about three more times this afternoon. Persistent young lady, I reckon."

Mike smiled at her, trying to make it a smile of conspiracy. Young lady. If only that were so, life would be a lot less complicated.

"You got another job yet?" She was hinting at the rent, no doubt.

"Not yet, Mrs. Burridge. Still looking around. Your money's on the table, by the way."

She shuffled into the room to collect her rent and mark his card as paid for another week. He wished she'd go. He wasn't in the mood to listen to her inane chatter or answer her not very delicate hints. Still, it was only common courtesy to tell her he might be away for a few days. It wasn't well received.

"Well, I hope you'll be sure to close the windows before you go. We don't want no burglars in here. And take your phone off, Mr. Southgate. My old man's on nights, and he don't want to be woken up all hours of the day with it ringing."

She left him to butter his toast, which had browned unevenly as usual; pale gold at one edge and charcoal at the other. He was eating it when the phone rang again, and because he feared his landlady's further annoyance, he broke the habit of a lifetime and rushed to answer it.

He couldn't believe the voice at the other end. "Mike—? I've been trying to ring you all day."

"Darren—you're in trouble—"

"What? No, no. Everything's fine. Mike, I need your advice."

"Darren, where are you?"

"Still down in Suffolk." He sounded slightly impatient. Or was he nervous? "Mike, I've decided to put my grandmother's flat on the market, only I've no idea how you go about selling property. There's no one else I can ask."

Mike hesitated. "Darren, will you tell me exactly where you are?"

"What's it matter? We can meet next week somewhere—"

"Darren, I got into your flat."

"You what! You mean you broke into my flat?"

Mike waited while the lad raged on at him, swearing and cursing: How had he ever trusted him, a bloody social worker, in the first place; he'd have the law on him; he'd kick the shit out of him. When he began to wind down, Mike interrupted: "Did you steal old Charley's money?"

"Did I do bloody what?"

"Darren, I was waiting for you outside the flat and I overheard his sister talking with a niece. There was over two thousand pounds in the old boy's place. They know you often drank with him and did shopping for him; they knew you were just about the only one he ever let into the flat, too, and so they thought you took it."

For a long while Darren didn't speak, though Mike could hear his breath, rapid and short like somebody who had been running.

"I took it," he said at last. "But I didn't steal it. I went round to his flat to see if he was okay. It was the night I usually met him in the pub on the corner, and when he didn't come in I got worried.

"I let myself in—Charley always kept his door key dangling from a bit of string inside the letter box—anyway, I let myself in, and . . .

"Mike, are you still there?"

"I'm still here."

"I went into the front room. The telly was on, but no Charley. I called out to him, but he didn't answer. Then I went into the bedroom and there he was—half in, half out of the bed. I felt his pulse. . . . I even got a mirror from the bathroom and held it in front of his mouth and nose, but he was dead all right. Probably had been for some hours. And then—" Mike heard a curious noise from him, like a gasp for breath, before resuming in a stronger, defensive voice. "Then I saw something sticking out from under the mattress, an envelope. I pulled at it and these pound coins came dropping out all over the floor. The envelope had a bundle of tenners and fivers, all grubby and creased like he'd been counting them over and over again. Yeah, I took it. So what? He wasn't going to need it no more, was he? And why should that cow of a sister of his have it? Charley always hated the sight of her. I reckon he'd want me to have it.

"Mike, I didn't steal that money."

Could you steal something that was already stolen? If those two women were right, old Charley had hardly come by the money honestly in the first place.

"No," Mike said. "But that was why I broke into your flat, to try and find out where you were. I wanted to warn you to stay away for a while."

"Yeah, well, you needn't have bothered. I'm going back north—maybe this time I'll stay there—"

"Darren, wait a minute. Listen to me. While I was in your front room I found a picture of Francie. You must have dropped it accidentally."

"I suppose it fell out of the album."

Another pause, taut and sharp as a length of fine, stretched wire. "Darren, you've got that girl with you, haven't you? You've got Nicolle Gurney."

"I don't know what you're on about? What girl?"

"The one missing from Wheatcliffe. Darren, she's the image of your stepsister."

"What the hell does that prove?"

"I know she's with you." He didn't add that he had been to Wheatcliffe-on-Sea, or that the girl's stepfather appeared to be making his own investigations.

"I didn't take her," Darren said quietly.

"But she is with you, isn't she? That's why you want to sell the flat. You can't come back because of her."

"If you really believe that, why haven't you gone to the police?"

"Because I think you have—I don't want to see you in any more trouble, Darren. I care about you. And I don't think you took the girl by force—"

"Force!" There was a tone in Darren Gillespie's voice that Mike had never heard before. Was this the same tone he had used to the young woman he tried to rape in Ipswich?

"Force? She attached herself to me. I couldn't get rid of her. Mike, she was covered in bruises. And her stepfather—I saw him; he was a right bastard. She wants to stay with me, and I won't let her go. I can look after her better than he or that gormless mother of hers ever could. I won't let her go. Ever."

"But Darren—listen . . ."

The phone at the other end was quietly, calmly put down.

At Benthill Fruit Growers in Norfolk, where many of the apples and pears grown in East Anglia went to be graded or put into cold storage, the eight-till-four shift was about to finish.

The young man looked at his watch. One more bin and he could clock off, go home to his dinner and a night playing darts at his local pub. He pressed a button on the control panel at his side, bringing the last bin of pears up the conveyor belt and locking it into position. Another button submerged the bin into a tank of water where the fruit began to float slowly to the surface, gently and without bruising, before flowing down the chute, washed free of chemicals as it went, to be graded by a team of young women, weighed and packed, and then sent off to supermarkets all over East Anglia.

The young man's girlfriend worked at the grader. Well, she wasn't his girlfriend as yet, but he was confident in the brash, arrogant way of a youth who has been doted on from infancy. Therefore, his eyes often turned to the window behind him where he could see the pretty head of his intended as she worked.

He was new to the job. New enough that he still liked to watch the process, fruit bobbing to the surface and reminding him of a game he'd once played at a children's Halloween party. Bobbing for these pears would be impossible, he thought; it would be at least a fortnight before you could easily sink your teeth into one.

They bobbled their way into the chute, like kids squabbling to get out of school at the end of the day, hundreds of them floating to the surface at once.

And then there was something red under the water; it looked like a piece of red cloth, and was gone, covered by the sea of green pears. The youth reached for the stop button, but paused. No, he was tired—too late a night last night—and was perhaps seeing things. He rubbed his eyes, glanced at the window where Mandy was at work. She never turned to look at him, which was vaguely worrying; if that normally reliable source was correct and she really did have the hots for him, surely she couldn't resist sneaking a look at him now and again? Why were women such trouble? They never said exactly what they thought or felt, preferred to make a guessing game of it. Understandable then that some men lost patience.

He turned back to the bin, and there it was again, larger now; almost certainly a piece of red cloth—silk, it looked like. Some careless picker, a woman no doubt, had dropped an item of clothing into the bin.

Then he saw her hand, beringed, floating to the surface as if in a greeting, while the rest of her body remained trapped by the weight of the fruit. He pressed the stop button, which raised the bin out of the water, and when he saw her hair swirling like a mass of brown embroidery silk around her white face, he started to shout and scream.

▽

12

Darren had never felt such affection for a place before, not even for his grandmother's flat, and he couldn't explain it, but returning to this town was like coming home. Darren, the great reader, thought that if there really was such a thing as reincarnation, then he must have lived before in Stoke-on-Trent. Hardly the most romantic place in the world, often included in the first division of national jokes, but it was where Darren would choose to settle. They took you at face value here, innocent until proven guilty, your past less important than your present and your future.

And Nicky loved it. "They don't understand me," she said, having gone to a newsagent's to buy sweets for herself and cigarettes for Darren, and stressing the East London half of her accent. "They fought I was Aus-tray-lian. Wouldn't let me 'ave the fags, Darren."

"Quite right an' all. Shouldn't 'ave asked yer, shrimp."

"Darren! That's brilliant! You sound just like Stan in 'Take the O'Neills!' "

Should he play on it? Despite his ideas of teaching her correct English, to speak like a little lady and not like a hobbledehoy, should he let whomever they came into contact with think they were Australian? The accent was similar. It needed a broadening of the vowel sounds, especially the long *A*, but a rounding of the *O* to give it an almost Germanic purity. Nicky would need little encouragement, though it was unfortunate that her precious Sunny Patterson had only a slight Australian accent.

"That's because she was born in England," Nicky, the expert, the Number One Fan, explained. "In Yorkshire, near where that bloke lived."

"What 'bloke'?"

"The one you gotta book about. Bramble Bront."

He corrected her, pleased that she had obviously looked at one of his favorite books.

"Where we gonna stay, then? How about that hotel opposite the railway station? That looked okay."

"Jesus Christ! We can't afford a place like that!"

The hotel she meant was way beyond his present means—and his experience. But maybe one day—one day . . .

"I'm fed up being in the camper all the time."

"I know. So am I."

"Darren—" She put an arm around his neck. "I like going round different places, but I want to be in a real house again. You know what I mean?"

"Yeah. I miss a real house, too. But don't you worry; we'll find a place soon. Nicky—?"

"What?"

"Nothing. You want some fish and chips? Come on, I'll show you Hanley. Got the best chippy north of London and wallys bigger than a Martian's—" He checked himself quickly.

"I know what you were going to say."

They found a wooden bench in the heart of Hanley to sit and eat the fish and chips; a kind of town square, surrounded by the ancient and the modern, the contrasts typical of all Stoke-on-Trent. A group of teenage girls in smart school uniforms went by, laughing and rehashing some lunchtime prank, and Nicky watched them, a curious expression on her face.

"See that place over there?" Darren said to distract her. "It's an indoor market. Proper stalls, just like Petticoat Lane, but all indoors. You can buy just about anything in there. They have some great clothes, too. We can do some shopping in a minute, if you like." Buying her friendship again.

"Okay. Darren, look at the sky."

He looked, wondering what she meant him to see. It was almost twilight, the sky a broad, deepening blue and quite cloudless. As they watched, a flock of birds passed low overhead, flapping and chattering, with the result that Darren had to throw several spoiled chips away.

Nicky laughed, looked up again. "That was a present for you. It's not like in London, is it?"

Now he understood. There was a red glow in the twilight sky over London; the glow from thousands of streetlamps, office blocks, and high-rise flats. The glow in the Staffordshire sky was pure, royal blue, with no hint yet of stars. He understood and was moved by what he saw as her sensitive, romantic nature to put his arm around her.

She stopped him effectively with the offer of a bite on her "wally"; "a Martian's prick."

"You watch your mouth. Come on if you want to go shopping, finish that up. They'll be closing soon."

He bought her two new skirts, a T-shirt with the slogan "Watch out! Here comes Trouble!" on the front, and the inevitable pile of pop magazines.

No one looked on them with curiosity or suspicion; the young man indulging his little sister, perhaps for a birthday treat. Why should they? Later, he would take her to the cinema, buy hamburgers for supper—and think about finding somewhere to stay. With the winter coming she wouldn't be able to spend so much time out of doors; and she was right, the camper was too cramped for comfort.

He was looking forward to Christmas. The first Christmas he would permit himself to enjoy for many, many years. And maybe they could afford to spend a few days in that smart hotel after all. There, they would surely have an enormous Christmas tree, and possibly other children staying with their parents; Nicky would have someone to play with. He told her this as another pacifying tidbit; one more attempt to buy her fidelity.

Oddly, she didn't seem excited, and when pressed on the

subject explained, "The first Christmas without me mum."

"I'm sorry, Nicky. I forgot. But I think she'd be pleased to know you'll be happy and enjoying yourself. It's what she'd want."

Nicky's adult self answered, "It's what all parents want for their kids, isn't it? I know I would. When I have kids I'm going to love them all equally. And if ever I was—was not gonna be there no more, I'd tell them to do whatever they wanted to be happy."

He didn't know what to say. So often she managed to startle him with this almost dual personality of hers: at first a silly child, immature for her age, wearing with her nonsense, and then so old and wise that it was unnatural in any youngster. He knew she had been through a lot. And kids of her age were like that anyway, weren't they? Barbie dolls one minute, makeup and boys the next, then back to Barbie.

"What was your mum like, Darren?"

"My mum? Well . . ." He had trouble remembering her—really remembering. There was this cloudy, nebulous image in his mind of an hourglass figure, her head piled high with a mass of brown curls: That was real enough, for he had a photograph to tell him so. But what had she been like as a person? As a wife and mother? Lukewarm was how one social worker described her, whatever that was supposed to mean. When she and his father first broke up, she had made it clear that she wanted custody of her son, but Gillespie would have none of it. Not that he particularly wanted the boy himself, and in later life Darren knew that, had he been a pet budgerigar instead of a child, they would have squabbled over him just the same and his father would have still kept him solely to spite his mother.

"Do you really think they'll let you keep him?" Gillespie shouted. "The hell they will when I've finished telling them about you and your bloody fancy man!"

After that, Darren's mother made only a halfhearted attempt to get her boy. Lukewarm. She finally disappeared with the "fancy man," and Darren never saw her again.

When his father went to prison, the social services tried, unsuccessfully, to trace her. Marsha could hardly be expected to take him on, the son of the man who had killed Francie, and so he was sent to the children's home.

He remembered asking someone there—it might have been the girl who worked in the kitchen; she was the only one he really trusted—why his mother hadn't come for him. Gran said it had been in the newspapers, even the nationals, so she must have heard about it.

"Perhaps she's abroad," he was told, "or perhaps . . ." They didn't finish, but he knew what they were thinking; his mother might be dead. He would have preferred to believe that at the time; it was less painful to think of her as dead than face the fact that she just didn't care. Today he felt sure she was alive and somewhere in the country, and he liked to dream that one day they would meet. He would be walking down the road and suddenly see her coming toward him. She wouldn't recognize him after all these years, of course, but he would know her. He would walk up to her, say, "Hello, Mum," and disappear into the crowd before she had a chance to respond.

"What was my mum like?" he repeated at last. "Nicky, I don't really remember. She was okay, I suppose."

"All right, if you don't want to talk about her . . ."

"I don't mind talking about her, but that would mean thinking about her. And it's the thinking I don't particularly want to do."

Nicky laughed. "Jonagold, you really could be my brother, d'you know that? You and me are exactly alike." And when he smiled back at her, "So, tell me about when you was a kid. What was Christmas like in those days?"

She made "those days" sound like the Dark Ages.

Christmas. Most people, or at least those who grow up within a stable family unit and with two loving parents, tend to roll every childhood Christmas into one in their memory. Darren could recall each of his separately and distinctly, up until they took him to the children's home, where he no longer cared about Christmas or anything else.

He tried to tell her about the Christmas stockings his gran used to put together for him. Not those horrid things you could buy at any store and that contain nothing but munch bars; the real, old-fashioned stockings that appeal to a youngster's five senses. Bulky packages to please both eyes and fingers, tangerines for a real Christmasy smell, something that rattled when you shook it, and half a dozen of those pink-and-white sugar mice with string for tails that you never saw these days. He tried to explain and describe this to Nicky, but it was too far beyond her experience.

"One year, I got a bike," he told her.

"One year, I got a bike an' all. Darren, we gotta get somewhere proper to live before Christmas."

"I know. That's why I've decided something, Nicky. I'm going to sell the flat in London."

"Is that what you've been trying to phone your friend about?"

"Yeah. He might have got himself another job and that's why he didn't answer before." He looked at his watch. "I'm going to give it one more try."

"No, don't."

"What?" He wasn't really paying her much attention.

"Don't sell the flat."

"And how do you suppose we're going to live if I don't? I'd hardly have enough on Social to keep myself, let alone you."

"Have you ever thought of getting a job?"

He stared at her. "Hey, what are you? A bloody social worker or something?"

"I don't want you to sell the flat. If you do it'll be because of me, and you'll having nothing to remember your gran by."

"Oh, Nicky." For the first time in days, he found himself comparing her with Francie.

"Do you like it, Francie?"

She examined his latest offering, a jewelry box with a ballerina in a pink tutu inside that pirouetted stiffly to the tune of "Beautiful Dreamer." To him, it was a sophisticated, beautiful object, the kind of thing girls who lived in great country mansions or even palaces might own and treasure.

"It's all right," said Francie, and placed his gift not on the dressing table where it rightly belonged, but on the window-sill. He misinterpreted her action at the time, telling himself she wanted to show it off: Nor did he understand when, having asked him if he thought it could be seen from the road below, she said it would "come in useful."

"Where did you get the money from! 'Ere, you didn't nick it!"

"No, of course I didn't. I sold my skates and my model cars." He waited for her to say he shouldn't have done it, that she didn't deserve it, and to hug him in gratitude.

Instead, she looked at him slowly, gave a simpering little laugh, and said, "Well, you're too old for skates and toy cars anyway."

"Nicky, I've been thinking of selling the flat for ages. It has nothing to do with you."

"But your gran—"

"I don't need a place to remember her. I don't even need things. She's up here"—he touched his forehead—"in my mind. When you really love someone and they love you in return, then you can never lose them." He hoped she would see some parallel with her own mother. "You can't hold on to the past through material things, Nicky. You have to think of looking after yourself and going forward.

"I'm going to sell the flat because it's best for me. That part of my life is over and now I'm ready to let go. All right?"

"Yeah, all right. You gonna phone now? Don't be gone long." She was hurt because he wanted to speak with Mike Southgate privately. Why? she had demanded earlier that day before one of his unsuccessful efforts to get through. And he couldn't tell her he was afraid that he might have to make some reference to his past that he'd prefer her not to hear.

"I won't be long. Don't wander off."

Darren had learned to trust her by now. If he told her not to do something, she would obey. Disobedience was so far confined to the number of hours she might watch television. He hurried down the road, turned right into Hanley's Pall Mall, where he knew there was a phone box at the end of the street. Passing the Theatre Royal, he was reminded of the promise he had made Nicky: that he would take her to Barnhearst to see Sunny Patterson in *Peter Pan*. He must think about the tickets very soon now or they may not be able to get seats until after Christmas.

How long would it take to sell the flat? He had an idea that a low price would result in a quick sale, and he would have Mike instruct the estate agents accordingly on his behalf. And would he need a bank account into which the money could be paid? He knew nothing of these things. There was his old savings account at Barclays, opened for him by his gran when he was nine, but that was all. So far, Darren had found no use for banks and building societies, realizing that monthly statements—written proof of his financial situation—would only serve to aggravate his neurotic tendencies where money was concerned. Mike would know what to do, though; he wouldn't laugh at Darren's ignorance, and previous experience told him that Mike would go out of his way to help. He was, therefore, overwhelmed with relief to hear the familiar voice at last answer his phone call.

When he left the call box he was trembling; shaking inside and out like an alcoholic after a bigger than usual binge. He almost collapsed on the steps outside the Theatre Royal, getting curious looks from passersby as well as one of the theater staff. They must have thought he was drunk, or certainly under the influence of some drug, and he remembered that he had reacted this way in Ipswich after he left the girl screaming and crying in the park. But in Ipswich he had only his own danger to think of. Now there was Nicky, alone on that wooden bench in a strange town where the shops were already closing for the day and local youths would soon be on patrol and looking for amusement.

What he had told Mike Southgate? That he was "still in Suffolk"; he remembered that and marveled at the intuition that had brought out that easy lie, for when Mike persisted with his whereabouts he guessed something was wrong.

He might have known old Charley's sister knew nothing of the hidden money, but Charley had never mentioned a niece.

The conversation after this blurred in his memory: the anger he felt because Mike had broken into his flat, his account of what happened the night he went to check on the old man and found him dead in the bedroom. Had he mentioned any future plans? He might have said something about returning north, but was sure he hadn't named any specific town. How could he remember now? All that mattered was Mike knew he had Nicky with him. What a fool—what a bloody fool he was to confide in anyone, much less Mike Southgate, that ex-social worker and archinterferer. Darren clenched his fists against his chin. He couldn't sit here another minute; he must get Nicky, take her away—to Scotland, Wales, anywhere.

People were looking at him, and that was the last thing he needed. He mustn't do anything, especially now, to draw attention to himself. He struggled to his feet, managed to walk slowly and not too unsteadily back along Pall Mall. Walking had always calmed him, helped him to think and reason, even when he was close to a panic.

"I care about you," Mike had said, and his voice wavered, almost broke. Now Darren knew. He understood why he so often felt uneasy when he was with Mike, why Mike seemed to have more interest in him than any of the other lads in the ex-offenders' group.

He wouldn't give him away—but he might come looking for him.

The revulsion Darren felt helped rouse him enough to hurry him along the street, up the main shopping thoroughfare to the wooden bench where Nicky sat patiently waiting for him. She looked so small, so lonely, her plastic carrier bag of new clothes from the indoor market clutched on her lap as she gazed at passersby, last-minute shoppers who had homes to go to.

The relief and joy on her face when she saw him was painful, reminded him of that first morning, so many weeks ago, when he almost deserted her in the café at Wheatcliffe-on-Sea.

"Darren, are you following me?"
"No, of course I'm not."
"Well piss off, then! Bloody little kid! Go on, sod off!"

"Darren, you said you wouldn't be long. . . ." She was near to crying, alone in a strange town.

"I'm sorry, Nicks. I had to wait for the phone."

"You get through? Is everything all right?"

"Yes." He wanted to gather her up, shopping and all, and carry her away. Instead, he grabbed her by the arm and led her down the street, past C and A's and into Hanley bus station.

"No," he said. "It's not all right." He bought her a hot chocolate drink from the vending machine. "Here, you're cold."

"Why isn't it all right? What happened?"

"My friend knows you're with me."

"So what? This chocolate tastes like cat's piss."

"Don't drink it, then. Jesus Christ, Nicky! Didn't you hear what I said? He knows you're with me."

She gazed at him steadily over the rim of her plastic cup. "What are we gonna do?" as if she couldn't honestly care less.

"I don't know. I just don't know."

"You're thinking of dumping me again, aren't you?"

Apparently she remembered that morning in the café too. But abandoning her had never occurred to Darren this time; he had made a commitment now and he would honor it.

"No, of course not. But I don't think we ought to stay in one place for too long."

"Does he know where we are?"

"No, but—"

"Well, there you are then. Besides, if he's your friend he'll keep his trap shut, won't he? You should've taken me with you. I could've put him straight."

"Nicky, you still don't understand, do you? You still don't realize how serious it is—"

She scrunched up her empty paper cup, swallowed a little belch. "What did you go to prison for?"

There were people waiting at most of the stands, workers on their way home, still a few teenagers in uniform who were probably late because of some after-school activity. He didn't think they were close enough to overhear, but he hushed the girl with a look.

"Well? Why did you? You've never told me exactly. You always change the subject."

"Okay. I attacked a woman. Satisfied?"

"Why did you attack her? Did you mug her?"

"Something like that. Now come on if you've finished your drink, let's get back to the camper."

She followed him silently for a few minutes, then, "Darren, are we near Newcastle?"

"What makes you think that?"

"There, look!" One of the buses displayed Newcastle as its destination, and Darren berated himself for his stupidity in bringing her through the bus station in the first place.

"It's not the Newcastle where you used to live," he told her. "This place is Newcastle-under-Lyme. Different altogether."

She looked at him distrustfully. "Where's the real Newcastle, then?"

"O-oh." His grasp of geography was not much better than hers, despite all his traveling. "It's about the same distance from here as Suffolk, only in the opposite direction. "Barnhearst," he added casually, "is much closer."

It worked. She wanted to be closer to the town where she would finally meet her idol, not further away. In his relief, he promised that they should go and look the place over as soon as possible—and buy tickets for the best seats.

Back in the camper with Nicky beside him he lit a cigarette and inhaled deeply. "Getting his fix," Nicky called it: Having read that two certain Australian stars were nonsmokers, she had decided that she too disapproved of cigarettes.

Darren closed his eyes and leaned back, a sign that he was making plans and she should please keep quiet for a minute.

He could never return to the flat again, much less attempt to put it on the market. Even if that disgusting little pervert Mike Southgate didn't go to the police, he was sure Charley's sister would. And he had been relying on money from the sale of the flat.

At last he switched on the ignition. "We'll go and see a film," he said. "Then we'll have hamburgers, and tomorrow we'll find somewhere to stay and I'll have the camper resprayed. I've got an old mate nearby who'll do that for us."

"Why?"

"Because Mike, the man I was trying to phone, might come looking for us. He knows I drive a blue-and-white camper, so I'm going to have it painted red and white."

Nicky considered. "Red and white is more common, I reckon. It's a shame, though. I like it the way it is. Darren . . . These mates of yours. Did you meet them in the clink?"

"No." This was the truth. Gary Stifani was someone he'd met on one of his excursions about the country looking for work.

But he was also thinking of one man he had met in prison: a man who had tried to hold up a small market-town bank with a replica gun.

He must have more money, and even though he had enough to last for a while, his old anxiety on the subject drove him to begin thinking and planning right now. But his immediate need was for cigarettes and a drink of some kind, and he pulled up outside an off-license.

"Can I come in with you?" Nicky asked.

Usually, he made her stay in the camper when he went shopping, feeling that people in shops were generally more observant than passersby in the street.

"Okay," he said. "Hey, let's see if they mistake us for Australians this time, shall we?"

Predictably, she found the idea irresistible. "No worries, Darren."

It was early for an off-license to be doing much trade; people usually think about getting in their night's supply just before television peak viewing time. All the same, he noted one or two adults among the kids who were choosing sweets or trying unsuccessfully to buy cigarettes "for me dad."

The size of the shop and the variety of drinks it stocked told him that this was a profitable business. But then, weren't all off-licenses profitable in a large town? The money in the till at the end of the day would surely run into four figures.

He bought two bottles of wine, forty cigarettes, and crisps for the aspiring actress, who played her part so well that another child, overhearing, asked her what part of Australia she was from.

"Melbourne," came the casual but friendly reply, pronounced in the Australian way, Mel'-bun. (Those fictional O'Neills had cousins in Melbourne.)

It was a real stroke of luck. Not only did Nicky have a perfect ear for mimicry, she really could act; the ordinary kid holding an ordinary conversation with her brother, and who saw nothing unusual in her accent but was just the slightest bit fed up with other people, strangers, questioning her. So long as she only played at being an Australian when he was with her to monitor the "script," they would be safe.

Mike was looking for a dark-haired young man with a plump child in tow, a blue-and-white camper. Even if he did come north looking for him and chance or something Darren might have said months ago and forgotten led him to Staffordshire, no one he questioned would remember the pair he described. Now all he had to worry about was money.

He paid for the goods and looked around the off-license one more time. No, not here, of course; he wanted to stay in Stoke-on-Trent until December, and a smart dog doesn't shit in its own kennel.

Besides, he had to buy the replica gun first.

13

"SHE WAS COVERED in bruises." That phrase kept coming back to Mike Southgate all through the night and the following day. A figment of the lad's imagination? Wishful thinking to excuse the fact that he had abducted a child who closely resembled his adored stepsister?

Perhaps, but through checking up on the story in the newspaper offices he learned that Nicolle Gurney had run away before. Mike's experience in social work taught him that a high percentage of second marriages turned out well where the children were concerned; kind and caring stepparents outnumbered the uncaring and the downright cruel. Still, there were men and women who couldn't look at the children of their partner's first marriage without bitterness and jealousy. Was Alan Ralph one of the latter?

By Ralph's own admittance he had shouted at the girl, she had run away before, and now Darren insisted she had bruises on her body.

What sort of person was Alan Ralph? Mike wouldn't judge from such flimsy evidence—he was under stress; kids run away on impulse after being denied a few privileges, and they fall over while playing—or from photographs of the lumbering, rather surly-looking man. God, he had enough to be surly about. Mike now knew, via the newspapers, where Ralph's flat was, and because of reward money offered by a local pub for information leading to Nicolle's safe return, also where the man regularly drank. Before he gave another thought to looking for Darren, he must contrive to meet the girl's stepfather.

"So, you're going away after all, Mr. Southgate." A half-question, half-statement from his landlady, who was cleaning the step.

"No, Mrs. Burridge. Just for the weekend."

"You're up early enough."

"Eight-thirty isn't what I'd call early, Mrs. Burridge. Even for a Saturday." He couldn't resist adding, "I may be going away sometime next week," but had to bite back, "Anything else you'd like to know?"

He could smell winter in the air already, though it was only October. But this had been a year of early seasons; the best weather came in May, and autumn seemed to begin in August. "The weather's topsy-turvy," Mrs. Burridge remarked, as she often did, adding that morning that "Old Mother Shipton was right with her predictions."

"More accurate than the forecasters on the box, then," Mike answered, vaguely supposing Mother Shipton was someone Mrs. Burridge knew at the bingo. "Well, I'll be off now. See you sometime Monday," and with his ancient airline bag holding a change of clothes he hurried away before she could detain him any longer.

He traveled by tube as always because, although a born Londoner, he tended to get lost on the buses. Like many other Londoners, Mike only really knew the parts of his city where he had lived, worked, and gone to school. These did not include Bethnal Green, although he had twice as a youngster been taken to see the Museum of Childhood and he well remembered the beautiful old church opposite the tube station. His general impression as a fourteen-year-old was that Bethnal Green was populated by young Pakistani men and old people of every race.

The room he had managed to rent for two nights—after much telephoning around—was a small and dusty one above a pub called the Dew Drop Inn. Dusty, though not actually dirty, but houseproud Mike felt compelled to do the best he could with a handkerchief before setting out to acquaint himself with the area. Probably he was the first guest to stay in this room for a long time, and the landlord's attitude seemed to confirm it.

"You'll tell me if there's not enough blankets, Mr. Southgate? Or if there's any draughts?" The extra money evidently came as a welcome surprise, too.

He told the man he was passing through London on his way north and wanted to spend a couple of days looking up old friends, adding that he used to stay in the area often as a child because his grandmother lived here. Like Darren, he could lie with perfect ease, but only when he considered it politic to do so.

Outside in the streets, he saw that his teenage impressions were mistaken. Certainly there were many elderly people: old women trudging to the market, old men waiting for the pubs to open, all the more lonely and isolated because this was a Saturday and the streets were swarming with kids and teenagers. Some of the youngsters were probably going to the Saturday workshop at the museum, the rest either off to the parks or dragged, unwillingly, after their mothers to help carry the weekend shopping.

This was where Nicolle Gurney had spent the past two years of her life: These were the streets and the people she knew. Chances were that some of these girls, laughing and pushing each other as they passed Mike, had played with her, were her friends.

He walked on, past the fire station, past the rows of small shops, the market square on the opposite side of the road where stallholders were shouting out the price of their tomatoes or trying to persuade the reserved British public to sample the ugli fruit. He had to ask directions to the road where Ralph lived, which somehow caused him embarrassment. That was why he lied to the landlord of the Dew Drop Inn; as if they might guess from thevery fact that he was a stranger why he was there.

"Down 'ere, turn left at The Beggar's Throne and there y'are," were the quick-fired instructions.

The Beggar's Throne. That was the name of Alan Ralph's watering hole, truly a "local" for him, the pub whose regulars had put up a reward for information on the girl's whereabouts. The painted sign above the door looked new. It depicted a blind beggar (the Blind Beggar of Bethnal Green? whoever he was) with an ecstatic expression on his face and surrounded by radiant light.

It was the pub's only glory. Entering the bar, Mike saw that any character the place once might have possessed had been destroyed and lost forever by the more popular amusements of late twentieth century. It seemed that no one these days could enjoy a drink without rock music blaring or a machine in which to gamble away their loose change.

Mike asked for a half of bitter. He would have preferred a large whiskey, but sensible of his precarious finances and still determined to help Darren, now was the time to economize. He took his drink to a seat by the window, where he could watch people going by. Surely, sooner or later, he would see Alan Ralph.

He made the beer last as long as he dared, almost an hour, then bought another. Customers were in and out all the time, most of them laden with shopping, all known to each other, but Ralph wasn't among them. Of course—he should have remembered; there was another child, a little boy. If he came into the pub at all it would be this evening when he could dump the kid on a sitter.

Mike finished his beer and left. He could see the flats, drab, late fifties, with a scrappy square of grass and a children's climbing frame in front, but he daren't walk past. The first time Ralph saw him it must be in the pub or somewhere like that. Instead, he turned back toward Roman Road, relieved to be one of the crowd again. He recalled reading that the boy was still a toddler, so he kept a lookout for a man with a pushchair or buggy. Though if Nicolle's stepfather was the sort of person Darren believed him to be, he was more likely to leave the kid with a neighbor—or even alone in the flat—when he went out.

He wandered back to the market, bought a hamburger that must do for both late breakfast and early lunch, then took it into the park to eat quietly, have a smoke, and think. Many of the trees here were bent and broken, dangerously fractured branches sawed off to give the tree a curious shape. Londoners who seldom went into their parks tended to forget the hurricane of '87. Darren had once remarked that the Suffolk and Essex countryside that he was familiar with had been changed forever, but in the city it might never have happened.

There were plenty of kids around, some having a kick-about with a football, others cycling or roller-skating along pathways. The only adults he could see were two women exercising a pair of spaniels and an old lady who, to his slight annoyance, came and sat on the bench beside him. He could sense her looking at him; a lonely old dear who wanted someone to talk to. He wasn't a social worker now, sod it, nor was he in the mood for conversation. But the natural compassion that led him into the Social Services to begin with took over and he smiled at the old lady.

"Getting cold now," he said.

"Yes. Soon be winter again. I dread the winter."

"Me too."

"Ah, but you're a young man. You shouldn't feel the cold. When your bones get as old as mine, love, you find it hard to move about and keep warm."

Mike nodded sympathetically. "What sort of heating have you got?"

"Central heating. Gas. But I only dare keep it on at night in January."

He gave her the usual advice he had been trained to give pensioners—she must keep warm; the Gas people would understand her plight and certainly not "cut her off"—adding that if she could save during the summer and buy a duvet it would cut her nighttime bills in the long run.

"One of them French things? Me daughter offered to buy me one, but I reckoned it'd be a waste of money. How can one cover keep you warmer than four blankets? Daft, if you ask me."

Mike, beginning to like her, even enjoying a return to his old role, managed to persuade her to take the daughter up on her offer. "You don't know until you try, do you? I'd never be without my duvet, I promise you."

The old girl smiled. She had a chimpanzee look about her eyes, a multitude of lines and creases in her face where her powder clogged, and her breath had a fruity smell. Mike noticed a bottle in her coat pocket, a half-size Bells, now probably containing draught sherry. She'd rather spend her money on cheap booze than food or heating. He had seen this so many times before.

"You're not from round here, are you?" she said.

"No. I've got friends here, though. I'm just visiting for the weekend."

She nodded, looking at him steadily. "Young lady?"

"Ye—no, not a girl. Have you lived here long?"

"All my life."

"Changed a lot, I suppose."

"Depends which way you look at it. There wasn't all the crime when I was a youngster. A bit of petty thieving here and there, one or two fights on a Saturday night, that was it. Now? You're afraid to go out after dark. And then there was that kiddie—though she wasn't taken from around here. . . ."

"Oh, yes, I remember." Mike offered her a cigarette, which she declined with a cough. "Went missing from the seaside, didn't she?"

"That's the one. Poor little thing. I don't suppose they'll ever find her now."

"Did you know her?"

The woman shook her head, felt for the bottle in her pocket, then thought better of it. "Can't say I did. There's so many kids come here to play and I know a lot by sight, but I can't honestly say I knew Nicky. Know her father, though. Well, sort of what you'd call nodding acquaintance really. I see him in the pub when I go in on a Friday night. 'Course, I didn't actually know his name until this happened."

"Really?" He didn't want to appear too inquisitive, too eager. "I suppose he must be frantic, poor chap."

"Well, he'd just lost his wife, too, so I reckon he felt that more. And Nicky was his only stepchild."

Was. Did they all think of her in the past tense? He must go carefully now, but he had to keep her talking.

"I remember reading in the papers that he's got another kid to look after. It must be hard for a man, bringing up a toddler all on his own." Mike feigned to be watching the young footballers.

"He manages. There's a child minder near him who looks after the boy while he's at work—sometimes when he's in the boozer an' all. Or he brings the kid in with him."

"Doesn't the landlord mind?"

The woman either forgot herself or now felt at ease with the talkative young man, and took a large, noisy gulp from her bottle. "Suppose he feels sorry for him. Well, everyone does, of course. After his wife died he used to be drunk every night. He's not too bad in that way now. One thing I did notice . . ." She shook her head sympathetically. "I saw him in the street the other day—last Saturday, it must have been—out shopping with the boy. He turned to look at every fair-haired kid that went by. Every girl about Nicky's age. Poor bloke. They say he doesn't believe she can be dead. Won't believe it. But after all this time . . . You know?"

A good actor, always aware of the public eye and therefore always performing—or a genuinely grieving father? Mike still reserved judgment.

As a kind of payment for the "interview," he let the old lady chatter on, reminiscing as old people will about her youth, the war, the changes she had seen; and he asked questions, laughing and sympathizing alternately. She finally accepted a cigarette ("I shouldn't, but what the hell?") and offered him a swig of the sherry. He declined at first, slightly repulsed by her whiskery chin and occasional dribbles. But she was insistent and he took a mouthful, its immediate effects reminding him that it was growing chilly in the park.

"You ain't the old bill?" she asked suddenly.

"No, no. I'm unemployed. What made you think that?"

"You asked a lot of questions."

"I'm just interested in people. Actually, I used to be a social worker."

That, apparently, was just one step down from being the law, and Mike's companion suddenly remembered that she had to go home and get changed for the bingo.

"Nice talking to you," he said stupidly as she tottered away toward the Victorian archway that was one entrance to the park.

Oddly, he was sorry to see her go, felt bereft of a friend. Women made good friends—when age or other circumstances precluded the sex thing. He glanced at his watch. Not long to go before the pub would be open again, if indeed it had closed at all; they didn't have to these days, he recollected. He was hungry again. A proper meal, the old meat and three veg, was what he needed and not the junk he had been living on lately. Back in Roman Road, he asked directions to the nearest fish and chip shop, that dish not apparently meeting his definition of junk.

It cost him two pounds, which was reasonable enough, and filled him more than the hamburger had. When he had finished eating, he headed back to The Beggar's Throne, greasy and quite content, which was strange when he reflected that Darren might have been lying to him.

They had switched on the television over the bar, a large-screen set with the brightness control set too high so that it strained your eyes to watch. Nobody watched it much, though, and the usual Saturday night rubbish droned on like piped Muzak in a supermarket. Eight o'clock passed and Mike was on his fourth half, weakening to the point where he knew he would soon be ordering a large whiskey. He was sharing a table with two old men and a fiftyish-looking woman who seemed to be the daughter of one and the wife of the other. They were arguing with each other, and the woman was getting the best of it.

"I'm really sick of this," she said, speaking without moving her lips, much like a poor ventriloquist. "Every weekend it's the same with you lot. Serve you right if I buggered off and got blind drunk every night like what other women in my place do."

One of the men muttered something inaudible to Mike and got a sharp "Huh! Fat bloody chance!" in retort.

It was then that the bar door opened and a tall, lumbering man with graying hair and a red face came in. He looked about him cautiously, almost nervously, before approaching the bar. Alan Ralph. Mike knew him immediately, felt that shock of recognition one experiences when coming face-to-face with a TV celebrity or royalty.

He might have been handsome once; a Little Lord Fauntleroy in boyhood, an Adonis in youth. Today he was a ruin; a sagging beer gut, boozer's complexion, prematurely aged. Yet his eyes were still attractive, even beautiful and compelling, though there was nothing remotely effeminate about the man.

His entrance had brought about a momentary subsidence of the general cacophony in the bar. They were embarrassed by him, perhaps even resented his being there, a reminder that tragedy can befall anyone at any time and therefore a check on their own Saturday-night fun.

The landlord served him with a large whiskey, and he took it and settled in the remotest corner of the room, shielding himself behind a copy of the evening paper. An approach wouldn't be easy, but something in Ralph's demeanor told Mike he would be there until closing time: You could tell by the way a man sat down in a pub how long he intended to stay. And from his seat he could put his glass on the bar for a refill without getting up. Alan Ralph had come out to get himself blind drunk.

The opportunity to make his approach came sooner than Mike expected when the argument between the woman and two men at his table suddenly took an ugly turn. With most eyes, including those of Alan Ralph, in their direction, what could be more natural than to empty his glass and move discreetly to the bar? A young girl served him with a large whiskey while the landlord attended to the rumpus, and it was the easiest thing in the world to catch Ralph's eye and ask, "Mind if I sit there?" Meaning the seat opposite.

"Free country," said Alan Ralph.

"I came out for a quiet drink, not to listen to someone's domestic squabbles."

"Don't blame you. They're always at it, that lot." He resumed reading his paper and Mike lit a cigarette. Mustn't rush it; let the conversation start naturally. Give it time.

He glanced at the man as often as he dared. Nicolle Gurney's stepfather. There was no cruelty in that face, no hint of malice, only a terrible weariness and a blank resolve—the expression of someone working the ancient treadmill. Though he turned the pages of his paper, Mike noticed that his eyes were mostly still, and if they did move along a line of print it was in a continuous, unnatural way. When someone is reading, their eyes will trace along smoothly for twelve or more words, then pause for a split second, maybe backtrack a couple of words before going on. Mike doubted the man had absorbed one single sentence.

At last he had to put the paper down, but as the noise level in the bar was back to normal he no longer needed a shield. He bought another large whiskey, this time handing over a twenty-pound note with instructions to "tell me when it's gone." Certainly the behavior of one intending to get smashed, Mike thought, making a point of looking anywhere but at Ralph. Then, on impulse, he said, "Mind if I have a glance at the paper?"

"Help yourself. Nothing much in it."

But surely something that would serve as a topic of conversation.

Politics—verbal scraps in the House, the rising crime rate, a vicar's wife running off with a local sixth-former, a woman's body found in a bin of pears somewhere in Norfolk. And, of course, the never-ending saga of the Poll Tax.

Mike made a kind of guffaw as a prelude, and Alan Ralph looked up, slightly inquiring.

"Bloody Poll Tax," Mike said. "If we'd all stuck together in the first place and refused to pay, they couldn't have done much about it. They can't put everyone in prison." It was the sort of comment he'd heard a hundred times over the past month.

"You paid yours, then?"

"I'm out of work. I don't see why I should pay anything."

"Your choice." Alan Ralph looked into his glass, appeared to fish something out—a bit of cigarette ash, perhaps—with his little finger. "I can't afford to get on the wrong side of the law."

"Well no one wants to get in that sort of trouble, of course. But when a law is so unfair—"

"Who says it's unfair?" The man hunched over his glass like a bear over its dinner. "I'm doing all right by it."

Mike swallowed his own drink along with his anger. That *I'm all right, Jack,* attitude made him want to lash out. He wanted to shout at the man, *What about the husband in a low-paid job whose wife can't go out to work because she has three kids to look after? What about the old woman who can't even afford to keep herself warm in the winter?* Perhaps this bastard was better off under the new tax if he owned his own place. And there was no wife whose bill he would also have to pay along with his own.

Then Mike saw that Alan Ralph's statement came from his bitterness. His wife was dead, his stepdaughter had vanished—perhaps she was dead, too. Why should he give a toss about anyone or anything now?

"The old people will feel it," he said quietly.

"I suppose so. Never given it much thought. To me, it's just one more bloody form to fill in." He drained his glass, banged it on to the bar. "What the hell? They're against you every bloody which way."

"You don't sound very happy for a Saturday night." Straightaway, Mike felt like kicking himself. But Christ! What else could he—a stranger—have said?

The response was a grunt, not incongruous with his bearlike appearance.

"Cigarette?" Mike offered (God, he'd nearly said "cancer stick") and he was surprised when the man accepted.

"You're not from round here," said Alan Ralph.

"No, just passing through. I knew the place as a child."

"Wife with you?" An odd question to ask an acquaintance of less than ten minutes, and Mike wondered, Was it so obvious? He dressed like most young men, but was there something in his face, the face that should have been handsome yet was instead unsymmetrical and plain, that announced the truth as clearly as if he'd had it tattooed across his forehead?

"I'm not married," he said, adding with a laugh, "Suppose I'm a late developer. Or an early one, depending on which way you look at it."

Alan Ralph had his refill by now, and he swallowed half in one gulp. "I married late," he said.

"Ah."

"She's dead now."

"I'm sorry. Recently?"

"A few weeks back." The second half of his whiskey followed the first, and he banged his glass down on the bar again.

Mike didn't know how to pursue the conversation, so he ordered another drink himself, paying for it with the last of his loose change and hoping it wouldn't be necessary to break into another fiver.

"You must miss her," he said at last, awkwardly, inadequately.

"I knew it was gonna happen sooner or later. She had cancer. I knew it was gonna happen."

"Still a shock, though."

Ralph nodded, wiped a pudgy hand across his red forehead. He was sweating.

"Got kids?"

"Yeah."

"Must be hard for you—"

"Hey, what are you? A fuckin' social worker or something? What's all these questions for?"

"I'm sorry."

Alan Ralph got through another large whiskey and ordered one more before he spoke again. He offered a cigarette.

"You're out of work, you say?"

"That's right. I'm looking around for something. Something in PR, maybe."

"Any qualifications?"

"Couple of GCEs, that's all. But I'll try anything."

Ralph nodded. "That's what I like to see; a lad willing to turn his hand to anything. Have a drink? Whiskey?"

"Thanks." Was this the man who covered his stepdaughter with bruises? But why not? What about that gently spoken bank manager from the south of England, the man who, according to his friends, "wouldn't hurt a fly," and who, two years ago, beat and shook his stepson until the child suffered a brain hemorrhage and died?

"How do you manage?" Mike asked, an innocent question, polite curiosity.

"Got a child minder for the boy."

"And what about—"

Their eyes locked. Alan Ralph had stressed "the boy," as if speaking of one of his children, but Mike had followed him in a tone that proved he knew there was another.

"Who are you?" Ralph said, but oddly enough not in a hostile voice. Then—and there was no mistaking the hope in his face—"Do you know anything? Have you seen Nicky?"

"No, I haven't seen her."

"But you do know something! Tell me! For Christ's sake tell me!" He started to rise from his chair, sank down again heavily, his drink forgotten. "You're a reporter."

"No."

"Then what? You've been watching me from the minute I walked in. You were waiting for me. You the police?"

"No. I used to—well, that doesn't matter. You've been down to Wheatcliffe-on-Sea, haven't you—Mr. Ralph? You spoke to the café owner."

"Look, I don't know who you are, or what you are, but if you've got something to say to me you'd better just come right out with it. Was it you who wrote that letter? Because if so, I can tell you now I've got nothing to hide."

"I don't know anything about a letter. All I know is"—taking a gambler's chance—"you have nothing to do with Nicky disappearing, and yet you're afraid of the police."

The man nodded, and it was as if he were making a confession: as if some terrible weight had not been lifted but slightly eased from his head.

"We can't talk here," he said, waving the barmaid away when she would have refilled his glass. He rose, folded the newspaper, and stuffed it into his jacket pocket. And Mike followed him out, conscious of all the blatantly hostile stares across the bar.

Alan Ralph led him not straight down the road to the flats where he lived but around the corner into a badly lit cul-de-sac. Before Mike had a chance to feel fear, or even wonder what was happening, he found himself lifted off the pavement and flung against a wall.

"Where's my stepdaughter? Where is she?"

"I don't know, Mr. Ralph. I honestly don't now." The words came on exhaled breath. His legs, dangling somewhere in space, were trembling and felt like cotton wool.

"You know somethin'!" Then calmly, softly, Alan Ralph said, "Tell me, or I'll kill you. I want the girl back. Tell me where she is." He let Mike's feet touch the ground but still held him fast against the wall.

"I don't know where she is, but I think I know *who* she's with—"

"Then she's alive. She *is* alive? Tell me!"

"I can guarantee she's alive, and being well looked after. Believe me, I want to find them both. I think I can find them, but I don't want the police involved. And I can't do it alone."

The hint of police involvement, another gamble, paid off. Alan Ralph shuddered. "We'll go to my place," he said.

14

ALAN HADN'T PLANNED to call at Mrs. Waterstone's tonight. The agreement was that he would leave James in her care until Sunday morning; in fact, the child spent so much of his time with her that he was beginning to think of her flat as his home and sometimes rebelled when his father came to collect him. Tonight, however, he was fast asleep, and Glynis Waterstone handed him over, warmly wrapped in one of her own blankets, without demur. She would still be paid for her services, after all.

Clutched in James's hand was a lump of rag-clad plastic, and anyone acquainted with the toy just might have recognized it as an Action Man in combat dress. Slung over his father's shoulder, the little boy grizzled with discomfort in his sleep, and Alan absently stroked his back. He was aware that every action, every flicker of expression on his face was being noted by the thin, fair-haired young man who, fit as someone of his age should be, had difficulty keeping up.

No, he wasn't the law. He didn't have the physique or the height; yet there was something of the do-gooder in him, and that made Alan more uncomfortable than he'd have been if suddenly confronted by half a dozen uniforms.

Neither spoke until Alan unlocked the door to his flat, switched on the lights and the central heating. The heater made a loud popping noise, which caused Alan's guest to jump.

"It always does that when it comes on. It'll soon warm

up. Well, you'd better sit down." And as an afterthought, "What do I call you?"

"Southgate. Mike Southgate."

"Southgate. I know an Eastgate. I'll get a drink." He put the child, now waking up, onto the floor amid a pile of toys. The flat was exactly as he'd left it that morning; clean, but with the "lived-in" look that is a polite euphemism for untidy. The kid's toys littered the place, and two armchairs were piled high with clothes and bed linen—one heap awaiting a wash, the other needing an iron. It was the best he could do, and as far as he could tell the living room smelled fresh.

There was a bottle of Bells in the sideboard cupboard, left over from the funeral; Alan seldom drank at home. The only glasses he had were brandy glasses and half-pint tumblers, and he selected two of the latter as the cleanest. His hands shook as he poured the whiskey, a nervous tension that didn't escape Mike Southgate's notice.

"I'll make some sandwiches," he muttered, a ludicrous suggestion under the circumstances. But this was what you did when you had company in the house, you gave them a drink and something to eat. It was part of Alan Ralph's upbringing, and not to offer refreshment would be, to him, like ignoring a lost child or an old lady who was being mugged. Had his guest been a police officer with a warrant for his arrest, he would have offered the same hospitality automatically.

The bread was new and soft—a Mighty White loaf, Nicky's favorite—and there was a tin of ham on the top shelf of the larder. The ham. He had been meaning to use it up for weeks, and he thought crazily, insanely, of wrapping what didn't go into the sandwiches in kitchen foil and giving it to Mike Southgate to take home with him. Lisa had bought two tins—on her last shopping trip, he remembered—one for her husband's birthday, the other to be saved for Christmas. The first had been eaten on the day of her funeral.

Perhaps other women, too, have returned from the shops unaware that they had just bought their own funeral tea.

Lisa, Lisa . . .

Alan took the food into the living room on a tray—just in time to see Mike Southgate, with James on his lap, lift the child's pullover to look at his back. No need to wonder what he was searching for.

"You won't find a mark on him," he said. "I never hit my kids."

"Never, Mr. Ralph? I'm sure you feel like it sometimes, though."

"Don't all parents?" He couldn't look at Southgate because, although he had never struck Nicky, he often slapped his son's legs.

"You never hit the girl?"

"Look, who the fuck are you to come askin' all these questions? *Are* you the law?"

"No, I told you."

"In that case"—Alan swallowed his drink in one go, took the child, and replaced him on the floor among his model cars—"you'd better start talking."

"I used to be in the Social Services—"

"Might have known it."

"Are you going to listen, or what?"

Alan clasped his hands between his knees and stared at the floor. He wasn't drunk, at least not by his definition of the word, but his thoughts rambled and swam, and it was his thoughts rather than the alcohol that blurred his vision and made him nod almost humbly, like a degraded prisoner. "Go on."

"I was a social worker. I began an evening group for ex-offenders, young men just out of jail, most of them simple robbery cases or R and V. One day, my boss told me about a lad named Darren Gillespie; she wanted him to join my group. His offense is irrelevant, but I can assure you that there was no child involved—"

"He's the one who's got Nicky?"

"Will you let me finish?" Southgate had an authority in

his voice that Alan hadn't noticed before, and his eyes glittered impatiently.

"Look, mate, I'm sorry but this is my kid we're talking about. She's the one that matters, not some sick yob. You were right when you said I was afraid of the law, and the reasons are no business of yours. But you don't want the police in on it either, or you'd have gone to them long before now. What would you do if I phoned them this minute?"

"I don't think you will, Mr. Ralph."

Alan rose, walked over to the telephone, and Mike Southgate watched; each ready to call the other's bluff.

Then young James, who had caught his sister's name and followed the exchange with rapt attention since, announced: "Nick's comin' home. Nick's comin' back," which he repeated over and over as a mysterious and magical chant. Once he began on one of his pet themes it was difficult to shut him up.

"Your kids are close?" Mike asked, his voice now deceptively soft.

"Not particularly. He's a funny little sod. Doesn't seem to give a toss about anyone or anything. It doesn't matter if you're pleased or angry with him; it's all one to our Jamie. Unnit, mate? Nicky's the only one who can do anything with him most of the time."

"She's fond of him?"

Alan shook his head, staring down at the boy. "That's the funny part about it. Lisa, my wife, first got ill after his birth, so Nicky blames him. It's nonsense, of course; just one of those things. Could have come on her anytime. But you can't really explain that to a kid. Nicky looked after him a lot of the time when Lisa got worse, buy only to please her mother, not because she liked doing it. She could be quite rough with him sometimes, but Jamie seemed to prefer her to anyone else. You heard him just now—he still asks for her." He glanced at the telephone, then at the child. Then he returned to his armchair and poured two more whiskeys. "What did you say the bloke's name was?"

"Darren. Darren Gillespie."

"All right. Go on." He'd give Southgate a chance. Just one chance, and then he'd ring the police. Nicky's safety mattered more than the fact that he might lose both kids right now. And among his swarming, half-drunken thoughts, there was one that stood out from the rest: His stepdaughter—because she was so like Lisa—was more important to him than his natural child.

"I wasn't keen on Darren joining the group at first," Mike said. "I already had too many of these lads, and limited time. Then I read his case history. It isn't a unique story by any means, but one of the most harrowing I've ever read."

Alan listened, his eyes on James once more. He guessed now the true nature of Southgate's interest in this young man, and though not easily embarrassed or quick to condemn, it was the sort of thing he preferred knowing nothing about.

"Darren's mother abandoned him when he was about five years old. As far as I can tell, she was the kind of mother a child is better off without, though Darren himself told me he was happy enough before she left. Later, his father remarried. The same sort of woman; thought more about going out and having a good time than looking after the house and her family. She had a child of her own, a daughter named Frances, or Francie as they called her. Darren adored the girl. She was older than him, beautiful—and what I suppose you'd call streetwise. They got on well together. Best friends. Though Francie often tired of Darren always trailing her, and something Darren once told me makes me believe she could sometimes be spiteful. Still, he loved her and used to buy her sweets and presents."

Mike paused, looking for a reaction, Alan supposed. Why didn't he just get to the point?

"Darren's father started coming home drunk. He was a possessive man, jealous every time anyone so much as looked at his wife. And though she was no better as a mother than his first wife—selfish, gormless, a slattern around the house—she had the looks to turn heads. Gillespie was pretty insipid where she was concerned. He got blitzed every night and instead of walloping his wife, which was probably what she deserved, he took it out on the children. Especially Francie." Another pause. "I can understand that, can't you, Mr. Ralph? I think a possessive man like Gillespie must find it hard to look at his stepchild without being reminded that there was someone else before him."

"I know what you're getting at," Alan growled, "but I never hit Nicky once. Never."

"It's not you I'm talking about, Mr. Ralph."

Alan looked up at him then. His eyes were wide, surprised, innocent-looking, rather how Alan imagined a cop's eyes would look when he was about to trick you into making a confession.

"Get on with it, Southgate. I haven't got all day."

"So, he began hitting the girl. One of the teachers at her school noticed bruises on her—not the kind of bruises a kid might get in a playground rough and tumble—and they reported it. Too late, though. That night, Gillespie came home drunk again. No wife—God knows where she was—only the kids giggling at some late-night smut on the television. He sent Darren to bed, then started on Francie. She gave him some lip, he lost his temper, grabbed an ornament off the mantelpiece, and struck her with it. She must have died almost immediately. And Darren saw the whole thing from the doorway."

Alan slapped his hands against his knees, poured another two drinks. "Okay, okay. So the boy had a rough time." It sounded inadequate, even flip. "But I still don't see the connection. I mean, what has all this to do with Nicky?"

"Darren has a flat in South London, left to him by his grandmother. But so far he's shown no interest in getting a steady job. He often travels about the country in a camper looking for seasonal work, apple picking and—Mr. Ralph. What is it?"

That was what Alan had been told by the barman at The

Shipmates' Arms at Wheatcliffe. So Southgate was genuine; this Darren was the one who had Nicky.

"Do you know him, Mr. Ralph? Have you seen him before?"

"I think I might have done. At Wheatcliffe. Bit of a loner, if he's the one. But go on. You haven't told me—why Nicky?"

"I needed to find Darren urgently, and so I—I got into his flat. There I found a photo of his stepsister. I'd seen a picture of her before, but now she reminded me of someone. Someone I'd seen recently on the television news. Mr. Ralph, your daughter bears a strong resemblance to Frances Gillespie." He fumbled about in his pocket, producing the photograph of Francie he'd found in the flat.

Yes, the likeness was quite startling. The same coloring: honey-colored hair, straight and soft-looking, green eyes. The same bone structure, the same pronounced widow's peak in the broad forehead. This child was older than Nicky, and there was something almost coquettish in her smile. What was it Southgate had said? That she could sometimes be spiteful? All children could be spiteful. Nicky herself had brought it to a fine art, especially where her stepfather was concerned: She really knew how to hurt. But Nicky had a motive. She resented anyone taking her dead father's place. Frances Gillespie's expression said something quite different.

"Pretty kid," Alan muttered, handing the picture back.

"Yes. I get the impression Darren has idealized her over the years, though. But at least you can understand why he was drawn to your stepdaughter? And I don't think he abducted her, Mr. Ralph, not in the accepted sense of the word. I mean, she's run away before, hasn't she?"

"Coupla times. Southgate—would he hurt her? You know what I mean, hurt her in that way?" He tried to explain; the boy Darren had a crush on his stepsister, but because of his age it was almost certainly of a romantic rather than a sexual nature. Now he was an adult. . . .

"I'm sure he wouldn't."

"And you think you can find him?"

"Perhaps. I know most of the places he's worked, the places he made friends, and I'm certain he'll return to one of those towns. The thing is, I don't have a lot of money. I don't own a car, and I'm out of work."

Alan rubbed his chin with his thumb and forefinger. It made a rasping sound. "If it's money and a car you need, then I can help. One thing, though, Southgate. Nicky comes first, and I go with you."

"Why have you changed your mind about the police, Mr. Ralph?" And when Alan didn't answer, "Darren rang me a little while ago. He rang because he wanted to sell his flat and didn't know how to go about it. I told him I'd found that photo on the floor, that I knew he had Nicky with him. He didn't deny it. And, Mr. Ralph, he said your stepdaughter was covered in bruises."

"Exaggerating," Alan shouted, getting out of his seat, his face a fiery red and wet with perspiration. "She had one or two, yes. But she's an awkward little sod, always walking into something, always falling off her damned bike. You can't wrap kids up in cotton wool, Southgate. If I had a quid for every time she came home with a bruise or a graze, I'd be a rich man I can tell you."

"So if you've nothing to hide, why don't you ring the police right now?"

"It's not what you think." He reached for the bottle again, shrugged when Mike Southgate covered his glass with his hand, and refilled his own. Someone had once told him it was possible to drink yourself sober, a stupid idea, yet Alan now felt clear-headed and capable of walking in a straight line had anyone asked him to do so.

"I did my best for that kid," he said. "Did all I could to get on with her. Bought her everything she wanted, tried to organize trips out so we could get to know each other, I even offered to pay for her to take dancing and drama lessons because she was so keen on it. Not a shred of gratitude in return. She just didn't want to know." He wiped his mouth on his cuff.

" 'Course, her real father—well, me an' him was chalk and cheese. I used to reckon that maybe, if I'd been more like him, Nicky would've taken to me more."

"You knew her real father?"

"Only by sight, not to speak to. He was younger than me, Lisa's age. Perhaps that was why it all went wrong; they married too young. In fact, if Darren Gillespie was the one I saw hanging around on the beach, the one I saw chatting with her before she came in for her tea, then he's not unlike Paul Gurney in the face. Younger, of course, and scruffier, but there's a certain resemblance. That would explain why she didn't run off when he approached her."

"You saw her talking to a stranger on the day she disappeared, and yet you didn't report it to the police?"

"How do you know I didn't?" Oh, he knew all right. Southgate must have researched the case very thoroughly before he came here. "You checked up through the newspapers, I suppose?"

"Easy enough to do, Mr. Ralph."

Alan searched through his pockets for cigarettes, and finding none reached for his spare pack in the sideboard drawer. He didn't offer them to Southgate.

"Before I say any more, just answer me one question. Why haven't *you* been to the police?"

"Because I don't think Darren could stand being sent down again—"

"He should have thought of that before he went off with my kid."

Mike Southgate continued as if he hadn't noticed the interruption. "I'm afraid of what he might do. He's an intelligent lad, well read and perceptive. He wouldn't hurt your girl. He was wrong to take her away, but I believe he really thought he was doing it for the best. And she must have been happy to go along with him, because he would never have taken her by force."

Alan reached for the whiskey bottle, then thought better of it, clasped his hands between his knees. He had to talk to someone; it was what he had needed so badly since Lisa's death, and it might as well be Mike Southgate.

"Okay. I'll tell you. You were right when you said didn't I ever feel like hitting the girl. I did feel like it. Often. She drove me to it, almost as if she wanted me to belt her one. But I never hit her. Not once. It was Lisa . . ."

Lisa, Lisa . . . It felt like a betrayal.

"It was a spur-of-the-moment thing. Lisa had a quick temper, but she was quick to be sorry as well. I knew she hit Nicky on occasions, and I told her about it. She used to say it was none of my business and she'd never hit her hard anyway. I believed her at first. And Nicky did use to come home saying she'd fallen over at school or fell off her bike. But I heard Lisa shouting at the kid; she'd asked for it for making her mother feel worse that she already did—and—and if she didn't behave, she'd have to go away."

Mike Southgate nodded. "And when you took the kids to Wheatcliffe was Nicky still bruised?"

"She had a few, but they were old ones, going yellow. When I asked her about them, she said she'd been in a fight. That would have been like Nicky, to defend her mother. Now I can answer your question, Southgate." He changed his mind about the whiskey, half filled his tumbler, and offered the bottle to Mike, who accepted this time.

"I'd seen this lad on the beach several times; sad, lonely-looking boy, scruffy and with swastika badges around his cap. Would that be him?" Mike nodded. "I suppose I noticed him because he looked like I felt. D'you know what I mean? Anyway, that afternoon, after I'd shouted at Nicky for being late, I saw him talking to her a little way off on the beach. I didn't tell the police about it when I reported her missing because—well, because of her bruises. And I'm her stepfather. They'd think I was making it up to get their attention away from me. I know it doesn't make sense, but it did at the time; I was confused—didn't know what to do for the best. As it was, they kept me down the station for hours. I was afraid they'd take Jamie away from me, too; put him into care or something. It would have been bad enough telling Lisa about Nicky, without that.

"Then this bloke from the café turned up. They printed that Photofit in the papers, and it was nothing like the lad I'd seen. So I never told the police about him because it didn't seem to matter anymore. And my wife was dying. . . ." He drew the back of his hand across his eyes. "That's the only reason I can give."

"I understand, Mr. Ralph. But you went to Wheatcliffe about a day before I went there. You discovered that the café owner thought the Photofit inaccurate, didn't you? Why not go to the police then?"

He believed him. Alan was sure Mike Southgate believed him. He got up, went to the sideboard cupboard, and drew out a buff-colored envelope, which he tossed at Mike. "Read them."

Read them. Alan knew all three almost by heart.

Murderor. Child murderor. we know what you did Alan Ralph well get you if the plolice dont first child murderor

Three "poison pen" letters, all in the same badly spelled, mainly unpunctuated hand.

And suddenly it was too much for him: the strain of Lisa's illness and death, Nicky's disappearance, the fear of losing both his children. Alan Ralph was close to a nervous breakdown, and he was aware of it. He didn't want to go to work in the mornings, he didn't want to look after James, to prepare a meal for himself, or even to wash. Sometimes he wanted to die. Tonight he took refuge in tears, hidden behind his great paw of a hand that covered his eyes.

Mike only needed to read one letter. "This is sick," he said, and Alan could hear him gulping at his whiskey.

"But you must see," Alan began shakily, using his cuff once more but this time to smear his eyes. "I want to find Nicky myself. If I can find her, reason with her, and persuade her to come home of her own will . . . if she wants to come back, then they can't do a thing about it. But if the police find her first—she'll never say a word against her mother.

And that—that person . . ." He indicated the anonymous letters, shaking his head, fighting his despair, wanting to believe this young man could offer him some hope.

"You said money and transport were no problem."

"No. No, of course not. I'd spend all my savings to get her back. I'd be doing it for Lisa. But I want to come with you, and I want to contact my sister—she lives in Wales—and get her to look after Jamie. It'll take a week or so because I'd need her to come here, look after the kid in his own home. Would that be all right with you?"

"Anything you say. I want to get into Darren's flat again if I can before setting off. I'll be looking for addresses, all the places he's worked before, all the friends he's made. That sort of thing. I can ring you if you'll let me take your number."

"It's on there." Alan nodded toward the telephone.

James had fallen asleep on the floor, and he gathered the child up in his arms and carried him to the bedroom. He was already in pajamas, put on by Mrs. Waterstone, and Alan laid him gently in the bottom half of a child's bunk bed. He was dry all night now, or he woke up if he needed to go and could use the potty by the bed unaided. Alan switched on the Mickey Mouse lamp, just in case, and was about to leave when Mike entered.

"Nice room," he remarked.

"Did it up myself. 'Course, we'd planned to move into a bigger place in a couple of years or so. Then they'd each have a room of their own. This is more Nicky's room." He looked around at the posters on the walls, mostly of Jason Donovan, the piles of books and magazines, the soft toys. "Look. Nicky did these."

There was a cork notice board on one wall, and pinned to it were penciled portraits of Jason Donovan, Kylie Minogue, and one or two other Australian actor-pop stars. Beside each drawing, Nicky had placed short biographies, gleaned from teenage magazines.

"They're good," Mike said politely. Good, but not outstanding for a child of her age. "There's one missing, though." He read a biography, carefully pinned beside the empty space.

Sunny Patterson was born in Yorkshire, England, in 1954, daughter of an Australian engineer and a Scottish nurse. She was christened Sarah, but the nickname "Sunny" was given to her by her grandparents because of the child's happy nature. In 1962, Sunny moved with her family to her father's native Sydney . . .

"Why is this drawing missing?" Mike asked. "Didn't she finish it?"

"Oh, she finished it all right. Best thing she'd ever done. Usually, she copied from pictures in her magazines, but this one she did from a—what d'you call it?—a freeze-frame on the video. Sunny Patterson in 'Take the O'Neills.' Lisa teased her about it, and Nicky tore it down." Alan opened a cupboard and drew out a box of videocassettes.

"I've recorded every episode of 'Take the O'Neills' since she went. She wouldn't want to miss it."

Mike admitted that he'd never heard of the show, or of Sunny Patterson. "A children's program, is it?"

"I suppose so. Though we all used to watch it. It used to make Lisa laugh." James lay quiet, deeply asleep, so he led Mike from the room, careful to leave the door ajar. "You'll have another drink before you go?"

"Okay. One for the road. I've got your number, by the way."

Alan swayed back to his armchair. He knew what he was going to do now. He would go along with this little queer, find Nicky, and persuade her to come home. And then he would ring the police, get that bastard Darren Gillespie put behind bars where he belonged.

Mike got to his feet awkwardly. He was stiff, his mouth dry, dehydrated, and his bladder felt as if it were bursting. It was daylight, almost ten o'clock, and he could hear people in the street outside. Alan Ralph lay flat out on the couch, snoring, his tongue visible, thickly coated, and vibrating slightly with each inhalation of breath.

Something apart from his full bladder had woken Mike, and on his way to the bathroom he noticed a Sunday paper lying on the doormat. He attended to his most immediate need, dampened his handkerchief and wiped his face with it, drank cold water from his cupped hands, and then, having reassured himself that Alan was still asleep, crept into the children's bedroom.

James was awake, out of bed and amusing himself by crashing a toy dump truck at every available piece of furniture. He looked up at Mike, greeted him in memory of last night with "Nick's comin' back. Nick's comin' back," and resumed his play. He had used the potty, but his pajama pants looked wet and he smelled slightly of urine. Mike smiled at him and went to study the cork notice board. He was drawn to the empty space—"Lisa teased her about it, and Nicky tore it down." Poor kid. It hurt when your mother or father held up someone you loved and admired to ridicule: Mike could recall a similar pain from his own childhood. He reread the biography beside the space where Nicky's master-piece should have been.

Sunny may be coming to the UK to do a panto at Christmas, if the dates fit in with her demanding schedule.

Sunny Patterson. It was a name he would later remember.

He studied the other pictures and posters on the walls, wondering for the first time, Who was this girl? Who was Nicolle Gurney? He tried to see her through Darren's eyes but found it impossible. But Darren would never hurt the child. He was a child himself when his life was so filled by Francie.

Mike returned to the front room and the sight of Alan Ralph, still sprawled on the couch, most of his shirt buttons undone and his snoring now as soft as that of a woman. He remembered the paper and went to retrieve it; he wouldn't leave until Ralph awoke because he wanted to recap the plans they'd made.

Alan seemed a decent enough man, far removed from the archetypal Cruel Stepfather. All around the flat Mike could see proof that both he and Lisa had been caring, responsible parents: The cupboard from which Alan had taken the whiskey, for example, was kept locked; a quick look in the kitchen revealed high cupboards where the bright blue Domestos bottle and other dangerous cleaning agents that might attract inquisitive small hands were kept well out of reach; there was a guard around the cooker top. Sensible parents who took every precaution.

And here was this troublesome adolescent, still missing her real father, resenting her little brother, bewildered by her mother's illness, and with a penchant for running away. No wonder her stepfather looked and spoke like a man on the brink of a nervous breakdown.

Was Nicolle Gurney an abused child? She had told Alan she'd fallen off her bike or been in a fight. It was common, almost the usual thing, for a kid to protect the parent inflicting the physical abuse. On the other hand, Alan was under so much stress. Who could blame him if he had lost his temper and hit the girl? Mike sighed and turned to the paper. Only Nicky herself could tell him the truth, and God knew where she was at this moment.

The newspaper was one of the "popular" ones, aimed at a readership who demanded scandal, bingo, and bare tits in preference to news. Mike leafed through it, reading such items as took his interest: a man who refused to pay his Poll Tax charged with beating up the bailiff; a fifteen-year-old boy taken into care after being seduced by his aunt and leaving her pregnant; the body found in a bin of fruit in Norfolk identified. This last he read only because he remembered the story from yesterday's evening paper and he was vaguely puzzled by the word *bin*. Mike knew nothing about fruit picking and supposed a "bin" to resemble the old-style dustbin. Darren could have enlightened him.

Darren. The name stood out in the column of print just as if it had been set in capital letters.

The woman whose body was found in a bin of pears at Benthill, Norfolk, on Friday has been identified as that of forty-four-year-old Therese Wallace. Therese, known as Terry, who came from Glasgow, had been strangled . . .
Police say they would like to question a young man calling himself Darren Lansdown or Landsdale, who left Elm Tree Farm, Defford, the day after Terry disappeared. He is described as average height, fair-haired and with brown eyes. He is believed to come from the Croydon area, drives a blue-and-white camper van, and is in the company of his younger sister. Police stress that the youth is not under suspicion, but may be able to help with their enquiries.

Mike swallowed a mouthful of whiskey straight from the bottle—what was left of it. Lansdown or Landsdale, that was the name Darren said he sometimes used. Fair-haired, as the Defford farmer described him, meant he must have dyed it in order to pass himself off as the girl's brother.

Not under suspicion, but it was too much of a coincidence. Was Darren Gillespie capable of murder? Perhaps, if he saw it as the only way out . . . if this woman, Terry Wallace, was sharp enough to recognize Nicky from the rather blurred photo she must have seen on the television news.

Mike sagged in his chair, overwhelmed by everything, much as Alan Ralph was, and only certain of one thing: The girl was with him by choice. For how else could Darren have mixed with so many other people and told so many lies unless Nicky was an ally?

Alan began to wake just then, grumbling his way to consciousness, licking the dry, white film from his bottom lip.

"Paper's bin then, has it?" he mumbled.

"Yes. I hope you don't mind. I just had a glance."

"Take it. Keep it. I don't read the papers much now. Don't even do the pools no more."

Mike folded it and stuffed it in his pocket.

Even if Darren had nothing to do with that woman's death, he must have heard about it by now, voracious reader that he was. And with Nicky to think of he certainly wouldn't be contacting the police to "help with their enquiries." No, he would get out of the area as soon as possible, perhaps go somewhere he had friends. Mike remembered that the lad seemed to favor Shropshire and Staffordshire, and he determined to get back into Darren's flat to take every name and address he could find.

And Alan mustn't know about the dead woman.

▽

15

THE MODEL WAS a realistic-looking Smith and Wesson .38, the weapon Ruth Ellis had used to shoot her lover. An interesting fact, that, Darren thought, reading from the box. All the same, he couldn't help feeling there was something wrong in a law that allowed such a "toy" to be displayed alongside the Airfix—even if the labels clearly stated "Not suitable for the preteens."

He had the thing assembled inside five minutes, truly child's play, and sat turning it over in his hands. Though he had never seen a real gun before, much less held one, he guessed that the weight, the feel of it was about right. Of course, an expert would know without even touching it that it was only a replica, but he wasn't likely to run into an expert. And this way no one would get hurt; there was no danger of any accidents. Darren didn't want to hurt anyone ever again, shuddered at the very thought of wounding another person and especially of spilling their blood. He was only going to do it because he could see no other immediate way of getting money.

Finding this place was a great piece of luck, and providing reference had been easy: two old friends willing to say Yes, they were So-and-So, a councillor, and So-and-So, a retired police sergeant—if the references were ever checked up, which Darren very much doubted. He had sat down and written two letters on two different types of notepaper, careful to disguise his usual hand on both. These would be sent off to the two friends and then reposted to his prospective landlord.

The two-bedroom flat was the top half of an ex–council house on the outskirts of Stoke-on-Trent. The owners, Mr. and Mrs. Cebrian, had done what they could to make the postwar house stand out from its council-owned neighbors. The result was just short of garish, and even Nicky, whose taste was hardly refined, declared the bright orange paint around the windows as "O.T.T."

Mr. Cebrian had been sent by his firm for six months' training with the parent company in the south of England. The opportunity meant promotion, a permanent position in Hampshire, and was too good to turn down; but it had arrived at extremely short notice, due to the sudden death of one of Cebrian's colleagues. There was a furnished flat awaiting them with a future option to buy, and the only problem was what to do with this place. Cebrian's elderly mother, who was almost blind, occupied downstairs in what her son described as a "Granny Flat." She refused to leave the area where she was born, or even to contemplate moving into one of the old people's flats two streets away. Her daughter would call in once a week, and home help could be arranged, but the old lady really shouldn't be alone in the house. The obvious solution was to rent out the upstairs rooms, giving his tenants access to the kitchen below and use of the washing machine.

Darren was the first to answer Cebrian's advert in the local paper. He gave Nicky two glasses of wine with her breakfast, knowing she had a particular taste for the stuff. "It'll go sour if we leave it any longer," he told her. "A treat for you."

When she fell asleep he drove to Cebrian's house, leaving the camper discreetly parked a little way down the road. He looked neat, clean-shaven, and fresh, ready to impress. Yes, of course he could provide references—by the end of the week, if that would be in order? His sister would be sharing the flat with him. She was an art student and he, Darren

Gillespie, was in the civil service. Mrs. Cebrian the elder would be kept an eye on; of course it was no trouble. A pleasure would be nearer the mark.

The old lady took an instant liking to Darren. "You're Australian, aren't you?" she questioned, leaning heavily on her walking stick and straining to see his face.

"Originally, ma'am." Ma'am seemed the politest form of address. "Our parents came over here when we were both very small. We're British citizens." Here was another piece of luck: The only other inhabitant of the house would be a half-blind woman who was a local and mistook his accent.

It was perhaps because of the old lady that Darren got the flat. She made her mind up Darren was the one she wanted in the house during her son's absence. She trusted her own intuition, she said, and there really was no arguing with that. They drank tea, and Darren answered questions with the lies that came so easily to him now. Could they meet his sister? Not today, he said. Not until next month—the Cebrians would be gone by then—as she was at her college and busily preparing for the annual exhibition.

"She's sharing a flat with another girl at the moment," Darren said, frowning in a distracted way. "And I don't want to pull the heavy Big Brother act with her, but this other girl isn't really the sort of person—well, I think she could be a bad influence on Vicky. You know, tempt her to go out every night when she should be studying or resting." Cebrian was beginning to look bored, as if he could have dispensed with the family details, but his wife and mother were nodding sympathetically. "So I've persuaded her to move in with me—if I can get a nice, clean flat. I feel responsible for her since our parents died. And"—with a smile at the old lady, whether she could see it or not—"it's what Mum would have wanted."

"Your parents are both dead?" asked Mrs. Cebrian the elder.

"Killed in a motorway pileup last winter. I expect you

heard about it on the news." Wasn't there at least one motorway pileup every winter?

"Well . . . now you come to mention it. John, don't you remember that awful crash?"

"Yes, Mother. I'm sorry, Mr. Gillespie. A terrible thing. Now, I would be asking three hundred and forty pounds per calendar month, the first month payable in advance. Subject, of course, to your references being satisfactory."

He was pompous, poor man, but the Cebrians had never done anything like this before. They were almost as innocent as Darren, and three of the party were correspondingly surprised when they found themselves shaking hands across the table and talking about drawing up a formal agreement.

Darren drove away, only to park again a few streets away from the Cebrian house. It was a shock to him to realize what he had just done. Three hundred and forty pounds a month was nothing; he had enough for the first month and would soon get the rest. The shock was because he had succeeded: a spacious flat, bright and clean, in a nice neighborhood. He lay his head on his arms over the steering wheel. Had he been right to use his own name? Certainly he couldn't call himself by his mother's maiden name anymore, not now he knew the police were looking for him in connection with Terry Wallace.

"Police expect to eliminate the young man from their enquiries, and request that he come forward in order for them to do so as soon as possible."

And he wanted to eliminate Terry Wallace from his thoughts.

He turned to look at Nicky, still fast asleep on the couch. Soon she'd have a real bed to sleep in, they'd have access to a proper oven, and he could cook her a proper meal, roast beef and Yorkshire pudding with all the trimmings, she'd like that.

He'd had the camper resprayed by an old friend, a local man who wasn't likely to ask many questions. Darren explained away the color of his hair in the same way he would explain it to any old friend he might meet. "This is my natural color. I used to think it was too bloody poofy, so I dyed it. I might dye it again," he added, aware that he must leave all options wide open.

Nicky took the news with less enthusiasm than he expected.

"How far are we from Barnhearst?" was her first question.

"About twenty miles. Probably a bit less."

"I thought you said we were going to have a look at the place? Get the tickets for the panto . . ."

"We are. Today. And if I can get this flat, we'll have a base. We can see the show again and again if you like."

Nicky brightened, took a folded sheet of paper from her handbag, the bag she'd had with her the night Darren took her to the fair and she followed him home.

"What's that?"

"A drawing. I had it up on my wall at home, but me mum . . ."

"Let's have a look. Hey! That's good! Best thing you've ever done." It was a portrait of the actress she so admired. "Shame you folded it."

"Yeah, it's spoiled. So I'm going to do it again. If I can get it just right, I might give it to her when we meet her. What d'you think?"

"Good idea. What was that about your mum?"

"Nothing. Well, she teased me about it. She was rotten. Rotten cow."

"Nicky, don't talk about your mother like that."

"Who cares? I hated her when she said—what she said." She bent her head low over the sketch pad, lightly outlining the new picture.

Darren felt a certain jealousy of her idols, especially Sunny Patterson, but he was also angry with Lisa Ralph. He would be careful not to make the same mistake.

"Nicky, if you really admire someone, if you think they're great, then what does it matter what anyone else thinks? You know better. Right?"

"Yeah."

"That really is a very good piece of work, you know. Did you copy it from a photo?"

"No, I did it off the video. The freeze-frame. That way, I could get her exactly the way I wanted. I'd like to be a photographer, Darren. I'd like to be like Lord Whatsisname and photograph famous people. He's my hero, Lord Thingy."

"Lichfield." Another idol. But it gave Darren an idea; another bribe. "A camera. That's what I'll buy you for your birthday. When is your birthday?"

"How about tomorrow?"

"When is it really?"

"July."

"Okay. Tomorrow's July."

Once in Barnhearst, Nicky wanted to find the theater straightaway, and it was she who stopped people to ask directions. The Victoria Theatre turned out to be a dilapidated-looking place sandwiched between a betting shop and a Chinese take-away, yet it could boast a couple of well-known names in the current production of *The Anniversary*. Darren peered through the doors into the foyer. The place was deserted, but he could see large photos of Sunny Patterson and Diana Dietz on display—"Coming Soon!"

"Not open yet," he told Nicky. "Come on, let's go and find a place that sells cameras. How about one of those Polaroids?"

"Not very professional."

"I know that. But it'll do to begin with. And you'll be able to see the results right away." He tugged her along the road, knowing that once she got a glimpse of her idol's picture she'd probably want to hang about until the place opened. And they couldn't afford to hang about drawing attention to themselves.

What would she want next? he wondered.

They bought the camera, plus five packs of film, flash cubes, and a battery, listened attentively as the salesman instructed them in its use. Nicky, of course, wanted to try it as soon as they got out of the shop, so he took her to a seat outside Barnhearst's town hall where the would-be Lichfield ordered him around and drew attention to them both anyway. While she was engrossed in watching her first four snaps develop on the bench armrest, Darren looked at the shops along the market hill. One of them, Collector's Items, interested him. He couldn't see the window display clearly from a distance, but they certainly weren't antiques.

"Look, Darren. Aren't these brill?" She had made him pose like a male model or a pop star, and the result in his opinion was stiff and unnatural. But she was happy with them, and keeping her happy was the most important thing.

"Yeah, brill. Come on, Nicks. I want to have a look at the shops."

"Aw!"

"Listen, if we're going to spend some time here while your Sunny's in town, we'd better get to know the place. Right?"

"All right." She trailed after him like a sulky child expected to help shop for groceries on Christmas Eve.

"Look, there's a Wimpy. We'll know where to come for something to eat."

"And there's a boozer. You'll know where to come for a jar, won't you, Jonagold?"

"Cheeky monkey." The "boozer," however, was not a pub but an off-license-cum-sweetshop, and it was right on the corner, offering an easy getaway.

Darren went in, bought a bottle of wine and crisps, and had a look round the place. It was quite a small shop, only one checkout and an elderly man at the till. Security seemed to consist of two notices: "Shoplifters will be prosecuted" and a poster of a snarling Doberman with the caption, "Guard dog on patrol at night." There were no cameras that he could see. The worst they had to fear, then, were nighttime break-ins and kids pocketing the Mars bars. This wasn't London, after all. He wouldn't even consider robbing an off-license in London.

At the checkout he exaggerated his accent, with the result that the old man asked how he liked England.

"Beer's too bloody warm, mate." He grinned.

"You should say grog, not beer," Nicky informed him once they were outside.

"That would be overdoing it. Eat your crisps."

The shop, Collector's Items, was two doors up from the off-license and specialized in model aircraft and ships, models of early telephones, crystal or wireless sets that actually worked, and limited-edition jigsaws.

"Dad bought me a jigsaw once," Nicky said, peering into the window.

"You mean your real dad or Alan?"

"Me real dad, of course. It was a thousand pieces and took us weeks to do. Me mum had a moan because it took up the whole dining table—and that was with the underneath bits pulled out. You had to go sideways to get out of the room." She sighed, suddenly lonely, he thought; missing her father. And that worthless mother of hers.

"I'll buy you a jigsaw," he offered. "We'll do it together."

While she was selecting one inside the shop, Darren looked around the shelves. He'd never been interested in model aircraft as a child, and all the Airfix kits complete with tiny paint pots that his grandfather sent him regularly at Christmas or on birthdays were discarded. It made him feel guilty.

Then he saw the replica guns: Remingtons, Lugers, Berettas, and the famous Colt Army 1873 .45-caliber-model. Each with a short history on the box, assembly instructions, and the warning that these were "Not toys. Not for sale to the preteens. Parental approval required before purchase by anyone under eighteen."

Useless, all of it. Replicas were used in hundreds of crimes every year, from robbery to rape. They may have blocked-off barrels and no firing pins, but Darren knew, through his indiscriminate reading, that replica guns are realistic down to their inner mechanisms: They could be efficiently converted by someone with the know-how into a weapon lethal not only to the victim but to the user, too. And here was this glorified toyshop selling the things as "collector's items." It occurred nationwide, and only when some outraged parent complained or kicked up a stink via their local paper was anything ever done about it. Darren felt sick to think that some teenager, needing money to feed a drug addiction, perhaps, might get his hands on one of these.

But he needed money himself. It would only be until after Christmas, or at least until after that wretched pantomime finished its run, and by then he would have some clear idea of what he should do. He was keen on finding a night job somewhere; ten until six, when Nicky would be safely tucked up in bed. How he would manage to catch up on his own sleep was a part of the plan he hadn't yet arrived at. Right now, he must have money.

He chose the Smith and Wesson, for no particular reason except that he liked the name, paid for it while Nicky was still looking at the jigsaws, and slipped it into the plastic carrier with the wine. Whatever happened, she mustn't see it.

She finally chose a five-hundred-piece puzzle depicting the Prince and Princess of Wales, "A limited edition—sure to become a prized collector's item," which came in the kind of tin one might expect to contain chocolate biscuits.

"Can we afford it?" she asked doubtfully. Money was a subject she touched on only periodically. The rest of the time she was like most kids, who seemed to think adults could just pluck lumps out of themselves.

"Of course we can," Darren told her carelessly. He looked at his watch. "Come on. Let's get something to eat, and then the box office should be open."

He had never bought theater tickets before, just as he'd never stayed in a hotel, dined out anywhere smarter than the corner café, or left the country. The Gillespies were the kind of people who seldom ventured from the way of life they knew and were comfortable in. Darren, too, might have settled for a factory job, spent his days in brain-numbing boredom and his evenings in the same pub, getting smashed with the same mates, if his reading habits hadn't intensified his already restless nature.

"A little learning," as his stepmother was fond of quoting, "is a dangerous thing."

Nevertheless, Darren had experienced few of the things most young men of his age take for granted. He had traveled about England looking for work and knew many towns and cities quite well, but he was a stranger to just as many situations because there had never been anyone to guide him, to explain. And Darren had the additional handicap—phobia would be nearer the mark, perhaps—of making himself look ignorant in public.

He approached the box office feeling as if he were about to commit a crime instead of buying two tickets for the panto. Fortunately, Nicky was engrossed in a leaflet she had picked up describing future events at the theater and didn't see him floundering.

"*Peter Pan,*" he said. "I'd like two tickets for the—" He nearly said Upstairs, but a sign above him came to his aid. "Two tickets for the Circle. The first available date, please."

The woman smiled. A motherly sort. "Let me see . . . Oh, you're in luck. Tuesday, the eighteenth, second house. How's that?"

"Fine." He paid her the fifteen pounds, only surprised it wasn't twenty-five.

Typically, Nicky complained because he'd been unable to get an earlier date, and though he'd promised himself to check her the next time she showed ingratitude, he let it pass in the relief that he'd actually got tickets at all.

"Can I have them, Darren?"

"Better let me keep them, Nicks. You might lose them."

"Aw, all right. But you guard them with your life."

"With my life," he said. "With my life." And he meant it.

He hadn't even looked at the gun again until today, but kept it wrapped in a plastic carrier and hidden away among his clothes. The Cebrians were gone, happy with their tenant and the impressive references he'd provided, everything signed and sealed and the first month's rent paid. This last made Darren feel his funds were dangerously low, though in fact he still had enough for food and next month's rent.

Nicky was at the kitchen table, busily working on her portrait of Sunny Patterson. She was taking her time with it, working herself up into agonies before putting pencil to paper, so determined to do a good job. At this rate, Darren rather doubted she'd finish it before Christmas. He could hear old Mrs. Cebrian's television blaring away downstairs. She was a bit deaf as well as blind, and sometimes forgot to switch on her hearing aid. Both these handicaps proved advantageous to Darren. She heard little of his comings and goings unless he tapped on her door with the shopping she'd asked him to fetch, and only commented that the "art student" was very small for her age.

With them both so fully occupied, Darren decided he couldn't put it off another day; he pulled the package out from among a heap of shirts and studied the instructions on how to assemble the Smith and Wesson. When he had completed it he turned the model over and over in his hands. Not only did it feel right, how he imagined a real gun would feel, but it also gave him a strange sense of security: a deterrent that would hurt no one, should he need to protect himself and Nicky.

Yet guns suggested death and dying, and there had been too much of that already: Francie, his grandparents, old Charley . . . and Terry Wallace.

He had shut that night at Elm Tree Farm out of his mind almost as one might shut out a vivid, recurring nightmare from waking life. But nightmares have a way of coming back to haunt you during the day: A chance remark, something seen on the television or in the street, and the full horror of the thing is upon you, enveloping you like a heavy black cloak. For Darren, it was an exasperated mother in the supermarket threatening to strangle her whining child, the sight of pears displayed in a greengrocer's window, the back view of any woman in the street with the build and hair of Terry Wallace.

He tried to reason with himself: He had done it to protect Nicky, to save her from being sent back to the stepfather she hated. Hundreds of people were murdered every week, weren't they? And for every murder there had to be a motive: financial gain, intolerable sexual jealousy, to shut someone up.

He wasn't the first person to take another's life.

No one would miss Terry Wallace. No one would feel more than a passing regret that she was dead, or be genuinely, deeply sorry. She'd had her followers, her cronies, but even they would forget her, find another leader, as women of their sort always do.

Terry Wallace was no better than that girl in Ipswich. They had both more or less asked for it.

Darren put the gun into a plastic carrier bag, along with an old pullover to disguise the shape, and slipped it under his mattress. Then he went into the kitchen to check on Nicky. She sat hunched over her drawing, pencil poised, evidently in one of her agonies to get the smallest detail right.

"Hungry, Nicks?" he said. It was only six o'clock, and they usually ate at seven-thirty. But she had only eaten a light lunch, eager to get back to her work, and had nothing but a Coke since then.

"A bit."

"You ought to give it a rest, you know. You'll get stale if you spend too long at it. How's it coming along, anyhow?"

"You can look if you like." She only let him look if it was going well and she was feeling pleased with herself.

He peered over her shoulder. "Oh, Nicky, that's wonderful! She's going to love it." It was, in fact, much better than the original that she had taken from the video.

"I've got to be so careful," she said, frowning. "Mustn't spoil it now."

"You won't. But you ought to rest—not spend too long at it in one sitting." He went on looking at the portrait. Why was this so remarkably good when every other drawing she'd done was what you'd more or less expect from a girl of her age? A labor of love, he supposed you'd call it, and with a pang of jealousy he wondered if she would agonize so were she working on a portrait of him.

"What d'you want to eat?" he asked.

"Spaghetti on toast, can we? Only 'Take the O'Neills' will be on soon.

Damn it, he'd forgotten what day it was. She wouldn't miss that for the world.

"Okay," he said cheerfully, "it won't take a minute. Clear your stuff off the table."

He gave her a glass of wine with her meal, placing the bottle in a metal litter bin—for the want of something better—filled with ice cubes.

"Wine with spaghetti, Darren?"

"Well, if we're going to eat Italian . . . When in Rome, and all that." The wine was German, but she wouldn't know.

"Why d'you let me have wine?"

"Why not? French kids drink it with their meals."

"But you don't let me have it every day."

"You're not used to it."

"It makes me sleep." She watched him steadily, accusingly, as he ate. "Do you give it to me when you want me to sleep?"

"Jesus Christ, Nicky! What the hell d'you suspect me of doing?" Sneaking off to rob an off-license was certainly not it. He wondered, Did she think he—*did things* to her—while she slept?

"Okay," he said, reaching for her glass, "don't drink it. I will, and you can have water from the bloody tap, if that's what you want."

Greed won over suspicion and she grabbed the glass from him. Probably she only thought he was going off somewhere without her and resented it.

She finished a second glass, settled down ready to watch her favorite show while Darren washed up. When he finished, he came to join her, a book under his arm and cigarettes in his hand, like someone intending to spend the evening quietly at home. Downstairs, Mrs. Cebrian's television seemed to vie with his in noise.

Nicky looked at the wine bottle, then back at Darren questioningly.

"You'll fall asleep," he reminded her.

"No, I won't. I'm used to it now."

"All right. Just this once." She seemed more alert than usual after two glasses. Of course, a child regularly drinking wine would indeed soon become accustomed to it so that it no longer affected her in the same way. Darren could remember the time when a quarter bottle of whiskey, his regular Friday-night intake, made him violently sick: Today he could manage a half-bottle without staggering (much).

Nicky giggled through the program. Gloria O'Neill, the eldest daughter, played by Sunny Patterson, had found herself a classy boyfriend and was determined to keep him and her family of degenerates apart. It resulted in her trying to pass off her mother, a slut in slippers and curlers and with a cigarette dangling from her lips, as the daily help; while her siblings were "some poor unfortunates" she had adopted. The boyfriend was suitably impressed, and it looked as if Gloria was going to be the bride of an English twit with a title and a stately home. But the show, for once, didn't end on a laugh. Mrs. O'Neill, fiddling with the curlers in her hair, stared at her reflection in the living room mirror, and a tear trickled down her wrinkled, over-powdered cheek:

"Oh, Glo! I didn't know you were ashamed of us. . . ."

When Darren turned to look at Nicky, she was flushed, surreptitiously swiping at her cheeks with the back of her hand.

"Nicks, what's the matter?"

"It's so sad, Darren. It's so sad."

"What are you blubbering for?" he said, misunderstanding. "She's still in the show, isn't she? You said they're starting another series next year."

"It's not that. Of course she's still in it. Gloria's boyfriends never work out. It's her mother. . . ."

This could be dangerous. He might have realized she hadn't yet recovered from losing her own mother in the few weeks since Lisa Ralph's death. She was at that curious stage in a child's development when she needed proof of something before she would believe it. Maybe this was a subconscious but natural reaction to years of being deceived with Father Christmas and the Tooth Fairy, thought Darren, who had lately begun to fancy himself something of an expert in child psychology. He was also, needs must, an expert on the fictional O'Neills by now.

"Don't cry," he said cheerfully. "Gloria's a social climber, but she'll always put her family first in the end. It'll turn out right in the next episode, you'll see. Here, let's polish off the plonk, that'll cheer you up."

It didn't, of course. She sniffled, gulped at her wine, stared stonily at the television screen, then fell asleep. Darren looked at his watch: seven-twenty. Past experience told him she would sleep for around three and a half to four hours, waking only with a slight thirst as a hangover. Very likely, she would be wide awake by eleven and demanding to watch whatever unsuitable late film was on the television. The Cebrians had a video recorder, the operating of which was still a mystery to Darren. Nicky, predictably, was blasé about the thing, and not averse to scolding him.

"I told you, Darren"—shoving the remote control under his nose—"the red buttons are for recording. Don't you touch them. This one's for play, that one's for winding it back. It's gonna take me a year to learn you."

Chastised for his ignorance, he hadn't bothered to correct her grammar.

He would rent a video this evening. Something suitable for a kid to watch.

He laid her comfortably on the sofa, found a blanket to cover her; paused with the blanket held up in his hands. She would soon need a bra, and then there would be periods to deal with. The latter would be no problem; she knew about her monthly flow, had even discussed it with him in relation to a growing tendency she had toward Equality ("How would you lot manage if you had to put up with what we have to every month?"). But a bra? Darren knew very little on the subject. He only knew it wasn't as simple as going into Woolies for a dozen white cotton size thirty-four. The wretched things had to fit properly. He could possibly take her into one of those cheap boutiques you found in most shopping precincts and hand her over to a sympathetic female assistant with the story of a bedridden mother at home. Every problem had a resolution if you only thought about it.

He looked at her once more. She was long-boned, still with a hint of last summer's tan on her hairless limbs. By the time she had finished growing, she would be of above-average height for a woman; perhaps as tall as Darren himself. He even imagined she had grown a couple of inches since she had been with him. Her hair was certainly grown, and she now tended to fuss with it in an adult way, wanting to wash it every morning and then sitting around with a towel on her head because the dryer would "ruin the ends." Yes, she was becoming a vain little madam. And she would grow into a beautiful young woman.

This wouldn't do. If he was going to get her a video before driving to Barnhearst he must get a move on. The video shop would want some form of identity, he supposed, and all he had was his driver's license and an old plastic library card. He hoped they would be enough.

Barnhearst was quiet that evening, possibly because there was a big football match on the television. People would already have bought their beer supplies and be settled in front of the box. This was something that hadn't occurred to Darren until now, though he knew about the match; he regarded it as an unexpected bonus. And a good omen.

He parked around the corner, pulled his collar up, and

tugged the old cap with the swastikas on it low over his forehead—not unnatural or suspicious, as it was raining miserably. Another idea he had thought of was to disguise himself with a scarf tied around the lower half of his face and then clutching his cheek as if he had a toothache. A good idea to use in the future.

He would have liked a large whiskey to calm his nerves, but it wouldn't be wise to hang around getting himself noticed. Pub landlords were notorious for remembering strangers, especially ones without the local accent. Instead, he thought about Nicky, recalling a conversation with her that morning.

"Time to dye your hair again, Jonagold."

"Why do you call me that? It makes me sound like one of Robin Hood's Merry Men."

"Yeah. Stealin' from the Rich to give to the Poor."

That might actually be worth a laugh in an hour's time, he thought.

There were two customers in the off-license when Darren entered: one an ancient old man who was asking for draught sherry, the other a young girl waiting by the checkout, probably for cigarettes. The man Darren had seen at the checkout before was nowhere in evidence, and a plump, motherly sort of woman seemed to be in sole charge.

He inspected the wine shelves, surreptitiously looking as he had before for security cameras, while the woman trickled draught sherry from a plastic barrel into an old lemonade bottle. That customer dealt with, she served the youngster with forty Embassy.

Darren's heart was pounding harder than he could ever remember it doing before, and his mouth felt dry. He had to remind himself that as yet he had committed no crime. The gun was still in his carrier bag along with the video he had rented for Nicky. He had money in his pocket. He was a bona fide customer.

"Can I help you, love?" The woman was smiling at him. They were the only two in the shop.

"Yes . . ." He approached the checkout, reaching into his bag. "I wonder if you could possibly"—out came the gun—"open the till." The woman obeyed automatically, almost as if this had happened to her many times before, and Darren, though he wanted to look at the money in the till, didn't dare take his eyes off her.

He held the bag open. "Put it in here—all of it," he said, remembering to maintain the London-Irish accent spoken by many of his old friends, and which he could imitate perfectly.

"Move away from the till," he ordered when she had finished. And he was careful that she saw him glance at the door and to the right, up the market hill; he did it twice for good measure. Then he ordered her to the back of the shop and to lie facedown on the floor. Had somebody else entered at that moment, they would have been sent to join her. But no one else came in. He swiped a bottle of Bells from the shelf and ran; he ran left outside the door and round the corner to the camper.

As he clambered into the driving seat and reached for the ignition, notes and coins tumbled from his bag and onto the floor.

16

Nicky was having another restless night, the third that week, and Darren tried to persuade himself that the wine was responsible for disturbing her sleep and that she would soon be back to normal. He refused to acknowledge the truth, much less accept it, which was that all his gifts, his love and care, he himself, could never be enough for her. She needed kids her own age to play with, and she needed a woman in her life. He guessed she would have liked to spend some time with old Mrs. Cebrian, but he discouraged it: The woman was half-blind, but sooner or later Nicky might do or say something in her presence that would reveal her true age.

He listened to her moving around in the room next to his for a while, then went in to her.

"Can't you sleep?"

She was sitting on the edge of the bed, halfheartedly flipping through magazines by the light of her bedside lamp. "You'll strain your eyes, Nicky."

"I had a bad dream."

"Ah, well, if you talk about a bad dream it usually helps."

"I don't know."

"How about some warm milk, then?" Milk was his grandmother's favorite remedy for sleeplessness.

"Yuk!"

He persuaded her back into bed and to talk about her

dream. "Was it about your mother?"

"No. Alan. I dreamt he was looking for me. He wasn't angry. Just sort of . . . upset. His clothes were all torn and he was filthy dirty—stuck in some sort of mud so he couldn't get out. It was like I was there. He was looking right at me—calling to me."

Darren nodded. "Did you really hate him so much?"

"Sometimes. Or I thought I did. Then sometimes, when me mam was having a bad day, I used to think he looked like a great bear. An old bear kept in a cage and too tired to growl anymore."

"That's sad." He loved her ability to speak in pictures. Whatever she chose to do in later life, he was sure it would be something creative.

"But he wouldn't really come looking for me, would he? And if he did, he'd be angry."

"Perhaps." He was going to lose her. Whatever he did, however many presents he bought her, however many places he took her for a treat, he would eventually lose her.

He sat on the edge of her bed, watching her, planning. It was December, not long now until Sunny Patterson opened in *Peter Pan*. While the actress was in England Darren felt he could keep Nicky with him. But he must resign himself to giving her up one day. He would take her back to London, leave her somewhere near her home, and just drive away. Perhaps he would come back here and, Micawber-like, see what turned up in the job line.

Looking at Nicky now, he couldn't believe he had ever thought her like Francie, or that he had ever wanted her to be like Francie. The strong resemblance was there, but they were entirely different characters. He was glad Francie was dead. Had she lived, he would have been forced sooner or later to accept her for what she really was: a spiteful, sly, deceiving little bitch. Maybe the elderly neighbors remembered her for her little acts of kindness towards them, but that was all an act—part of the image she created for herself. No, maybe he was being too hard on her. She was no worse than a million other kids, and that was what he found so hard to forgive.

Francie was not the little saint he had made her, but an ordinary, heartless teenager.

"Darren, don't!"

"What?" He shook off his thoughts. "Don't what?"

"Don't look at me like that."

"Didn't know I was looking at you like anything." He rose abruptly from the bed. "Try and sleep."

He went back to his own room, which was much smaller than hers, more of a glorified broom cupboard, and had little space for his clothes and books. There was no table lamp in here (not even a table to put it on), so he had to use the ceiling light. He kept the money in a paper bag under his mattress, just as old Charley had done with his savings. There weren't many of the grubby, battered notes left now, but alongside what remained was a wad of tenners and fivers, totaling 740 pounds, his haul from the off-license. Darren now had over a thousand pounds in cash; a comfortable figure that would have seen him well into spring were he following his old lifestyle, for he had always been careful with money. Even with Nicky and his ever-growing tendency to buy her anything she so much as looked at in a shop window, he could still manage for some weeks. But already he was feeling his old anxiety, that he wouldn't have enough, that he would run out if any emergency arose before Christmas. And the answer was to look for another off-license.

At half past three, he went in to check on Nicky. She was asleep, a frown on her worried face; possibly she was dreaming again. Darren sat on the floor beside her bed as he used to do before she learned that her mother had died. Afterward, he would sleep beside her on the camper bed, outside of her covers. He missed that. He missed the smell of her hair, the warmth of her. And he missed carefully maneuvering his position late at night when he could feel her breath on his face.

What did she mean earlier on when she told him not to

look at her "like that"? Whatever it was, he knew he would never be able to fall asleep next to her again.

The next afternoon, she wanted to be allowed out on her own. There was a park nearby, but it was deserted, as the schools hadn't yet broken up for Christmas.

"Tomorrow," old Mrs. Cebrian said when he asked her. "I think they break up tomorrow. I suppose your sister's term is already over?"

"Yes. Well, I'd better be off—"

"I thought I heard her this morning." She leaned on her walking stick with both hands, peering into his face with an openmouthed, questioning smile. For the first time, he noticed that her gums looked diseased, almost decaying, and her breath smelled rotten. "She makes more noise than a kid."

Darren thought an explanation was in order and, as usual, a story came easily to him. "I know. She's never had much self-confidence, you see; and last year, just as she was making new friends, getting more independent, our parents were killed. Poor Vicky. It's just as if she's going back in age five years."

"Well, that's understandable, I suppose. If she ever needs someone to talk to, another girl"—she laughed, leering at him—"I'm always here."

"I'll be sure to tell her."

As he left her, he wondered if his accent had slipped a little.

He let Nicky go out, warning her that he would expect to meet her by the park gates at four o'clock; then they would go and get fish and chips for an early tea. She took her bag with her, which was unusual when she went off to play somewhere, but Darren wasn't worried; he knew she had very little money on her, possibly just enough for the bus fare to Stoke-on-Trent railway station. There were trains to Euston every hour, but she'd never get past the barrier without a ticket. Besides, she would never run when the chance to meet Sunny Patterson was a matter of days away.

Just to be sure, he checked the money under his mattress. It was all there, as was Nicky's portrait of the actress, carefully placed in a folder on the dining table. She wouldn't leave without that.

He spent the time getting the place tidy; vacuuming, dusting, cleaning windows; then he handwashed some of their pullovers. Nicky wanted to wear her favorite, a dark blue one, to the theater, and so he took special care with it, washing it inside out and separately the way Gran used to do with woolen garments. He had bought her a warm jacket, which was what she had on today, but she really ought to have a good winter coat. Money again. But he told himself that a winter coat was not "spoiling" her, it was a necessity. He, too, needed something a little more suitable against the cold than that rag of an anorak he'd been making do with for the last three years. They should enter the theater in style; the cherished offspring of professional people; fond elder brother and adoring little sister.

Money. He would get more, and before the week was out. Tonight, before he lost his nerve.

At ten of four, he combed his hair, rinsed his face, and went to meet her. She was coming not from the park but along the street where there was a row of shops.

"Where've you been?" He tried to keep the anxiety from his voice.

"Oh, just lookin' around."

"Did you meet anyone? Speak to anyone?"

"No. Darren, can I have four fifty?"

"Four fifty? What for this time?" He was already reaching into his pocket.

"There's a new 'Take the O'Neills' annual. I've just seen a kid with it. Can I, Darren? Please!"

"All right." It would keep her quiet for the rest of the day, he thought. "Where do they sell it? At the newsagent's?"

She knew where the shop was, of course; had probably been staring in the window for the past half hour. He tried to recall his own idols when he was her age, wanting to relive a little of the excitement by sharing hers. But perhaps girls were more prone to this hero worship than boys. At any rate, the only name, the only face that stood out in his memory was that of Francie.

"The 'O'Neills' annual?" frowned the newsagent. "We did have a load of them in, but they're all gone. I reckon everyone's sold out of them. Been going like the proverbial hotcakes, they have." Darren couldn't see Nicky's face, but her disappointment must have been acute, for the man seemed suddenly concerned. "Hey, don't you fret. I'll be getting some more in. Now, let me see . . ." He had a computer behind the counter, and he tapped at the keys with the pride and importance of one who has recently mastered a new skill. "December eighteenth. That's when they'll be in. Come back then, love."

"The eighteenth," Nicky said. "That's the day we're going to Barnhearst."

"Okay. I'll keep it for you. What's your name?"

"Gillespie." Darren answered for her. He bought a copy of the local paper, which came out weekly, and forty cigarettes. He wanted Nicky out of the shop quickly: Excited, and then disappointed, she couldn't keep her mouth shut, and even then she had to twist out of his grasp to plead, "You won't forget, will you?"

" 'Course not, love. I'll make a note of it now."

He gave her wine with her fish and chips, and, combined with the fresh air and excitement, it soon made her fall asleep. The paper, which had a large circulation, devoted two pages to national news. There was nothing new on the Terry Wallace case, which didn't surprise him; the national news value of that story was simply the circumstances in which her body was discovered. The local section reported:

Police are no nearer to discovering the identity of the man who robbed an off-license in Barnhearst last week. The youth, who threatened an assistant with a gun before forcing

her to hand over the contents of the till, is said to speak with
a London-Irish accent, is fair-haired and of average height.
On the night in question, he wore a grubby cap decorated
with silver badges. . . .

That was one item he must dispose of.

The video he chose to rent that evening was *Look Who's Talking*, as Nicky hadn't seen it before—one of the few she admitted not to have seen. And as he left the shop he was oddly relieved to pass a youth, just entering, with fair hair and a filthy cap. There were a lot of them about, after all.

He drove to nearby Saltinghouse, a small town he remembered from his previous stop in the area. The off-license here was smaller than the one at Barnhearst and sold only beer, lager, and spirits, no wine. Again, the woman on the checkout seemed to be in sole charge of the shop. Again, security seemed to be limited—in this case two mirrors placed so that whoever was on the till could also keep an eye on browsing customers. It took robbery to bring some of these people to their senses and have modern security equipment installed, so in the long term he was actually doing them a favor. Better to lose the evening's takings than a vanload of spirits and fags.

This time there were more people in the shop, and he had to hang around for ten minutes, studying labels until they were gone. It was then two minutes to closing time, so surely anyone too idle to walk to their nearest pub would have been here by now? The woman in front of him had a small child in tow, a little boy sucking an ice lolly, and as Darren watched, a piece of the lolly dropped on the floor and the child began to wail. His mother paid for her lager and dragged him from the shop.

"Ice lollies in this weather! I ask you!" remarked the checkout woman. "Some people have no sense. Well, what can I do for you, love?" She looked at her watch, impatient to lock up.

"Yes, I was wondering if you could"—out came the

gun—"hand the money over. All of it. In here—" Holding
open the plastic carrier containing Nicky's video.

"Look, love, I—"

"Shut up! Just give me the money and I won't hurt you."

She obeyed, not mechanically as the woman in Barnhearst
had, but swiftly, like a child ordered to pick up its toys or go
to bed.

"Right, now move away. Go on! Down the back there and
lie on the floor."

She began to move away from the till, but then she lost
her balance, slipped on the lump of melting ice lolly, and fell,
banging her head on a shelf.

For a few seconds Darren couldn't move. He stared at her
chest, watching for the rise and fall of her breathing: He
couldn't detect any movement.

No, not another death! Please, God, no . . .

"Hey! What the hell happened?" A young man, who must
have heard the crash of her fall, came running from a door
at the back of the shop. He saw the gun and started to back
off, hands in the air. "Oh, hey, look here . . ."

"She slipped," Darren said. "She slipped, I tell you! I didn't
touch her—I wouldn't hurt her—" He ran from the shop,
clutching the carrier, to the safety of his camper around the
corner.

Nicky sensed there was something wrong. He picked at the
salad she had prepared, didn't even question her activities
while he was out, and it wasn't until she sulkily cleared the
table and sat to finish her portrait that he remembered he
had left her fast asleep.

"The telly was on," she said. "It woke me. Darren, where
were you?"

"I went out to see an old mate."

"Why didn't you want me with you?"

"You'd have been bored. His flat smells and there's no
telly."

"Oh," somewhat mollified. "Then why didn't you say so?

I don't mind sitting here watching the telly. There was no need to dose me up."

"Nicky! That's not true."

"Yes, it is. You're afraid to leave me alone with the old dear downstairs in case I tell her who I am."

"Would you do that?"

"Why should I?" But she wouldn't look at him, said she was still hungry and began to nibble on a chocolate biscuit; it was her favorite evasion tactic, taking advantage of his Jewish-mother attitude toward feeding her. This time, it didn't work.

"Do you want to go home?"

"I don't know. Sort of. I mean, I'd like to see everyone and then come back with you."

"That's impossible. I'll take you home anytime you like. Right now, if that's what you want." He added, "Only you'll miss Sunny Patterson."

"Darren, couldn't I phone Alan? Or write to him?"

He hesitated. If he said no, those restless nights would go on. And perhaps to deny her would be a form of mental cruelty. He could supervise any letter she wrote and some-how have it posted elsewhere. "I suppose so."

"Good. Darren—I already did. . . ."

"You what? You phoned him? How—when?"

"When I was supposed to be in the park. I didn't phone him. I tried to, but some woman answered—I think it might have been Alan's sister; it sounded like her; so I put the phone down. Then I bought some envelopes and wrote to him. Don't worry, I didn't say where I was or your name. And I cadged a stamp off some bloke outside the post office."

"God Almighty, girl! Haven't you heard of postmarks? And what do you mean, 'some bloke'? How many times have you been told about strangers?"

"I didn't have no money left."

He gave her a short lecture, which may or may not have sunk in, then let her watch the video while he hid his latest haul. Even if that woman was okay, this was the last time.

*   *   *

The woman *was* okay. Just. She had severe bruising and swelling, and slight amnesia, which the doctor said would pass. She would be kept in hospital for a few days, then released into the care of her husband, who was making a nuisance of himself with the police, demanding they go out and "catch the animal" instead of plaguing a sick woman with questions she wasn't in a fit state to answer.

"He was fair," she told the police. "I remember that much. And he had beautiful eyes. Beautiful, but frightened. I'm sure he didn't push me, or touch me at all. I must've slipped."

This last was borne out by a pool of melted ice lolly police found on the shop floor.

"But he had a gun, Debs," her husband said. "He would have hurt you if he had a chance. Why are you trying to defend him?"

"I'm not. He's done wrong and of course he has to be punished. But—I don't know. He was so young, so frightened. . . ."

"You'll be saying next that he could have been our own son."

The woman sighed. She wished he'd go home and let her sleep away her headache. She couldn't remember what she'd had for lunch that day, or what clothes she'd been wearing any more than she could describe the clothes the youth had on. But there was something more important that she was trying to recall. Something as teasingly elusive as a name on the tip of the tongue.

On the day she was released from hospital, as her husband was driving her home, it suddenly came to her. She insisted on stopping at the police station.

Twenty minutes later, Inspector Baker-Smith had a team of men visiting every video rental shop in the area. He wanted the names and addresses of anyone who had hired *Look Who's Talking* on the night of the robbery. And he would check every shop in Staffordshire if necessary.

◁

17

"A MESSAGE FOR you, Mr. Ralph," said the landlord of the pub where Alan and Mike were staying. He read slowly, ironically—he thought they were a pair of queers—from a slip of paper. "Your sister called. She says she's got a letter from Nicky and will you call her back straightaway."

Alan was already halfway to the phone, Mike at his heels. A letter from Nicky. Even if she didn't say where she was, there would be a postmark—a positive lead at last.

The woman answered after one ring, evidently as agitated as her brother. "I haven't opened it yet."

"Then open it, for Christ's sake, woman!"

"The postmark," Mike urged, and Alan repeated it.

"Stoke-on-Trent. Oh, Al! However did she get all that way?"

"Never mind how, just read the bloody letter."

Stoke-on-Trent. Mike didn't know the place, except that it was large enough to be the haystack for Darren Gillespie's needle.

"Dear Uncle Alan," read the woman. "I'm all right. I hope you are all right. I heard about Mum. I'm with my friend. We have a flat where it's nice and quiet and there's a park. Don't worry about me. With love, Nicolle Gurney."

"She never called me uncle before," said Alan. "She never called me by any name if she could help it. Are you sure it's not a hoax letter?"

"No, Al. It's her handwriting. I compared it with some in her room. You know the way she does **her letter** *E*, like a

number three back to front. Al, should I take it to the
police?"

"No! That's the last thing I want you to do. A flat in
Stoke-on-Trent. I'll find her."

Mike knew he would. If he had to knock on the door of
every flat in Stoke-on-Trent, he'd find her.

"Where it's quiet and there's a park," Alan said thoughtfully when he had put the phone down. "Wouldn't that
suggest the outskirts of town rather than right in it?"

Mike had never seen him like this before: tense, excited,
too restless to sit and eat his dinner. He wanted to leave for
Stoke-on-Trent that night.

"It's no good bolting off this minute," Mike told him. "It's
a large place. We've got to plan it thoroughly. Did you pick
the pictures up?"

He produced two photos of Nicky, enlarged from the snap
Mrs. O'Reilly had given him. They were a little fuzzy, but a
good likeness. In the morning, Mike said, they would leave
for the town, find a place to stay, and buy a couple of street
maps. Then they would split up, Alan taking the car, Mike
using the bus, and work their way methodically round the
outskirts of the town. They would show the photo to
shopkeepers, park attendants, lollipop ladies, anyone who
came into regular contact with children.

"Don't forget other children," Mike advised. "And don't
forget to watch out for the camper—blue and white with
orange curtains."

It would take days, and Mike was beginning to wonder if
Darren was really so important to him after all. But finding
the girl was everything to Alan Ralph; he, Mike, couldn't let
him down.

They planned late into the night, mainly because Alan
was too restless to sleep: Hyper was what the Americans
would call it, Mike thought, watching him. He supposed,
because they were now on first-name terms, that they were
friends. An odd alliance: the young, effeminate man and the
older, very masculine Eastender. The only thing they had in

common was a taste for good Scotch whiskey—and the tendency to overindulge it. Yet Alan had a gentleness one might not expect to find in—Mike hesitated to say—someone of his class, a man with his background. The child, Nicky, didn't know when she was well off. If only Mike's own father had been like him, tolerant and understanding, willing to listen and accept.

Alan's attitude toward Darren was gradually changing, too. He had stopped referring to him as "that man" or "your friend" and now called him "the boy." It was his idea that whoever found the pair should do nothing until they could approach them together.

"I know I can persuade her to come home of her own free will," he said. "I'm sure of it. After all, she did write to me."

His hope was inextinguishable; Mike only hoped the brat was worth it.

In the morning, they studied the maps Mike bought, noting the parks and play areas around Stoke-on-Trent. The task seemed even more insurmountable than before, but there was Alan, confidently suggesting a starting point, ready to get on with it. Enthusiasm like his was the purely infectious sort, and Mike had no choice but to follow where once he led.

The days were long and tedious. Mike hadn't understood just how many people owned campers before nor had he realized that one doesn't go around questioning children for very long before a fist-happy father turns up. He should have known better, of course; him an ex-social worker. And, dabbing at the cut above his eyes—the child's father must have worn a signet ring—left the area before the police should turn up.

After that, he was careful before approaching a child, or he only questioned children with their mothers. Three days into the search, and his copy of Nicky's photo was beginning to look dog-eared and grubby. Mike's flat was spotless, but he was the sort of person who found it impossible to keep the contents of his pockets in order. He must have gone into hundreds of shops—newsagents, sweetshops, cafés, and toyshops—with that photo, as Alan had on his side of the town. Every night they met up at the pub where they had rented a room, with nothing to report.

"A bloke at the chippy thought he'd seen Nicky," Alan said dismally one evening. "But she was with a woman. A redhead. And I've been thinking about something. You said you think the boy's dyed his hair. Couldn't he have changed Nicky's too? If not the color then the style?"

Mike had to admit that it was possible. "But I don't think so. Remember? He took her with him because she reminds him of Francie."

The older man was tiring, though he would never admit it; trailing the streets of an unfamiliar town, probably often meeting with a hostile response to his questions, was too much for him. He was graying when Mike first met him, but now he looked worn and haggard. Alan was exhausted.

"Why don't you have a rest tomorrow?" Mike suggested.

"No, I'm going on. I can't give up now."

"Look, if they've got a flat they won't be going anywhere. He's got friends here, contacts who'll help him find a job. You can afford one day's rest, and I'll phone you straightaway if I find anything. Anything at all."

Alan nodded. "All right. Just one day. I'm so tired, Mike." He laughed, the first time Mike could remember him laughing. "I guess I'm just not used to all the fresh air."

Mike was careful to discuss his plans for the day, pointing out on the map the quiet, residential area he was going to visit. "There's a park and a few shops, but I think it's mostly council houses, not flats. Still, we have to cover it."

In fact, there were no flats as far as he could tell. One or two large houses set back from the road and hidden by laurels, quiet, tree-lined streets occupied by First-Time Buyers, and those postwar council houses the color of suet pudding that can be seen all over the country. The park was almost empty. There were a couple of people walking their dogs, but it was too cold for children to be playing there. One of these people, an old lady, had a mongrel tied on a length of string. The dog appeared well fed and lively, a young animal, while its mistress was too thin, too fragile-looking. Mike watched her for a few minutes, the steam of her breath coming in short, rapid spirals, quickly evaporating. Then he approached her; gently, not wanting to alarm her, and showed her the photo.

"I don't know," said the old lady, shaking her head. "They all look the same to me. It's like a uniform, isn't it? They all dress the same, all do their hair the same. You want to call in the newsagent's down the road there. That's where all the kids go. He'll be able to tell you."

Mike thanked her, would have liked to give her a couple of pounds, but he needed what little money he had for food and emergencies.

She was probably right about the newsagent, he thought, entering that shop. They stocked a good many teenage and pop magazines and had a sweet counter, one of those parents' nightmares where a child might spend half an hour picking out fifty Ps' worth of penny chews. But with so many kids in and out all the time, how could the shopkeeper remember one?

Nor did he remember her. Not at first. Mike had to wait while he argued with a woman over her paper bill, served another with cigarettes, and shouted to his wife in the back room to come and lend a hand. He frowned, rearranging some Crunchies that had tumbled from the display counter.

"Show me that picture again. . . ." And when Mike, with a flutter of hope, of premonition in his chest, handed over the photograph, the newsagent nodded. "Yes. Yes—it could be her."

"You've seen her? Where—I mean, when?"

"Look, are you the police or what? Otherwise, why are you looking for her?"

"I'm not the law. She's a runaway. Daughter of a friend of mine." And with the recollection of that Defford fruit farmer,

"She may be with a young man claiming to be her brother."

"Not a fair-haired boy? Dark eyes?"

Mike felt a curious fluttering again under his ribs. Darren . . . so near now.

"You have seen them, then?"

"A few days ago. I can't say *what* day, mind. I remember them because the girl was so upset when I told her I didn't have any more 'O'Neills' annuals left—"

"You mean that Australian thing, 'Take the O'Neills?' "

"That's the one. We had two dozen of them, but I reckon I sold the last copy no more than a few minutes before this kiddie came in. Close to tears she was when I told her. Wait a minute . . ." He tapped out something on his computer. "That's it. I remember now. I told her I'd have some more in on the eighteenth and she asked me to keep one for her."

"The eighteenth? That's today—and she hasn't been in yet?" My God, they could walk in at any minute.

"She won't be in today, that's why she was so anxious I keep her a copy. That's the day they were going to Barnhearst, she said. I remember that particularly because the boy started to look agitated, like it was a secret and he wanted her to shut up."

"Barnhearst? Are you sure?" Mike had a list of addresses, taken from the London flat, of all Darren's friends, and he was certain none of them were in Barnhearst. Why on earth had they gone there?

He was on the wrong side of town. Catching a bus here meant traveling right across Stoke-on-Trent and having to change at Hanley. It was going to be a tedious business, and Mike doubted the wisdom of embarking on what might well prove a wild-goose chase.

"Are you sure?" he repeated.

"Of course I am. I don't recall everyone who comes in here, or what they say, but I don't forget having to disappoint customers, especially a nice little girl like that one. If you were a shopkeeper, you'd understand."

Chastised, Mike left and headed for the bus stop.

The journey was slow and uncomfortable. Mike, who had long limbs, always became acutely aware of his knees and elbows whenever he sat on a bus; fat old women laden with shopping bruised his elbows and used his knees to part support their bags of groceries. It was strange, but as he sat there, staring out of the window at the unfamiliar streets, he found that he was unable to picture Darren in his mind. Though he had only seen two photographs of Nicky, he could picture her quite easily, while Darren's features eluded him. Somehow, that made him terribly uneasy.

He gazed dully at the town, wishing to be somewhere else and thinking that people in this part of the world were extremely fond of erecting statues. The locals were friendly, but you had a job understanding them, especially the older ones, and if you used the word "mate," they thought you were Australian. Why had Darren come here? There was little work, and surely this must be the coldest place in the country.

"It's going to snow," the woman next to him remarked, and he told her he wouldn't be at all surprised.

There was little shelter from the wind at Hanley bus station, and he had to wait half an hour for the Barnhearst bus, sitting on one of those seats that fold up to make more room and designed, no doubt, by someone with a very narrow backside. He was hungry, but all he dared spend on food was fifty pence, not enough for a sandwich these days, and he didn't want to sponge off Alan any more than he could help. He had to leave enough for his bus fare back today, plus a couple of ten-pence pieces in case he needed to phone. He resigned himself to dining on a bag of chips; at least they would be hot.

The town was small, surrounded by sprawling houses and industrial estates and covered with the sort of mist people mean when they talk of the rain being in the air. Mike soon began to feel chilled, and his hair, darkened to the color of wet straw by the damp, kept falling on his cheeks and coldly sticking there. His feet felt wet, too. Trainers are not meant to be waterproof, but they are the most comfortable thing to wear if one is going to be walking around all day long.

Mike went to the job center first, sure that Darren must have been looking for temporary work—perhaps as Father Christmas in one of the stores. But they had no Gillespie (or Lansdowne or Landsdale) on their register. So why come to Barnhearst? What was there here to attract him? One or two more statues, one or two more shops selling Staffordshire china—all right for those who could afford it—and almost everything five pence dearer than elsewhere. A bag of chips cost him fifty-two pence, where it would have been forty at home, and then the woman wrapped them so clumsily that he dropped some. What a dump. What a godforsaken dead-'n-alive hole.

All the while, he was looking out for Darren and the girl, overtaking every fair-haired lad so that he could see his face. Reluctantly, he decided to start calling in the shops with Nicky's photo. Even if they had only come to the town today, surely they must have gone into at least one shop? Then he saw the Victoria Theatre.

It was the kind of theater found throughout the provinces: tumbledown, needing a face-lift, and never getting it because these days grants went to the enterprising people who walked around East Anglia carrying a telegraph pole or laid bricks in a haphazard pile and called it Art. Mike, unlike Darren, was a frequent theatergoer when he could afford it, and had once even considered becoming an actor himself. But he was a realist. He knew he was only moderately talented, that his face was hardly memorable, and that starring in the annual school play was not quite the same as performing before a paying audience every night. He sighed, full of regret for all the things he could have done, all the things he might have been.

Peter Pan was the current production at the Victoria. Of course it was all panto at this time of year, but imagine a place like this putting on *Peter Pan*. There must be two performances today, because although it was only three o'clock there were coaches parked outside. Mike went closer to see if there were any well-known names in the show. There were: Diana Dietz—and Sunny Patterson.

That was why they went here, then. He was taking her to see the woman Alan said was her idol. Perhaps even now they were in the theater, or would they be coming for the evening performance?

He felt he had no choice but to wait across the street and see if they came out with the rest.

They were early. Darren wanted to eat, but Nicky would have none of it. She was too excited.

"We can go round to the stage door now, can't we? I mean, I know it's only five, but she must be there. Darren, we can, can't we?"

He gave in, as usual. That portrait was going to get battered and grubby if it wasn't handed over soon—why on earth had she taken it out of the folder? He offered to carry it for her, but this went down as well as the suggestion that they eat.

"You haven't lost the tickets, have you?"

"No."

"And you've got a pen?"

"Yes."

"And paper?" She wanted an autograph.

"For the billionth time—*yes!*"

"And for the *zillionth* time, don't exaggerate." She laughed, too bold and too loud, buoyed up on her excitement.

The street was quiet, Victorian in character, and Darren noted with something like rising cheerfulness that there was a pub opposite the stage door. He could grab a pork pie or something.

"Darren, I'm scared!"

"What? What d'you mean you're scared? All these weeks it's been nothing but Sunny, Sunny, bloody Sunny, and now you're here you're *scared*?"

He'd had no idols as a child, couldn't understand. But his

qualms about buying theater tickets didn't extend to barging in the stage door and dragging Nicky behind him.

A gray-haired man sat in what he could only think of as a cubbyhole, reading a newspaper; elderly, but ready to deal with anyone who had no business being there.

"My sister," said Darren, thrusting the girl forward, "has a present for Miss Patterson."

"Well, now. What have we got here, eh?" He inspected the drawing. "Say! That's what I call a real work of art, young lady. But you've just missed her. She's gone for her break. D'you want to leave it with me?"

Nicky shook her head. Awed, for once, into silence.

"No, well, it'd be best if you gave it to her yourself. She's really going to love that, you know. Tell you what, she'll be back—oh, let me see—between quarter and half past six. You come back then. All right?"

Another nod, and Darren had to propel her out.

Once outside, she found her voice again. "Darren, shouldn't we buy her some flowers? Wouldn't that be the right thing to do?"

"I think the right thing to do would be to get something to eat. My stomach thinks my throat's been cut."

"Aw, that's got whiskers on it. Can't you give me some money for flowers while you go and eat?"

He should have done that. He should have handed her a tenner and let her go alone to the indoor market while he went for a hamburger. Instead, he dragged her to the Wimpy and more or less force-fed her ("I'm not having you fainting on me halfway through the show"). Then they bought carnations, three dozen of them, at the market: multicolored blooms that had very little smell and would probably wilt within a few hours. But Nicky was satisfied with them, thought the arrangement tasteful.

"So they should be at that price."

They still had time to spare and Darren was inclined to dawdle, looking in shop windows. He didn't want to stand outside the stage door too long in this weather, though Nicky appeared not to notice the cold. She looked so lovely in her new blue coat; what his gran would have called a proper little treat. He'd wanted to buy her a matching hat as well, but she would have nothing to do with it. He was disappointed but knew it was useless to force it on her; she'd probably contrive to lose it at the first opportunity.

He let her walk a little way ahead so that he could watch her. So lovely . . . If only things could be different. Was it really all those weeks ago when he had first walked behind her just like this at Wheatcliffe-on-Sea? And if he could turn the clock back to the few seconds before he saw her face clearly for the first time, would he take refuge in a shop doorway and just let her disappear into the crowd? No, probably not. And if he had to give her up, he would do so and try not to have regrets.

He knew the woman in the off-license was all right, so he wouldn't have her on his conscience. As for Terry Wallace . . .

That was when he saw the young man in the phone box. He stopped, stared in disbelief, then siezed Nicky's hand and led her down a side street. "I need a quick drink," he said.

A large one.

18

"DARREN, IT'S QUARTER past six. Hurry up!" Nicky, her arms full of flowers and one hand carefully clutching her drawing, led him back to the grimy side street and the Victoria Theatre's stage door. "You don't think we've missed her?"

"No, of course not. But you can go and check if you like."

"Aren't you coming?"

"No, I'll wait over the road." The doorway of the Curtain Up pub was almost opposite the stage door. He'd wait there.

"Why aren't you coming with me?"

He couldn't explain that he was almost sure the man he had seen in the phone box was Mike Southgate, or why he longed for the safety of being inside the theater.

"It's those damned flowers," he said. "They make me want to sneeze. Now go on, I'll be just over there."

His first impulse on seeing Mike was to take the girl and leave Barnhearst immediately, but he could easily imagine her reaction when told she couldn't meet her idol after all. Even now that a small doubt had entered his mind—how could Mike have traced him here?—instinct told him he should keep out of sight until it was time to enter the theater. Only anxiety for Nicky kept him standing where he was.

He had a notion that most actors were self-absorbed; charming enough before a crowd of fans, impatient and offhand with an admirer otherwise. No doubt Sunny Patterson would be surrounded by autograph hunters after the show, but how would she react beforehand to one adoring adolescent with her carnations and her offering of artwork?

Darren waited, intending to intervene if the woman gave her Number One Fan less than the reception she deserved, while Nicky, having inquired at the door and finding herself in plenty of time, signaled him an okay.

The street was quiet, though once or twice somebody opened the stage door to look up at the sky: Heavy snow was forecast, so possibly there was some concern over coach parties. Darren lit a cigarette, drawing deeply on it, then, realizing the smoke would give him away, put it out again.

At just on half past six, he became aware that Nicky was watching someone further down the road, stamping her feet the way she always did when she was excited or agitated. She started forward, changed her mind, and leaned back against the wall, clutching her flowers.

Darren saw a young woman stop, heard her say hello, and Nicky's shy, "These are for you." Odd to see Nicky looking shy, to hear her so in awe—and painful, too.

At first, Sunny Patterson failed to impress him. She was "actressy" in her dress—a long black coat with the shoulders heavily padded and the sort of boots that would hardly sell for less than three figures—and in the way she said "For me?" and clasping the flowers theatrically. Somewhere he had read or heard a theory that actors never stop acting. Though she spoke softly, with only the hint of an Australian accent, her voice carried clearly to him across the street.

"Are you going to see the show?"

"Yes."

"Who are you with? Surely you're not on your own?"

Darren was unable to hear the girl's reply, but she couldn't help turning to him and he dodged out of sight. When he looked once more, Sunny Patterson was studying Nicky's drawing.

"That's wonderful! But you haven't signed it. . . . Oh, yes, artists always sign their work. Didn't you know that? Come on, we'll go and find a pen, shall we?"

Nicky turned to him again, smiling in delight and triumph, and Darren was forced to watch her being led away by a stranger.

Nicky taken by a stranger.

It was unlikely the woman recognized her, or had even heard the name Nicolle Gurney, but he spent five minutes in utter terror until the door opened and Nicky came out. He heard the girl's voice clearly this time: "I will. Yes, thank you, Sunny. I will," and one last glimpse of the actress waving her good-bye. He didn't think the woman had seen him but couldn't be certain.

"What did she say to you?" he asked when Nicky joined him, eyes lit up with love as they were whenever he gave her yet another present.

"She said my drawing was wonderful, but I hadn't signed it."

"Yes, I heard all that. I meant, what did she say to you when you were in there."

"Introduced me to Ned—he's the doorman and he gave me a chocolate—and got me to sign the picture."

Sign the picture. Oh, God! He'd heard her say, You haven't signed it, but he'd never given it another thought.

"What did you write?" he asked, trying to keep the alarm out of his voice.

" 'To Sunny, with love. Nicky Gillespie.' Was that okay, Darren? You don't mind?"

"Mind? No, of course not. I'm your brother, right?"

"Right. Darren, we'd better go round to the front now. Sunny says she has to hurry and change—oh, and guess what? She says—well, I asked for her autograph and she said if I came back afterwards, she'd find me a really good picture and sign that. Can we, Darren? Can we?"

It would be past ten o'clock by then, and there would be a crowd of kids clamoring for autographs. And maybe, just maybe, he was mistaken about the man in the phone box.

"Well, of course we can," he told her. "That's half the fun of the theater, going back for autographs later. Come on, then. Let's find our seats and get settled. I'll buy a program, shall I?"

"Please! Oh, Darren, she was so *sweet*!"

Sunny Patterson hesitated inside the stage door. She wanted to peer out but daren't, and instead called the door manager.

"Ned, look down the street and see if you can see that child, would you?"

Old Ned did so good-naturedly. Miss Patterson was such a nice girl; always had time for a chat. "Just turned the corner. She's with the young man I saw earlier. Her brother, she said. Is there anything wrong, miss?"

"I'm not sure. You say they were here earlier?"

"That's right, miss. When you went for your break. I told them what time you'd be back—there *is* something wrong, isn't there?"

Sunny Patterson bit her lip, frowning. "Ned, when 'Take the O'Neills' first started showing over here I began to get some very odd letters, postmarked London, from someone signing himself 'Roger.' At first, it was the usual kind of stuff; he admired my work, and so on. But then I was getting letters from him every day—he was in love with me, wanted to marry me. . . ."

"That's the kind of thing you have to put up with a lot, I suppose," said the old man sympathetically.

"Yes, but then it started to get really weird, Ned. Frightening. He sent me a ring—it looked Victorian and valuable— and of course I sent it back. Then he wrote to say he was getting a room in his house decorated—*for me*." The actress shivered. "Every night I wonder, Is he out there? And every night when it's my turn to go out for autographs I wonder if he's standing there behind the kids."

Ned understood her fear. "But why do you think this young man was him?"

"He was hiding in the doorway of the Curtain Up over the road. I only noticed him because Nicky kept turning to look at him. When I looked too, he dodged out of sight. Ned, isn't it possible he could have bribed the child to come to the door?"

"You're really worried, miss?"

She nodded, glanced at her wristwatch: It was time to change for the second performance.

"All right. Look, I'll ring the police and explain the situation. They'll send someone."

When Sunny Patterson had gone to her dressing room, Ned phoned the station. Brother and sister, the girl had said. But they didn't really look much alike. Suppose this young man was the one who had been frightening Miss Patterson with his sick letters? And yes, he could have bribed the kid to come to the door. Ned told the police all this, surprised at the interest they showed. When asked, he recalled that the child's name was Nicky. Nicky what? He didn't know, but the girl had signed a drawing for Sunny Patterson. Ned got young Jason to run to her dressing room, and soon the answer came back.

"Gillespie," Ned told them. "Her name's Nicky Gillespie."

"Darren, she was so *sweet!*" Nicky repeated. This went on until they had found their seats, in the third row from front in the circle, "Sunny said," and "Sunny told me"—as she recalled another detail from the brief meeting. Around them kids screamed impatiently, some for Sunny Patterson, some for Diana Dietz, who was playing Wendy.

"There's going to be lasers," Nicky informed him, reading the programs.

"Lasers?" He gazed blankly toward the stage, the blue velvet curtain, uncomprehending. He didn't want to talk. All these other people sitting around him—talking about "Take the O'Neills" and "Whitecross Ways," nagging or pacifying the kids—how could they hear each other? It was like being a small boy again, sitting beside his mother, light-headed, waiting for curtain-up. There was a loudspeaker on their left, and when the orchestra struck up at twenty past seven the noise stunned him. A sign of old age, he thought, smiling as

Nicky and what seemed like ten thousand other kids began clapping and stamping in time. Noise, so much noise all around. "The Second Star to the Right," themes from the two TV shows. But as he became accustomed to the din, he felt himself growing tense with excitement, just as he had all those years ago when his mother sat beside him and still cared enough about him to take him to the panto.

By the time the curtain rose, he was ready to shout and applaud along with everyone else: ready to laugh at Mr. Darling, who couldn't fix his tie, ready to boo when he slipped his medicine into Nana's dish. Nicky's hand touched his briefly when Peter appeared on the windowsill looking for his lost shadow; she turned and whispered something to him, but it was drowned in the general shouting for Sunny Patterson.

The audience, having greeted their favorites, more less settled down, saving their energy perhaps to boo Captain Hook and egg on the crocodile. As Peter led the Darling children away to Never Never Land, blue and white lasers flashed across the theater. Darren watched Nicky, studied her face in the pulsing lights. God! He'd never get her out of here. As far as he could tell, her eyes were on Peter. Sunny Patterson, her light brown hair fastened under a green cap that matched the rest of her costume, appeared to fly through the night sky, the lasers representing stars, followed by the three children in their nightclothes.

Had Francie ever been to the panto? At fourteen, she would have turned her nose up at the very idea, called it kid's crap. But had she ever been? Had Marsha, like Darren's own mother, taken Francie to the theater in the days before her own wishes and desires took precedence over the happiness and security of her child?

Perhaps he could arrange tickets for another day, he thought, his hand momentarily brushing against the replica Smith and Wesson in his inner pocket that he had been too afraid to leave in the flat. Christmas Eve would be perfect, but failing that he had until mid-January, when *Peter Pan*

ended its run. Nicky would love to come again, he was sure
of that long before the interval.

Never Never Land had her almost paralyzed in her seat.
The Lost Boys being tailed by the pirates, in turn followed
by the redskins, who, with their seminaked bodies gaily
painted, were the most colorful group of all. The kids booed
and hissed Captain Hook, darkly handsome in his Charles
the Second–type attire, wolf-whistled the proud and beautiful Tiger Lily, shouted at the crocodile, which was an
awesome and lifelike monster guided by remote control
offstage.

And now even Darren could appreciate a little of Nicky's
admiration for Sunny Patterson. He remembered the woman
he had seen outside in the street: soft-spoken, not much
taller than Nicky, almost fragile. On the stage she seemed
another person, taller, confident and powerful. He stored
these impressions to share later with Nicky.

But the last he was ever to see of the girl's idol was in the
final moment before the interval.

Wendy had been lifted to safety by Michael's kite, leaving
Peter alone on stage. Arms defiantly outstretched, he declared:

To die will be an awfully big adventure!

as the curtain fell.

"Darren—Darren . . ." She didn't know what to say,
hardly knew how to express what she felt, except by throwing
her arms around his neck.

He responded by kissing her before he could stop himself;
kissing her mouth in the few seconds before the houselights
went up.

"Darren—don't do that! Don't—"

"It's all right, Nicky. I won't hurt you. I love you,
Nicky. . . ."

"Darren—*no!*" She pushed him away: He was sweating,
numb with the horror of what he had just done. But

surrounded by shrieking children, he was sure the incident had gone unnoticed.

"I'm sorry," he said, looking not at her but at the stage. "I'll buy you an ice cream, shall I? A strawberry split?"

He couldn't look at her. Couldn't think of anything except that he had somehow betrayed her. In a daze, he made his way up the stairs of the aisle, eyes not quite focusing on the uniforms ahead of him. One was the crisp white and black of a young woman selling ice creams—a strawberry split; she liked strawberry splits—and beside her, two men in the uniform of St. John's Ambulance. Maybe they always had medical assistance on hand in large theaters, or maybe this was special because of the lasers. Darren didn't know. All he saw now were the men in police uniform standing by the exits.

Mike Southgate signaled to the police officers, some of whom were armed, indicating they were to keep back and give him a chance to reason with the lad. They were reluctant to do so, however, because they believed Darren had a gun.

Now Mike felt he had made a mistake in telephoning Alan Ralph, and had only done so because he'd promised as a friend.

"I know where they are," he told him. "Right now, this minute. I'll explain it all later, but he's brought her here to Barnhearst to see Sunny Patterson in the panto. Can you get here right away?"

"Southgate," Alan growled. It was the first time he had addressed him by his surname in a fortnight. "Southgate, you lied to me. You told me he wasn't dangerous."

"*What*? He isn't. I don't understand. What—"

"It's here in today's paper. He's held up two off-licenses, that's what. They traced him through the ID he used to rent a video, though he used a false address. He's the one they want in connection with that murder in Suffolk. *And he's got my kid!*"

Useless to try and persuade him not to call the police. If only he'd kept his mouth shut, waited . . .

Now Darren, halfway up the aisle, saw him. He stopped, their eyes met, locked in recognition, Darren's expression revealing his sense of betrayal.

I thought you were a friend. Why have you done this?

Already, some members of the audience had noticed something wrong and were stopping their children from running for ice cream.

Darren looked at the police uniforms, then ran back to his seat at the end of the third row and grabbed the girl by her arm. Mike could see that she was shaking her head, distressed, but not apparently afraid. He wouldn't hurt her; Mike was certain of that. He must care about her a lot to have her so well dressed and have brought her to the panto to see her idol.

Yet he obviously intended to use her as a shield, for he had one arm across her chest, holding her close to him as he pushed her up the aisle, while the other groped in his inner jacket pocket. So he was armed after all.

When he waved the gun over her head several people screamed, their voices almost drowned by the general racket. Somewhere, Mike could remember reading about crowd chain reaction, where one person in a panic was capable of alarming a hundred others in a matter of seconds. This was happening now across the circle; people either getting down onto the floor behind their seats, trying to reach the further exits, or merely screaming.

Darren was holding the gun close to the girl's head, but not pointing it at her; possibly she couldn't even see it. Briefly, he waved it at the officer in the nearest exit, who moved slowly aside to let him pass, concern for the girl being paramount.

Mike followed at a distance, his hands slightly raised, palms outward, calling to him. "Darren! Darren, calm down. Stay where you are. Let's talk about it."

But he continued to back out through the exit, taking quick glances over his shoulder and now keeping the gun pointed at Mike.

"Stay back, Mike!" he warned. *"Stay back!"*

For the first time, the girl seemed to realize what was happening and she shouted too, defending Darren.

"You leave him alone! Don't you come near us! Tell Alan I want to see him. I want to talk to Alan!"

Mike caught a glimpse of Alan downstairs in the foyer; he was being restrained by two policemen and hadn't heard. The girl called out something more—it sound like "Alan" and "Sunny," but Darren clamped his hand over her mouth and dragged her backward into the ladies' powder room. He pushed the door with such a force that it remained open, and his expression seemed to say he felt he had just made a terrible mistake. Not that it would have mattered; from what Mike could see and what he guessed about the position of the room in the building, there was no other way out.

The powder room was brightly lit and smelled of scented soap, but no one else was yet in there because the curtain had scarcely fallen on the first act when Darren left his seat. Mike stood in the doorway facing the lad, who was back up against the far wall, still clutching the girl. He looked terrified, and Mike knew how dangerous that could be.

One of the officers called to him to move out of the way.

"No. No, give me a chance." He thought he heard one of them moving behind him—reaching for his gun?

Mike spoke very softly, reassuringly. "It's all right, Darren. It's all right. Let Nicky go now. I know you wouldn't hurt her, but *they* don't know. Let her go, and I promise they'll keep back while we talk. How about it, Darren? A deal?"

The boy shook his head, held the girl more tightly to him. "No. Let us both out of here and I'll leave her somewhere you can find her."

Mike turned to one of the officers, who shook his head. Of course, it was an unreasonable request.

"Then let me take her place, Darren. Let me come over to you"—raising his arms higher—"and let her go. I know you wouldn't hurt her. . . ."

He must have loosened his grip, because Nicky twisted under his arm, looked up into his face.

"Darren, I want to see me Uncle Alan. I want to go home."

Mike, quickly wiping perspiration from his upper lip, saw a change come over the lad then: Something seemed to drain from his face to leave him forever.

"She wants to go home, Darren. You wouldn't hold her against her will, would you? I know you love her and care for her because she reminds you of Francie. But she's not Francie, Darren, she's Nicolle Gurney and she doesn't belong with you."

"Francie let me down," he said, eyes on Mike, but not focusing. "I used to think it was the other way round, that I'd betrayed her by not telling anyone Dad hit her. I used to say I'd get even one day. I'd find Dad when he got out of prison and—I don't care anymore. I'm glad she's dead. I didn't want to hate her, and I would've in the end, you know. . . ."

Mike nodded. "But you don't want to hurt Nicky—"

"*I won't hurt her!*"

"Then there's no point in holding her. Let her go, Darren."

He saw him hesitate, trying to come to a decision, and instinct told him to keep silent for a moment. Was the gun real, or just a replica? Perhaps one of the officers, a ballistics expert, could tell. He knew there was someone immediately behind him, but daren't turn or even move lest it should panic the lad. Nor did they show yet that they were armed.

Suddenly Darren spoke to the girl. "Do you want to go?"

"Ye-es, but—"

"Then go. *Go on, go!*" Still keeping the gun pointed at Mike, he pushed her forward.

As she got to the doorway someone reached for her, but she twisted away, trying to turn back.

"Darren—"

The sudden movement alarmed him, and he lowered his hand so that the gun was momentarily pointed at her.

The shot sounded like an explosion in the small room,

but it hadn't come from Darren's gun. He lay on the floor with blood flowing from his chest, soaking his shirt and making a bright crimson pool on the white vinyl tiling. The girl screamed, tried to run to him, but Mike held her fast, her face in his chest so that she shouldn't see.

"Get an ambulance!" he shouted over his shoulder. "He wouldn't have hurt her. He was afraid—*but he wouldn't have hurt her!*"

"He had the gun pointed at her, Southgate," said the voice behind him. "We couldn't take a chance."

"I don't believe it's even a real gun." Mike thought the blood had stopped flowing. Perhaps this was for the best. Darren would face a long sentence this time. Perhaps he would rather be dead.

Someone stepped past him, knelt at Darren's side, touched him, and shook his head. "Get the girl out of here, Southgate. There's nothing you can do for—" He nodded at the boy's body.

Mike looked one last time, then led Nicky away. Alan Ralph was no longer in the foyer, so probably the police had persuaded him to wait outside. There were two ambulances parked across the road, a number of panda cars and uniformed men, but he couldn't see Alan. The girl walked unsteadily, so Mike supported her through the door.

"You'll feel better in the fresh air," he said, the first time he had spoken to her. She didn't reply.

A young woman wearing stage makeup and with a heavy black coat draped over her costume rushed forward.

"Is she all right?"

Vaguely, Mike recognized Sunny Patterson, and the girl broke away and ran to her. It was then that Alan got out from one of the cars and ran lumberingly across the road. It must have pained him to see his stepdaughter being comforted by a stranger, but Mike couldn't think of that just then. All he could think of was Darren and how he, like so many others, had let the lad down.

I thought you were a friend. Why have you done this?

As he watched, Nicky gradually released her hold on Sunny Patterson and allowed Alan to lift her into his arms. He carried her back across the road and was guided by a WPC to one of the ambulances. The girl would probably be treated for shock.

Mike, the actress, and several curious bystanders watched the vehicle, escorted by a police car, slowly move away. As it turned the corner, the first flakes of snow began to fall.